THE SURROGATE

LYNN KATZ

Black Rose Writing | Texas

ISBN: 978-1-68433-682-1
PUBLISHED BY BLACK ROSE WRITING
www.blackrosewriting.com

Printed in the United States of America
Suggested Retail Price (SRP) $18.95

The Surrogate is printed in Garamond Premier

F
KATZ
LYNN

blisher, Black Rose Writing does its best to eliminate reduce paper usage and energy costs, while never experience. As a result, the final word count vs. page count pectations.

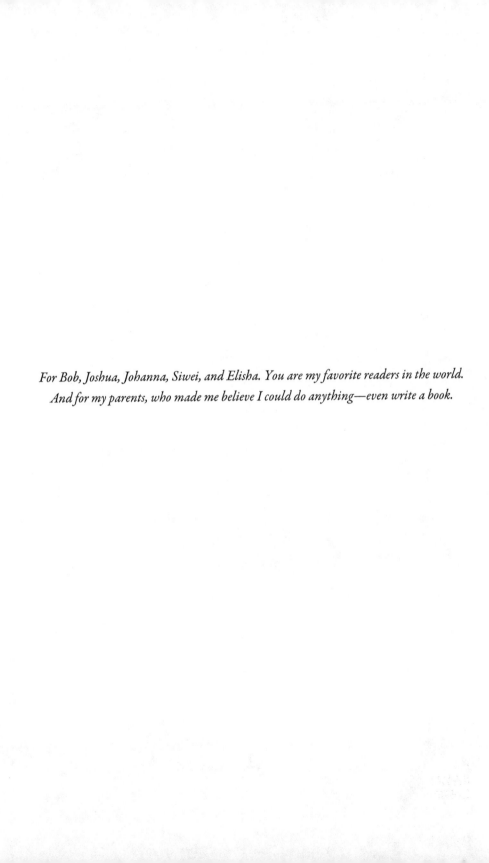

For Bob, Joshua, Johanna, Siwei, and Elisha. You are my favorite readers in the world. And for my parents, who made me believe I could do anything—even write a book.

THE SURROGATE

"The purpose of life is not to be happy. It is to be useful, to be honorable, to be compassionate, to have it make some difference that you have lived and lived well."
—Ralph Waldo Emerson

PROLOGUE

Florida was her first mistake. It was impossible to ignore those cheap hotel prices. And the low airfare. Besides—with a finicky window air conditioner in her one-bedroom Hartford apartment, she thought, *August in Key West might be nice.*

Ernest Hemingway was her second mistake. In all fairness to Hemingway, there were other writers' homes she might have chosen that particular summer. And she could have avoided Key West by following that writer's footsteps across the Atlantic Ocean all the way to Paris.

In the end, it came down to mistakes more substantial than Jenn Cooper's choice of summer vacation and decisions more consequential than any dead writer's house. In the end, she had only herself to blame.

CHAPTER 1

The heavy rain had turned into a persistent drizzle by afternoon. I abandoned Duval Street for the relative calm of a side road and meandered through unpaved back alleyways. Random raindrops made dents in the puddles. As I closed my umbrella and pulled at the hood of my rain poncho, the ding of a bell pierced the thick air. Before I had time to heed the warning, a bicycle flew by, and an arm brushed against my shoulder. Losing my balance, I slid sideways into a muddy rut in the road, somehow managing to remain upright. *Damn!*

"Sorry," a man called, his bicycle brakes screeching. He disembarked, turned his bike around, and trudged closer to where I stood in my footbath of warm rainwater. "Hey, Jennifer. Whatcha still doing here? I thought ya left town," the man said, staring at me, squinting. "Almost didn't recognize you in that...whatever it is you're wearing," he said, laughing.

I squinted back at him. Did I know the man? He didn't seem familiar. Wedged firmly between the tacky mud beneath my feet and curiosity, I stood in that puddle racking my brain. *Who was this man?* He stared directly at me as though we were old friends. He was about my height, perhaps in his forties despite his leathery skin. He wore a baseball cap, cargo shorts, and a red, rain parka. I was certain I'd never seen the man before.

He tilted his head. "You okay, Jennifer?" The only person who'd ever called me Jennifer had been my mother who passed away years earlier. My high school students called me Miss Cooper. My work colleagues referred to me as Jenn. Never Jennifer. So, who was this guy? "What are you up to?" he asked. I had to say something, but for the life of me, I couldn't come up with the right words or any words for that matter.

I studied his face, looking for clues. I tried to lift one foot, embarrassed by the sucking sound of my sandal pulling away from the mud. I considered asking the man his name. I should have cleared things up right away, corrected his mistake, told him that my name was Jenn Cooper not someone he thought he knew. Someone else named Jennifer.

At the time, standing there in the alleyway, my ankles encased in an unforgiving mixture of dirt and water, fusing me into a state of inertia, it seemed easier to answer the man's question. I had no energy for a conversation about mistaken identity. And yet, I struggled to articulate a reasonable answer to his question. What *was* I doing here?

"I'm leaving in a few days. I need to get home," I said. Not knowing what else to say, I erred on the side of the truth. "School starts in less than two weeks." That should have set him straight, or at least it should have helped him figure out he had the wrong woman, the wrong Jennifer.

"That's too bad. Hope this visit wasn't a complete waste of time for ya." He smiled, knowingly. "I thought you'd try to get in touch with me again. You look exhausted," he said. "Call when you get back. We should talk, okay?" Then the stranger on the bicycle winked at me and waited for a response. I had to say something. Anything to end this nonsensical small talk.

"Well, good to see you," I said, clearing my throat, glancing at an invisible watch on my wrist, willing the man to leave me in peace. He shook his head, peering at me from beneath the brim of his baseball cap. As he took off on his bicycle, he waved goodbye and rang his rusty old bicycle bell again like a six-year-old child. I watched him weave around ruts and puddles, disappearing, and then reappearing again, narrowly missing pedestrians and a few random Key West roosters as he made his way down the unpaved road.

I tried to shake off a sudden wave of panic and confusion brought on by my strange encounter with the man on a bicycle. I pushed forward and continued wandering the familiar Key West neighborhoods. My legs ached from walking miles in thinly soled sandals now soaked and muddy. I desperately needed a new pair. First, I needed to rest my blistered feet and shrug off the weight of dread pressing on my shoulders like an invisible barbell.

The rain picked up, and again I covered my head with my thin poncho. My hair stuck to my damp neck. I reached inside the hood, trying to smooth the frizzled ends of hair against my sweaty scalp. As I traipsed up and down the streets of Key West's commercial district, I glanced at the shop windows, half-heartedly searching for a new pair of sandals and some flint to spark my creative fires. Two weeks in Florida and I hadn't managed to write one word, not a sentence, not even an outline for the novel I promised myself I'd start this time. It was supposed to be a working vacation, and I'd squandered the time.

I stopped in front of a gallery and glanced at my reflection in the glass window. I almost didn't recognize the ragged woman looking back at me, tired, haggard, lost. I pulled the hood of my poncho away from my head again, scrounged in my straw bag until I found an old scrunchie, and deftly smoothed the hair off my neck into a quasi-ponytail, as if that might help my mood. Meanwhile, the Old Town neighborhood started to crowd up, as boisterous partiers gave up on capturing another picture-perfect sunset at Mallory Square.

I tried to shake my encounter with the stranger who acted as though he knew me. I'd never considered myself an irresponsible drinker, not even during my college days. But I wondered, *Was it possible I had too much to drink one night? Was it possible I had no memory of a drunken encounter with a random guy? Was this what a blackout felt like?*

But why did he refer to my trip as a potential waste of time? The man's question felt like a slap across my face. "You need a thicker skin," my mother used to tell me. Why did I care what some stranger thought? Why did I care what anyone thought, for that matter? My dead mother. My dead father. What did it matter? And yet I heard my father's voice poking at me from beyond the grave. "Those who can, do; those who can't teach." Determined to prove the dead man wrong, I'd wasted another summer vacation. Key West, Florida. Another town, another writer's home. Another futile attempt to begin drafting that novel I'd dreamed about for so many years.

I limped down a narrow street, wincing from the sting of blistered heels. I had to get off my feet, and so I stepped into one of the less crowded bars. Aptly named The Back Alley, the place had a few empty tables and plenty of vacant stools at the bar.

I collapsed onto the stool at the end of the bar. Slipping my wet sandals off my feet, I closed my eyes and sighed at the feeling of release. I startled when I sensed someone sliding onto the vacant stool adjacent to mine. I glanced down at long, tanned legs, and I angled my body away from the sudden intruder. I smelled her cloying perfume suggesting roses and desperation. I was tempted to move to the other end of the bar, but a bartender slid a menu in front of me and I felt trapped. I pushed the menu away. "No thank you. I'll just have a drink."

"So, what will it be tonight?" I ordered a Key Lime Martini and swiveled my stool away from the woman next to me. I focused on the singer strumming his guitar on the small stage.

When my drink arrived, I leaned into the martini glass, stealing several swallows of the foamy tartness, and then I took a few more sips. I decided I liked this pretentious drink. I licked the sweet and sour taste from my lips. Not that I'd ever been the martini-type. But this was Key West, and I believed in the adage *When in Rome.* I thought about visiting Rome someday soon. Or possibly Paris. Hemingway loved Paris.

I pulled a journal out of my soggy, straw purse and opened it to the next blank page. I scrawled reminders: *Buy Key Lime juice. Paris next summer?* I'd begun a new journal when I first arrived in Key West. A to-do list and a resting place for images, character sketches, story ideas for my novel. Possibly a final resting place. A graveyard of ideas. Entries separated by bullets. Pages and pages of bullets.

As I scribbled, I couldn't shake the presence of the woman next to me. I felt her eyes drilling holes into the side of my face. I slipped my journal and pen back into my bag and gulped down the rest of my first martini. The bartender caught my eye and raised his brows communicating in that universal bartender language. I nodded yes. I wanted another drink. I promised myself I'd slow down. I'd take my time with the next martini.

Along with her perfume, I smelled the loneliness drifting from the woman sitting next to me, hungry for conversation, preparing to pounce. I turned back to the singer on the stage and then risked a furtive glimpse in the woman's direction. Just a glance. The glance became a double-take, and then I found myself staring too. It was rude, but I couldn't look away.

I felt the blood draining from my face, and the sweat on my neck turned icy cold. I blinked my eyes repeatedly, waiting for my brain to catch up with the image before me. I continued staring into the woman's face, a complete stranger sitting next to me in a random bar in Key West, a few days before the end of another disappointing summer vacation. But hers was no stranger's face. It was my own face. My mirror image. Except for one problem: I wasn't looking into a mirror.

CHAPTER 2

The woman's face was identical to mine. And as she spoke, I studied her mouth. My mouth. "Oh. My. God. Who... are...you?" the woman whispered, pausing between each word. "I feel as though I'm looking at my own reflection in a mirror." Her whispery voice was nothing like mine, but we were thinking the same exact thoughts.

"I know. This is crazy," I said, trying to make sense of what I was seeing. There were obvious differences. Our clothing, our hair, her make-up. I rarely used make-up. I glanced down from the woman's face to her pink slip-on sandals with those flashy interlocking Gs—that Gucci trademark. This woman sitting next to me had made an effort to look fashionable, despite the weather. She wore a short, linen trench coat, belted at the waist. As for her hands, the sparkling diamond ring and wedding band on her left ring finger flashed like a neon sign. This woman appeared wealthy and unlike me, she was married. Behind the superficial differences, I recognized the high cheekbones, the deep-set brown eyes, the olive skin tone. The likeness terrified me—right down to the dimple on her right cheek that peeked in and out when she smiled. I'd always hated that dimple. A genetic gift from my father that caused uninvited comments.

"Is it possible we're related? Are we identical twins, separated at birth? What are the odds of that?" I asked, thinking there might be a scientific explanation for something that seemed inexplicable. The woman laughed at my questions. I wiped my clammy hands on my skirt and then used my cocktail napkin to blot beads of sweat from my upper lip. Sitting next to my doppelganger on a barstool in Key West, my legs quivered uncontrollably. Suddenly the woman grasped my wrist.

"Listen, this is crazy, but I think you're the answer to my prayers. Follow me, there's a table in the back." Her voice was urgent and left no room for argument. I stood up too quickly and then paused, waiting for the room to stop spinning. With the stranger's hand tugging at my wrist, I slipped into my soaked sandals and clutched my second martini. I held onto the stem, trying not to slosh even a drop of the liquid onto the floor.

After a few steps, I tugged out of her grasp, forcing my double to release my wrist. I shuffled behind, observing the slope of her shoulders, the way her trench coat clung tightly to her body. Our height seemed about the same. I studied the back of the woman's head, the gentle movement of her caramel-colored mane with summer blond streaks, tame and shiny. Nothing like my dull brown, dry, unruly mess, now stuffed behind my head in an elastic scrunchie. I searched for more differences, something, anything, a distinguishing characteristic. The woman clutched a frosty, glass mug filled with a golden liquid. I'd never developed a taste for beer. There was something.

We sat in the back, far from the stage. I could barely hear the singer. "So, how tall are you?" the woman asked. An odd question to ask a stranger you've just met at a bar.

"Five feet four inches," I said, taking a gulp of my drink. The woman grinned, flashing her white teeth and that one dimple.

"Me too. But that's an average height, right? I know plenty of women who are 5'4". Can I ask how much you weigh? We look about the same size." The woman's eyes roamed away from my face, evaluating the top half of my body. She must have wondered about the shape concealed under my loose-fitting clothes. Despite the alcohol clouding my thinking, I realized the questions were too personal, and yet, refusing to answer didn't seem to be an option.

"130 pounds, on a good day. You?"

"125. But I have to be careful. I work out three times a week with my trainer." The woman spoke in hushed tones, studying me as though I were a specimen under her microscope. "Do you work out?"

"Not really. I take walks sometimes. When the weather cooperates. I swim a few times a week at the Y when I can."

The woman continued probing, asking more questions about less obvious physical characteristics. *Any tattoos?* No. *Piercings?* No. *Surgeries?* No. *Scars?* No. By the time I drained my second martini, my legs stopped quivering.

I studied the woman's facial expressions as she spoke. They morphed seamlessly from surprise, to hilarity, to curiosity, and back again. I scrutinized the unfamiliar fine lines around her eyes when she laughed. Did I have fine lines when I laughed? Not that I laughed very often. There was nothing humorous about teaching freshman English to high school students year after year.

And then, suddenly, it dawned on me. We had something else in common beyond our physical appearance. The unsettling encounter from earlier in the day—was that the missing piece of the puzzle? The man who thought he knew me. The man who called me Jennifer.

"Listen, this is going to sound strange, but I think we have something else in common. My name's Jennifer Cooper, but people call me Jenn. Is your name Jennifer too?"

The woman tilted her head, her eyes widened. "Yeah. Jennifer Moriarty. My God. How in the world did you know?" I told her about my encounter with the man on the bicycle.

"I can't believe this. What did he look like?" she asked.

"Nice looking. I'd say he's in his late forties, muscular, wore a baseball cap, kept ringing this annoying bicycle bell." Jennifer laughed when I mentioned the bell.

"That was Floyd. An old, dear friend of mine. I can count on Floyd for anything. Very loyal, completely trustworthy. He runs a bike touring company in town. What did he say exactly?" Jennifer wanted details. I shared Floyd's comment about hoping the trip hadn't been a waste of time, about wanting to talk when she returned to Key West.

"And what did you say? Exactly what did you tell him? It's important." She sat up straight, leaning in, her mouth unsmiling now, the dimple disappeared. "Did you tell him he had the wrong woman? Did you set him straight?"

"No, I didn't know what to say. It was embarrassing. He took off before I had time to explain who I was." Jennifer sighed and melted into the back of her chair. She smiled again, as though relieved by how I'd handled the situation.

"This is too much," Jennifer said. "We look the same, and we have the same name? This is beyond perfect." I didn't think any of this was even close to perfect.

"So, what questions do you have about me?" she asked. "I'm an open-book, so ask away!" I grabbed a lock of hair that had escaped my scrunchie, suddenly feeling self-conscious. I twirled it around my finger, a habit that often served to calm my nerves. Thinking up questions felt unnatural. Small talk had never been my forte.

"So, Key West," I asked, finally. "How did you end up living here?"

"Actually, I live in a suburb of Miami for most of the year. We own a small vacation home here in Key West," Jennifer said. "It's what they call a conch cottage? A little place that's been in my husband Jim's family for generations?" The way she ended her sentences, as if she were asking questions, reminded me of my students who had that particular speech pattern. I'd say, "Are you asking or telling me?" Somehow, with Jennifer, it sounded vaguely southern and charming.

I didn't need to come up with more questions. Jennifer was a small-talk pro. She had plenty to say about her husband, a successful businessman, and about her two teenage sons. She kept busy enough with volunteer work at a local hospital, Yoga, and Pilates. Her personal trainer. "Really, the Key West cottage is the perfect escape. It's my haven," she said. "My family almost never comes, so I have the place all to myself." I couldn't help comparing our lives. I had nothing in common with this person other than our appearance. And our first name.

"What about you? What do you do in Connecticut?" Jennifer asked, studying my face.

"I'm a high school teacher, freshman English," I told her.

"Lucky you!"

"No, not lucky. I'm getting tired of my job. I dread going back to school. It takes so much effort to motivate kids these days," I said, pulling at my scrunchie and stuffing it into my straw bag. "They expect you to entertain them, and use technology with every lesson. And my colleagues—don't get me started. Especially those eager first-year teachers determined to save the world. I suppose I used to be like that when I was starting out." It was probably the martinis, loosening my tongue. I stopped twirling my hair and tucked it back behind my ear. "And if it weren't so sad, it would be funny, watching those ninth-grade boys with their acne and gangly limbs, trying to fit in, trying to be cool. Those poor boys don't stand a chance."

"I know exactly what you mean, with two adolescent sons of my own. Boys have it so hard at that age," Jennifer said. "But I have to ask, of all the summer vacations you could have planned, why Key West? I mean, August isn't the best month to visit South Florida."

That's when I tried to explain how visiting writers' homes had become my school vacation standby, so unlike my teacher colleagues at Dickinson High School who traveled to exotic locales, to historical ruins, to mountains and lakes and spas and European capitals.

I remembered the very night last March, sitting at my dining room table that served as a make-shift desk. I had a stubborn habit of wasting hours researching dead writers' homes—anything to avoid my own writing. That was the night I planned my next summer vacation where I'd find the inspiration needed to launch some serious writing. Key West, Florida. Ernest Hemingway. That was the plan.

"What have you been up to for two weeks in Key West? You must be going out of your mind with all this rain," Jennifer said. I smiled, recalling my very first day when I walked from my cheap hotel to the beautiful, limestone residence on Whitehead Street in the heart of Old Town, eager to visit the gardens and rooms where Ernest Hemingway created his magic. Something inside me needed to share the experience with her. I needed Jennifer Moriarty to understand.

"My tour guide must have been in his late twenties. He'd read all of Hemingway's books and stories, and he shared anecdotes about the six-toed cats, the wives, the sons, his friends, the swimming pool fiasco."

I tried to describe my out-of-body experience, looking into Hemingway's study. My tour guide understood. I didn't expect anyone else to appreciate what happened to me, and yet that's what I craved from Jennifer Moriarty. Understanding.

"See that typewriter?" the guide had asked. "That's not just any typewriter folks; this is the actual typewriter Hemingway used." I stood in front of the other tourists in the small group, as close as I could get to the roped-off study. I gazed at the sunlit space above the carriage house, this sacred room lined with books and mementos of the writer's travels. My eyes were drawn to Hemingway's desk in the center of the room, and I couldn't look away. The tour guide continued with dramatic flair. "Ernest Hemingway pressed his fingers on those typewriter keys. His DNA is probably still there. Imagine his smudged fingerprints, existing in perpetuity on the metal keys." I tried to convey the young man's religious awe of Hemingway's study.

"I know it may seem strange," I said, trying to convince her. "I basked in the glow of that typewriter, soaking up the details of Hemingway's writing life, the number of words he wrote every day, his physical pain, the way the light shone through the windows. I inhaled it all as if I were a drowning woman breathing in the Hemingway air, desperate for life, for salvation, for purpose. Ridiculous, right?" But Jennifer didn't laugh at me. She nodded her head, hanging on my every word.

"You know, I've been coming to Key West since Jim and I were married twenty years ago, and I've never visited The Hemingway House."

"Oh, you should go, definitely. Especially if you love Hemingway." As soon as I spoke the words and saw the look of amusement slide across Jennifer's face, I realized my mistake. I doubted Jennifer loved Hemingway. I doubted Jennifer would feel Hemingway's presence the way I had felt his presence outside his study above the carriage house.

I'd never been a religious person in the traditional sense of the word, nor was I prone to hearing voices. I believed in coincidences, not miracles. But I'd felt something profound at the door of Hemingway's study. A sense of urgency washed over me, clinging to my skin like a veil. My time was running out. *Is that what Hemingway felt?*

It was most likely the martinis that made me enjoy myself in this Key West bar. I liked Jennifer. It was easy for me to talk to her. We had little in common, other than our uncanny resemblance and our first name, but I felt a connection that had nothing to do with taste in literature. Nothing to do with life choices.

At some point, I looked up and noticed two burly men approaching our table from across the room. One man moved with a swagger, as if he had been riding horseback all day and couldn't quite get the hang of walking on land. The other man had spent too much time in the Florida sun. His scarlet face was partially peeled, and he grinned widely as he sashayed between tables. Half cowboy, half rodeo clown. "Let me handle this," Jennifer said as they drew closer.

"Twins!" the rodeo clown bellowed. "Just our luck, Joe," he said to his drinking buddy. "There's one for each of us," he said. "Unless I'm seeing double. Am I seeing double, Joe?"

"Yeah, you're seeing double, you asshole," Joe said, propping up his drunken sidekick. Then he turned to us and spoke with a pronounced southern drawl. "What can we get you?" he asked. "Whatcha drinking tonight?"

"No thanks," Jennifer said, scowling. I slunk lower in my chair, trying to disappear. I smelled the fear wafting from my own body, or maybe it was the revolting scent of the drunken men. I twirled a lock of hair and let Jennifer do the talking. My new friend probably had more experience with unwanted attention from obnoxious men.

"Ah come on, don't be that way. We love twins. Don't we love twins, Joe? The night's young, and you two aren't getting any younger," the sunburned man countered with a lascivious grin. Did he really believe that such a nasty comment might help his case? I cowered in my seat then looked around for the nearest exit.

"Let's get out of here," Jennifer whispered. We pushed our chairs back from the table, and we stood to leave, moving together as if we were one person.

"Hey, where you going? It's party time ladies," one of them said, smacking his hands on the table. Despite her reappearing dimple, Jennifer's cold smile did nothing to mask her disgust. "If you don't walk away right now, you will regret that decision. Get the fuck away." Jennifer's hand drifted to her purse. Slowly she turned the clasp and slipped her hand inside, her gaze never leaving the man's face. What was she looking for in that purse? Did she carry mace with her? Although Jennifer's tone of voice was calm, her vague threat seemed a bit stronger than the situation warranted. Nevertheless, it worked, and I admit I stood a little straighter, proud to be with someone who had the courage to defend herself. The drunken duo left in a huff, muttering a few disparaging remarks. We watched as the louts sauntered away, bumping into chairs and people until finding another pair of potential admirers.

"Jesus, what jerks—can you believe that? Listen, Jennifer, let's—"

"It's Jenn. Please, call me Jenn, not Jennifer." I didn't know why that mattered to me, but I felt the need to differentiate myself. I was already learning to be more like Jennifer—I was learning how to stand up for myself.

"Listen, Jenn. Let's get the hell out of here. We're going to my cottage. I'm getting hungry and we'll be more comfortable away from these drunken losers. It's an easy walk, less than a mile from here. I have cheese and crackers. And I make a terrific Key Lime Martini." I was already feeling the effects of my drinks, and another martini was a terrible idea.

"I don't know. I mean, I'm leaving Key West in a few days, flying back to Hartford, and I need to start getting ready, you know pack my things. I shouldn't get to bed too late."

"I'm not taking no for an answer. Besides," Jennifer stopped walking when we reached the bar. She looked right into my eyes and grabbed my arm. "I need your help. You really are the answer to my prayers. This is important." Part of me wanted to say no. Part of me wanted to walk away and never look back. But my curiosity got the better of me. What could be so important? How could I help this woman? Nothing made sense. Although I did welcome the idea of a walk in the fresh air and some food to soak up the alcohol. Besides, Joe and his sunburned rodeo clown had meandered to the far end of the bar, and now they were shooting unfriendly glances our way.

"OK. But I can't stay for long." Jennifer dismissed my tentative offer to share the bar bill and grabbed a bunch of twenties from her wallet. She left the money on the bar in front of the stools where we'd first met. She didn't wait for change. I followed closely behind, dragging my umbrella and my tired feet into the alley. I remember whispering the words under my breath, "Curiosity killed the cat." But rather than filling my heart with dread, the words made me smile as I stroked the dimple on my right cheek.

CHAPTER 3

"Wait," I called out, reaching for Jennifer's arm as we navigated the back streets. I felt dizzy from the drinks, the heat and humidity, and being with a woman who had passed as my identical twin. Rather than clearing my head, the walk filled my brain with the fog of dreams, a fantastic landscape.

"Jennifer—Are you real? Am I experiencing some drunken hallucination?" I asked, leaning on my new friend for support. "Did that bartender put something in my drink? Am I delusional?" I'd forgotten what it felt like, having someone to lean on.

"I don't think you're hallucinating. If you are, then I am too. We're almost there. Put one foot in front of the other." I followed Jennifer's advice and concentrated on walking. I focused on breathing and staying upright, knowing she was there to catch me if I stumbled.

"This is it, home sweet home." Jennifer led me down a short garden path, toward a two-story conch house set back from the street. The porch lights illuminated the floor to ceiling windows and louvered, black hurricane shutters. Both stories of the cottage were graced with wide porches stretching the width of the home. I tried to read the brass plate next to the door. I could tell it was from The Historical Society. Although the letters were blurry, the date was clear. The well-preserved house had been standing on this small plot of land since 1890. "This cottage has been in my husband Jim's family forever."

Thinking about generations of Jim's family caused a deluge of new questions to flood my mind. I staggered to the door. "So, did a member of your husband's family ever drink whiskey at Sloppy Joe's bar with Hemingway? Any of Jim's relatives ever sail to Cuba with him? Maybe Hemingway took a member of Jim's family fishing in his boat," I said. I wasn't trying to be funny, but Jennifer laughed. "Or, maybe they rocked in their rocking chairs together, right on this very porch, petting a six-toed cat, dreaming of Africa, or the next big adventure." I may have been slurring my words.

"Hmm. I rather doubt Hemingway and Jim's relatives traveled in the same circles. But to be honest, I never thought to ask him," Jennifer said as she opened the front door.

A blast of central air conditioning welcomed me as I entered the cottage. I looked around the foyer and stepped into the living room, taking in my new surroundings. Jennifer turned on two porcelain lamps and the overhead fan. I sank into an armchair and removed my sandals without thinking.

"Oh, my god, I'm sooo sorry," I said. My speech was definitely slurred. "I tracked mud into your beautiful home. I should have taken my sandals off outside on the porch."

"Not to worry, the maid comes twice a week." A maid. *How nice*, I thought. Then, *Of course, this woman has a maid.*

Jennifer got to work in the kitchen. I heard the refrigerator door opening and closing, the musical tinkling of glasses, and I realized I was famished. I hadn't eaten since a late breakfast around eleven o'clock that morning. Other than a cup of strong Cuban coffee earlier that afternoon and the martinis, I was running on empty. I tried to focus on the abstract painting above the fireplace, a swirl of greens and yellows and oranges that made the room spin even faster.

Jennifer carried a silver tray into the living room and set it upon the antique trunk in front of the matching armchairs. I admired the artful arrangement of cheeses and a French baguette, sliced mango and pear. I eyed the two glasses and a frosty, cold bottle of something promising.

"I'm out of limes, so no more Key Lime Martinis for you. Do you like Prosecco?" Jennifer poured and handed me a glass. I glanced down, distracted by the flash of her diamond rings and then her fingernails.

"Your nails are perfect. They look like little shells," I said. They were pearlescent pink and professionally polished. I'd never been one to waste money or time on manicures or pedicures.

I reached out to hold one of Jennifer's hands and studied her nails a moment longer. The color was subtle. I let Jennifer's hand slip away, and I nibbled on a slice of mango.

We sipped our Prosecco and fell back into an easy conversation comparing our lives, our looks, our families, our likes, and dislikes. And then, regrettably, we moved onto the topic of our taste in fashion. Looking back, that moment was our first critical encounter with Robert Frost's two roads diverged in a yellow wood. With each fork in the road, my doppelganger strolled deeper and deeper into a forest of bad ideas, luring me into the thicket with a trail of captivating clues. And I did nothing to stop her. Like an innocent victim in a twisted fairytale, I followed blindly.

"What size do you wear?" Jennifer asked.

"What size? Do you mean shirts?"

"Sure, what size shirts, dresses, jeans, everything?"

"Mostly Size 8. I like my clothes loose though," I added, although it was obvious. I was dressed in my vacation uniform; a pair of baggy, black pants, elastic waist, topped with an oversized gray T-shirt. When it came to color, I'd always relied on a neutral palette. Gray, black, beige. My double on the other hand, favored bold colors. She'd left her form-fitting trench coat in the foyer, and I admired the outfit underneath. Her neon-green, V-neck shirt fit her like a second skin, cut low, closely hugging her body. She wore a tight cotton skirt that stopped more than a few inches above her knees. The tropical design, bold with splotches of pink, green palms, yellow flowers matched the abstract painting on the wall. The overall effect wasn't my style, but Jennifer looked amazing. Right down to her perfectly painted, mother-of-pearl finger and toenails.

Was that the moment Jennifer suggested the idea of switching clothes? Or did that happen the next day? The timeline of events blurred like a photograph unfocused, distorting into unrecognizable, pixelated memories. I held out my fluted glass for more of the bubbly wine.

* * *

I clawed my way out of another end-of-vacation, back-to-school nightmare—those uninvited August visitors that soaked my sheets and coated my skin. This time I dreamed I was standing at the front of my classroom, wearing old sweatpants and a tight T-shirt with no bra. The shirt had a humiliating message written across my chest in bold letters: *Teachers do it with class*. I scrambled to find my lesson plan in a collage of random papers and file folders layering my desk. The students waited for me to begin, their brazen sneers judging me. Their teacher wasn't prepared for the first day of school and they all knew it. One student started to laugh. Others began pointing to the message on my shirt, mocking me. The entire class joined in the laughter as I crouched in the corner of the room, squeezing my eyes shut, like a toddler who thinks, *If I can't see you, you can't see me.*

Other than my back-to-school nightmare, I'd slept quite peacefully in one of the twin beds once used by the Moriarty sons. Although I had no clear memory of what happened after too many glasses of Prosecco the night before, I imagined it took very little arm-twisting to convince me to spend the night in Jennifer's cottage. I was probably in no condition for the walk back to my hotel. With the extra bedroom in the cottage, it made sense for me to stay the night. That's what I told myself.

Mostly awake, I reminded myself that despite the nightmare, I'd prepared for the beginning of school weeks before I left for my Florida vacation. Although I dreaded the end of summer and the start of another academic year, my lesson plans were ready. They included the same assignments, the same novels I'd used to teach 9th Grade English the year before. I had a curriculum to follow, and I didn't completely blame my students for their lack of appreciation for what the district deemed "good literature." I had about as much choice in the matter as they did.

Not ready to face the day, I let my mind wander to last year's most promising student, Addison Morris. Last spring I'd caught him in the school library, searching online for a plot summary of *To Kill a Mockingbird*. Incredulous, I'd confronted him. "Addison, tell me why you need this? Why can't you simply read the book?"

"It's boring, Miss Cooper. Besides, I don't have time, too much homework," he said.

"Addison, *To Kill a Mockingbird* is considered a great novel, it's anything but boring, and besides, summarizing each chapter of *To Kill a Mockingbird* happens to be your homework too."

"Yeah, but, Miss Cooper, reading a great book, that shouldn't *feel* like homework, right? Don't you want us to love reading? All these assignments you give us, the character analyses, finding themes and connections to our own lives, summarizing chapters. I know you mean well, but really, they're boring assignments. And the books you make us read, they're really old." I'd tried not to take Addison's comments personally. I'd been working on developing a thicker skin. It was a mistake to be overly sensitive when teaching teenagers.

But the fact was, I had a professional obligation to teach the curriculum the district provided, and I was required to follow the syllabus. My own evaluation depended upon it. Homework and written assignments were mandatory. Even if I wanted to, I couldn't give my students free rein to read whatever they wanted to read. Many kids would read nothing at all. The more promising students, like Addison, might choose poorly written bestsellers or Young Adult novels peppered with vampires, designed to entertain, rather than great classic literature that might encourage them to think beyond their own small worlds.

I untangled myself from the damp sheets and turned my freed body to face the wall. I had to admit, I understood why my students were unwilling to struggle over the meanings of archaic words or attempt to navigate awkward sentences. I understood that for most of my students, freshman English was irrelevant. They probably viewed me as another dull English teacher, an anachronism, posing stoically at the front of a classroom filled with marred desks and chairs, day after day, year after year, with neither purpose nor end in sight. They knew the truth about me; their teacher wrestled with boredom too.

I tried to drift back to sleep, shaking off thoughts about Dickinson High School. I hovered somewhere on the spectrum of oblivion. The light seeped into the room like a vapor and penetrated the thin shade of my closed eyelids.

Tap tap. Tap tap. I tried to ignore the persistent knocking on the door. *Tap tap tap.* The sound reverberated around my head, like a pinball thrust from bumper to bumper in one of those old pre-video-game machines. I flipped onto my back and covered my eyes with my arms. I felt as though someone was trying to chisel a hole deep into my skull. *Tap tap. Tap tap tap.*

"Jenn, are you awake?"

"I'm awake now," I groaned. I glanced at the clock on the dresser. It was half-past seven. The door creaked as Jennifer opened it a crack. "Come on in," I said, covering myself again with the damp sheet. Jennifer bounced into the room, sliding onto the matching twin bed. She was already dressed for the day, looking too perky and acting too energetic for this early in the morning. How did my double wake up looking so rested and glamorous? *What was her secret?*

"We're going to have fun today," Jennifer said, her voice too loud. "First things first, though. I bought coffee and croissants from Chez Jacques. It's still cool enough outside to eat breakfast on the porch. There's a robe for you, and don't worry—it's clean." Jennifer pointed to a white terrycloth robe hanging from a hook on the back of the bedroom door. I hardly cared about the cleanliness of the robe given the foul state of my own body. "After we have our breakfast, we'll plan the rest of the day, okay?" I didn't know what she meant by "plan the rest of the day," but I had no other pressing matters, and my curiosity clawed at me like a playful cat. I pulled myself up and leaned uncomfortably against the cold metal headboard. I'd keep an open mind, at least until my morning coffee.

"Okay, as long as I'm back at the hotel by six or seven o'clock at the latest," I said.

"No problem. See you downstairs."

"Wait," I said. "What did you mean? Last night? About needing my help? What was so important?"

"Later. We'll talk later." Jennifer grinned, exposing her dimple. My dimple. And then she started singing a random song about being on the road again as she closed the door behind her.

CHAPTER 4

I wondered how much longer I'd have to wait to learn what was really going on with Jennifer Moriarty and what she'd meant about needing my help. How could I be the answer to her prayers? It made no sense. But she was right about one thing: first things first and that meant coffee.

I pulled my body out of bed and sniffed my armpits, repulsed by the scent. God, I was in desperate need of a shower. I slipped the terrycloth robe over my grungy shirt and underwear. I tried to run my hands through my snarled hair but my fingers became tangled in the ratty nest. I needed my scrunchie. *Where was it?*

There were no mirrors in the room, thank god. Only the two twin beds, a small dresser with a clock, a lamp on the nightstand. The whitewashed walls were spotless. The window shades were a yellowing rattan. The bedsheets and lightweight blankets, a creamy eggshell color. Everything fresh and simple in that room. I longed to crawl back into bed, to remain in that pristine room all morning, to prolong the feeling of contentment, of comfort. But Jennifer waited for me, and I needed aspirin with my coffee.

As I made the bed, I realized I was looking forward to spending more time with a woman I had known for a few waking hours. I looked forward to breakfast on the porch of the cottage. I'd forgotten what that meant, to look forward to anything at all. And despite my headache, I felt myself smiling as I navigated the steep, rickety wooden stairs to join my doppelganger on the front porch.

* * *

After breakfast and a much-needed shower, I sat in the kitchen, waiting for the bleach and conditioning solution to turn my dull tresses into a vibrant, shiny, full-bodied head of hair, with "highlights and lowlights, and multiple shades to add dimension and play up facial features," making me look more youthful. That's what the promise on the back of the boxed, hair coloring kit assured the consumer. Jennifer promised something a bit different, something Nice-and-Easy couldn't promise. That hair treatment would make me look even more like Jennifer. That was the point of the experiment, and although I didn't understand why it was so important to her, I went along with Jennifer's idea of fun.

Jennifer held up a small mirror so I could admire her work. Slices of foil, folded over random locks of hair, graced my face like a lightweight crown. She was enjoying herself, experimenting on me, her new friend, with this do-it-yourself method of hair coloring. She danced around the kitchen and sang along with Beyoncé songs blasting from the home's invisible audio system. I realized Jennifer would never trust her own precious hair to a drugstore kit. But that didn't trouble me. It was only hair.

"Okay, lady. We need to wait forty minutes for the solution to work," she said, referring to the directions on the box. "Let's play a game." Jennifer turned the music down low with a click of her remote.

"I'm not really a game-playing sort of person." I didn't know what Jennifer had in mind. Trivial Pursuit? Pictionary? Not my thing.

"You'll like this one, trust me. It's called Two Truths and a Lie." I knew all about that game. The rules were simple enough. One player shares three statements about herself. Two factual statements, one lie. The other player has to guess the veracity of the statements. Janet Rousseau from the English department played that game to introduce herself to her students at the beginning of each school year. The kids usually guessed wrong. Even though she was only in her thirties, Janet was a grandmother of five. She'd married a man in his sixties with three adult children.

She never told her students that part of the truth. Her actual lie was a lie of omission.

I considered the merits of playing this childish game with Jennifer. It was a way to pass the time while my highlights cooked; an innocent strategy to learn more about my double's life. I still had questions that might have been too personal to ask directly. "Okay. Fine. But you go first." I wondered how revealing, how deep into her private life Jennifer would be willing to go.

"Fantastic! This will be fun, you'll see." Jennifer positioned her bare, perfectly pedicured feet on the edge of the kitchen table. Her hands cradled the back of her head. "Here goes. Two truths and a lie. One: My husband and I have an incredibly happy marriage." Jennifer's poker face revealed nothing. "Two: My son, Martin, is very shy, but he's a brilliant computer geek. Three: I always wanted to be a teacher." I knew which statement was the lie despite the lack of clues on Jennifer's face. There was a tone of wistfulness in her voice as she mentioned her marriage—it was obvious. I decided I wouldn't go there. I didn't care about winning the game and didn't think Jennifer cared about winning either. Perhaps both of us wanted to share information. Perhaps both of us wanted to swap our secrets with a seemingly harmless stranger. Yeah, I could play *that* game.

"I'm guessing that last statement is the lie. You never wanted to be a teacher, did you?"

"Wrong. I always wanted to be a teacher." Jennifer removed her feet from the table, replacing them with her elbows, and she cradled her chin in the back of her hands. I enjoyed watching her as she breezed through space slowly with the grace of a dancer. "I used to play school when I was a kid. I'd line up my stuffed animals on my bed and read books to them. I'd give them homework assignments. My mom bought me this little toy blackboard for my birthday one year. I loved it," she said with a regretful lilt in her voice.

I knew other teachers who claimed to have a similar professional calling. For me, teaching was a fallback profession. My dad liked to quote George Bernard Shaw; *Those who can, do; those who can't, teach.* I never believed I had the talent to make it as a writer. I took the safer route, teaching. A paycheck. A pension. "What happened? Why didn't you become a teacher?"

"During my junior year of college, I fell in love. My husband is ten years older than I am. Jim is old-fashioned in some ways. He wanted me to stay home to raise our kids. He had plenty of family money and a successful business. Jim convinced me it was for the best. He had the career, and therefore I didn't need one. Now it's too late," she said. Gazing out the kitchen window, Jennifer's eyes glistened.

"It's not too late," I said, trying to shift the mood. "I've met lots of second-career teachers. I can think of four colleagues of mine, stay-at-home moms who decided to pursue a teaching career after their kids left for college." Jennifer had stopped listening. She seemed eager to move on from the teaching career she never pursued.

"Do you want to guess again? Or should I tell you the lie?"

"Let me guess." I fake-frowned, tilting my head to one side. I pretended to struggle with my choice. "The first statement? Your marriage?"

"You guessed it. My marriage is the lie. We don't have a happy marriage, Jim and I." I wanted to know more about that topic, but I didn't probe. I was afraid she'd think I was being nosy. I waited, hoping she'd say more, and Jennifer didn't disappoint.

"We're on the verge of a legal separation," she said. "He's rarely at home as it is. He comes to the house from time to time, to pick up clothes, or occasionally to spend the night. My son, Martin, believes he's traveling for business. That's what Jim tells us. But I know better. He needs time away from me, and I don't really blame him. He's sorting things out."

"I'm sorry, Jennifer," I said.

"Don't be. I mean, it is what it is, right? Ours is not the first marriage to fail after a good try. And who knows—we can still patch things up. There's hope." She shrugged her shoulders. "And now it's your turn, Jenn. Two truths and a lie." I wanted time to process what I'd heard and to come up with three of my own statements, but Jennifer was drumming her fingers on the table and staring at me. I inhaled deeply and as I exhaled, allowed unfiltered thoughts to emerge from some dark, subconscious hiding place.

"Okay. Two truths and a lie. One: I want to write a novel, but I don't have time to do it. Two: I haven't had sex in about eighteen months. Three: My father encouraged me to be a doctor." I surprised myself, mentioning my nonexistent sex life. *Why would I tell anyone, let alone a stranger, about such a private matter?*

"The lie has to be the second statement. Please don't tell me you haven't had sex in eighteen months." Of course, Jennifer would guess the no sex statement was the lie. I was almost too ashamed to admit the truth, but what the hell, I decided to play by the rules.

"That statement is true," I said. "Regrettably, unfortunately, unhappily true."

"Oh, Jenn, I'm so sorry."

"Don't be. As you said, it is what it is, right? Guess again," I said, moving the game forward. I had no desire to reveal more details about that topic.

"Okay. The doctor statement is a lie, right?"

"Yeah, that's the lie. My father didn't encourage me about anything. In fact, he discouraged me all the time. About everything."

"What do you mean? Give me an example." Jennifer was interested in what I had to say. She cared. She wanted to know me, to really know me.

"Here's an example," I said. "I must have been seven or eight. My folks had taken me to visit Emily Dickinson's homestead. My mother had bought me an anthology of Emily Dickinson's poetry. On the way home, I memorized the words of one poem. I recited the lines aloud, waiting for my parents' accolades."

"What was the poem?" Jennifer asked. "Do you still remember it?"

"I do. Let's see. . .

If I can stop one heart from breaking,
I shall not live in vain;
If I can ease one life the aching,
Or cool one pain,
Or help one fainting robin
Unto his nest again,
I shall not live in vain.

"My mom was impressed. My father didn't say a word. 'Don't you like that poem, Daddy?' I asked. God, I hungered for his approval. 'It's not my favorite,' he said. I wouldn't let it go. 'Daddy, haven't you ever stopped one heart from breaking?' Not a word from my father. He turned the radio louder. I leaned toward the front seat. 'Did you hear me, Daddy?' He ignored me and so I kept pushing. 'I guess you've lived your life in vain,' I said. All I wanted was his attention. Wasn't that the point of memorizing the poem?" Jennifer was truly listening to me, hanging on every word. I felt like I was on a stage, under the bright lights, enjoying my adoring audience of one.

"Ouch, oh dear, I'll bet your father freaked," she said. "What did he say?"

"Oh god, he was furious. 'That's enough, Jennifer,' he snapped at me. 'Besides, any idiot can memorize a poem.' That's what he said. That's what he said to his only child. He called me an idiot."

I'd never forget those words. They slashed deep, leaving a scar to help me remember the pain. *Any idiot can memorize a poem. But not any idiot can write a poem.* I'd show my father what I could do. I wasn't an idiot.

Jennifer had a pensive look on her face, as if she understood my pain. "So, is that when you started visiting writers' homes?"

"As a matter of fact, Emily Dickinson's house was my first writer's home, the first of many. And you know, the words of that poem haunted me. They still haunt me. *I shall not live in vain, I shall not live in vain.* God, listen to me. It's pathetic. I believed I'd stopped blaming my father years ago for every misfortune in my life. I thought he was off the hook for my bad choices. But here I am, all my petty complaints come pouring forth from some subterranean well of discontent. Why am I telling you all this?"

"Because you can trust me. That's why," Jennifer said. And at that moment in time, I believed her. Yes, she was someone I could trust.

We were deep into our individual childhood grievances when the timer went off. My hair was ready, my transformation launched, and the day was still young.

* * *

At four o'clock that afternoon, Jennifer and I stood side by side in the downstairs powder room, in front of a large antique mirror hanging above the pedestal sink. The overall impression was striking. We may have looked as if we were separated-at-birth twins the moment we met. But now, we were practically clones. Hair, eye makeup, bronzer, lipstick, one of Jennifer's silk blouses unbuttoned much lower than I'd ever dared, completed the look. The Jennifer look. Jenn Cooper had shed the dull chrysalis trapping her for decades. A second, magnificent Jennifer Moriarty had emerged from the cocoon.

We gazed at our reflections in awe. Back and forth, from one face to the other. Then for some inexplicable reason, Jennifer started to giggle. Soon we were both laughing uncontrollably, clutching our stomachs, and gasping for breath, staggering back into the living room, as if intoxicated.

"Stop, stop, please, stop, it hurts," I cried out as I tried to catch my breath. Neither one of us could explain what struck us as so comical that afternoon. But somehow it didn't matter. We were both laughing with abandon and experiencing a unifying moment. *Is this what true friendship feels like?* I wondered.

"I don't want to leave this cottage," I said, finally settling down. I let my eyes roam around the living room. "I want to *be* that other woman in the mirror. The woman with the great hair. The woman with the cottage and two sons, and a marriage that needs a little patching up," I said, admitting to myself and to Jennifer the truth that had momentarily consumed me. "Hey. I might be able to patch up that marriage of yours, if you'd let me." Jennifer started to laugh again. Yes, I wanted to be that woman. The woman who could laugh at anything or nothing at all.

"Oh, Jenn," Jennifer said, once she too had caught her breath. "There may be one small problem. I mean, you haven't had sex in eighteen months. Do you think you're ready to patch up someone's marriage? But, you know, you don't have to go back to Hartford tomorrow. In fact. . ." Then she sat up and peered into my eyes. Her expression was serious. "Don't go back to Hartford tomorrow. Stay." She practically whispered the words. "I need you here."

"I can't stay," I laughed. "I have a job. I don't want to, but I have to go back."

"Do you?" she said. "Do you really have to go? What if. . ." Suddenly, Jennifer grabbed my arm so tightly the pain made me wince. There was something dangerous in her voice, a cold seriousness in her eyes that startled me. There was something in the way she said, "What if. . .," that lifted the hairs on the nape of my neck. I sat up, pulling back from Jennifer's grasp. Sensing my discomfort, she unclasped her hand and quickly grinned, her eyes dead-of-winter cold.

"What if. . . we have a wonderful dinner tonight to celebrate our new friendship," she said, slowly. "What if we have our own little party, get takeout food from the best restaurant in Key West, play a few games, and then I'll walk you back to your hotel by ten o'clock." *How do I say no to this woman who wants to celebrate our friendship?* I rubbed my arm, trying to erase whatever doubt or discomfort I may have felt moments before.

"Oh, Jennifer. I don't know."

"What if. . . we play Truth or Dare after dinner?" Jennifer asked. Truth or Dare? An odd choice for two grown women. Even more childish than Two Truths and a Lie. Almost creepy. I really was in no mood for another silly game, but I didn't want to offend my host. I'd be leaving soon, and why not maintain the friendship, such as it was, even long distance? Maybe I'd return to Key West during my February vacation to escape the New England snow and ice. Jennifer might want me to stay with her right here in her cottage. I still had to pack, and check out of the hotel, and get a good night's sleep before my trip home. Jennifer must have sensed my reluctance. I needed convincing.

"I know, I know. It's a silly idea. I haven't played that game since high school. But why not? Please, please, please say you'll stay!"

Already under her spell, I ignored the truths and the lies within Jennifer's proposal. *What if* I'd paid attention that night? *What if* I'd followed my instincts to run like hell? I'd ask myself those questions over and over again. Hindsight is 20/20, but all the clichés in the English language couldn't erase what happened next.

CHAPTER 5

We sat across from each other on the living room floor, separated by the antique trunk covered with takeout containers and a pitcher of Sangria. In between mouthfuls of Jamaican Jerk chicken, spiny lobster sauté, and skillet corn salad, Jennifer explained her rules for Truth or Dare. "I can't believe you've never played. What did you do for fun in high school?"

"Fun? I didn't have fun in high school. I mean, I read a ton of books. I suppose that was fun. Saturday night study groups with the other kids taking honors and AP classes. Really, all I cared about was keeping my grade point average up. At the time, I thought that was important."

"Oh, poor you! Studying was definitely not my idea of fun in high school. My friends and I would play Truth or Dare all the time when my parents went out. We had plenty of my dad's vodka to loosen us up," Jennifer said.

"Truth or Dare? I don't know. I mean, what's remotely fun about eating raw eggs or talking about your most embarrassing moments? You consider that fun? I call it silly."

"Silly is good, Jenn. Trust me. You need more silly in your life." Jennifer had a point. My life was devoid of silliness. "Let's try it. Don't be a party-pooper. Besides, if you don't like it we can stop and do something boring. We can read books if you'd like. I bet I can find a book or two around here someplace."

"Fine. I'll try it," I said, filling both goblets with more of Jennifer's homemade Sangria.

"You can even go first. Do you want Truth or Dare?" Jennifer pushed. "Pick one."

"Truth."

"Okay. Truth it is. I can ask you anything. And remember, you have to answer honestly. Ready?" I nodded, although I didn't feel the least bit ready. "How much money would it take for you to agree to switch lives with me for one month?" Jennifer asked. I must have swallowed the wrong way because I started coughing and spat a mouthful of partially chewed chicken into my napkin. I held up my finger to let Jennifer know I wouldn't choke. I simply needed a moment.

"Where did that crazy question come from?" I asked when I was able to speak again.

"What do you mean?" Jennifer asked. "It's not crazy. Everyone has their price, right?"

"Switch lives? No way. Never."

"$1,000?"

"Are you serious?"

"Okay, $10,000?"

I laughed and took another swallow of Sangria. "Jennifer, you're insane. Besides, it would never work."

"A million dollars? Admit it—you'd swap lives for a million dollars. It would only be for one month."

"The truth?" I stopped laughing.

"Yes, the truth. That's the whole point of this game."

"Okay. Not even for a million dollars. I wouldn't swap lives with you."

"What if I told you that I needed you to do this for me? What if I said it was a matter of life or death?"

"Not funny, Jennifer. Be serious."

"Now I'm offended." Jennifer pouted, her hand fluttered at her throat. "What would be so terrible? I have a wonderful life." The last thing I wanted was to offend her, a generous woman who had shared her home, provided delicious meals, and offered her friendship to me. Jennifer had given me a memorable ending to a forgettable summer vacation. I didn't want to fight with her over a stupid game.

"It's not that I wouldn't be tempted. I mean, it would be fun. Wearing your amazing clothes, living in a beautiful house—two homes as a matter of fact. And having time to start my novel." I picked up my fork and pushed the last of my chicken to the side of my plate, suddenly losing my appetite. "And it would be a great way to avoid all those back to school teacher meetings. But we'd never get away with it." Jennifer shook her head, ready to jump in and contradict me. "I know, I know, we look alike. But there are differences. The way we talk for example. Our voices are completely different."

"Your voice is deeper than mine, that's true. I love it. Very sexy," Jennifer said, lowering her voice to sound more like mine.

"Ha! Sexy? I'm not sure about that. And what about our accents? There's a slight difference. And speaking of accents, why don't you have more of a southern accent?"

"Most people who live in South Florida aren't native Floridians. Didn't I tell you last night? I grew up in the Midwest." There was plenty about our conversation the night before that I didn't remember. "Mostly, my accent's mainstream American, like yours, Jenn. We don't sound that different. But forget it. Let's get back to the game." I was happy to move on.

"Your turn, Jennifer. Truth or dare?" I asked.

She leaned back against the pillows propping her body up against the couch. "Truth."

I thought for a moment. What truth did I want to know about Jennifer? I wanted to know if Jennifer had been serious about swapping lives. No. Impossible. She couldn't have been serious. And what would be the point of bringing it up again? I looked at Jennifer sitting across from me, studying her perfect nails. What was she thinking about? And why in the world would a wealthy, classy woman with whom I had nothing in common other than our physical appearance, want to spend time with me? What was in it for her, this bizarre relationship? I wanted to know that too. Where were Jennifer's hidden imperfections? A woman who worked at being physically flawless, what was her Achilles heel? Other than the problem with her marriage, she seemed to have the perfect life.

Finally, I came up with a question for the game. A question that proved to be more important than I could have imagined. Jennifer's answer to my question would haunt me, even after I got to the bottom of all the Moriarty truths and lies. I asked the perfect question.

"What keeps you up at night?" Jennifer gazed up from her reverie.

"What do you mean?" She crossed her arms over her chest.

"You know. What do you worry about? What do you fear most? What keeps you up at night?"

"Oh, that."

"Yes, that. And it has to be the truth." I waited. Jennifer frowned at an invisible imperfection on her perfectly polished thumbnail. She twirled her goblet with the other hand, making the ice cubes clink against the glass.

"Well, I'd have to say, my son. Martin. I worry about him." I waited for more, but Jennifer seemed ready to leave it at that. Martin. She worried about her son, Martin.

"He's the shy one, right? The computer geek?"

"Yes." She made the ice cubes clink again and seemed mesmerized by the sound.

"Why does he keep you up at night?"

"He's fragile. Nothing like his older brother, Jason. Jason's confident, has lots of friends. He's an amazing athlete, solid student, an all-around great kid." Jennifer's eyes turned misty, her smile dreamy. "Poor Martin. He struggles so much." She looked up, worried, wanting to be sure I understood. "Oh, don't get me wrong. He's smart. He's probably even smarter than Jason. Just. . . introverted,

I guess that's the right word to describe him." And yet, clearly, she worried about Martin. He kept her up at night.

"That's not necessarily a bad thing. I'm introverted," I said. "For me, it was always about books. I'd hide away in my bedroom reading, not simply because I loved books, but also because I was shy around other kids. Right through high school." Jennifer nodded her head and grimaced.

"And look how you turned out!" Ouch. I tried not to take offense, but Jennifer started to giggle at her own little joke. The shrill laughter sounded forced, overly dramatic, and it continued for too long. At some point, I attempted to join in, tried to feign a smile. But listening to Jennifer carry on, I felt the hairs on the back of my neck lift again.

Jennifer stopped laughing as suddenly as she had begun. "I probably worry too much." She tilted her head to one side. "Martin will be fine. Just like you." She refilled our glasses with the last of the Sangria.

We carried our dishes and empty takeout containers into the kitchen. I rolled up my sleeves and leaned against the sink, ready to wash. Jennifer clamped her hand firmly on my shoulder, turning me toward her. "Maid's coming tomorrow. Leave the dishes. Go relax in the living room, and I'll make us hot tea. It's a special blend; and then it's time for something different, don't you agree? It's time to get serious."

I looked into my double's eyes, and the coldness I saw made me want to run, to get the hell out of that Key West cottage and never look back. As the room began to spin, I grabbed onto the kitchen counter, trying to steady myself. Jenn's hand felt like a bruise on my shoulder. I tried to shrug it off but her fingers dug into the soft flesh. My clammy hands, still gripping the edge of the counter, were about to slip.

"We've had enough truth for one night. It's time for a dare," Jennifer said, with a sinister smile. The words smashed into me like an ocean wave, knocking me down onto the kitchen floor. Jennifer picked me up under my arms and half-dragged me into the living room where I slipped into an armchair, waiting for my cup of tea. Jennifer's special brew. Waiting for whatever came next.

CHAPTER 6

"Miss Jennifer? Are you awake?" At the sound of an unfamiliar voice, I cracked open one eye. The cheerful words penetrated the bedroom door and the thick fog of sleep. "Miss Jennifer, do you want me to clean the bedroom now? Should I come back later?"

I turned my head a few inches to the right, as I tried to take in my surroundings. This wasn't the Key West two-star hotel room I'd inhabited for the past few weeks. Black and white photographs adorned the walls. Sunlight filtered through the slats of the shutters, branding the white comforter with thick gray bars. This wasn't the narrow twin bed I'd slept in the night before.

"Miss Jennifer, are you awake now? Do you want coffee?" The accent was Spanish. Too quickly, I shifted my horizontal body to an upright position and immediately felt the room spinning. I tried desperately to fit the puzzle pieces together to form a reasonable explanation for my whereabouts.

"Okay," I moaned, wondering but not caring who might be on the other side of the door. My head felt ready to explode. Coffee was exactly what I needed, and it didn't matter who was willing to bring it to me.

"I'll be back in a minute!" Turning my head a few more inches to the right, I squinted to block the sunlight shooting daggers into my brain. My eyes focused on a green T-shirt and tropical patterned skirt laid out neatly on a blue velvet lounge chair near a window. The skirt seemed familiar. These weren't my clothes. *Where were my clothes?* More importantly, where was my phone? My head pounded. Flashes of jagged lights pulsated around the perimeter of my left eye. I didn't remember having too much to drink the night before. I vaguely recalled what a real hangover felt like, and these physical sensations were different.

Struggling to pull myself out of the bed, I looked around for a bathroom. As blood rushed to my feet, I caught sight of my reflection in the mirror hung over a rattan dresser. What in god's name was I wearing? I didn't own silk anything let alone this black, transparent slip of a nightgown barely covering me. Suddenly, as a wave of nausea wracked my body, I worried I wouldn't find a bathroom in time. I sank to the wood floor and dragged myself on hands and knees in the direction of the voice I'd heard moments before.

I opened the bedroom door and heaved my body into the narrow hallway. I lurched to the bathroom at the end of the hall getting there just in time. Partially digested bits of food exploded like lava, burning my throat and leaving a wretched taste in my mouth. After rinsing my mouth with cold water, I was able to walk upright back to the bedroom. Jennifer's bedroom. How had I ended up in Jennifer's room?

I slid back onto the bed as jagged bolts of lightning around my left eye continued to pulsate. I vaguely remembered the details of Jennifer's farewell dinner the night before, a meal that proved to be too rich. Jennifer's recipe for Sangria didn't mix well with a takeout dinner of spiny lobster and jerk chicken. And was there key lime pie for dessert? That combination must have made me ill.

The hammering in my head amplified as the commotion of Key West's rooster population provided a raucous morning concert. I looked around the room again, searching for my phone. A collection of glass, perfume bottles shimmered on a chest of drawers, but there was no phone. My eyes tried to focus on a small, antique writing desk across from the bed. There was an old-fashioned quill pen and what looked like an envelope propped up against a quaint, crystal candelabra. Something was written on that envelope. Blurred letters. *What did it say?*

I slipped out of bed again, my head still pounding. I pushed the rickety chair away from the desk and sank into its cracked leather seat cushion. I leaned in, peering at that envelope until the letters stopped vibrating. Four letters. My name in capitals. JENN. I pulled a handwritten note from the envelope and carried it back to the bed. I read the message once, then again, and a third time, trying to make sense of the words.

Thanks for taking this dare. You're a lifesaver. And I mean that literally. We can do this. Everything you need to make this work is in my purse or car. I have everything I need. See you in one month. Passwords: JENN or jennifer'spassword.

Don't call me. I'll call you.

XXOO
Jennifer

What the fuck? What dare? What in god's name did Jennifer mean, See you in one month? Nothing in her letter made sense.

More knocking on the door. "Miss Jennifer, coffee time."

"Come in," I called out, hiding the note in my palm.

The door opened, and an excessively upbeat, heavyset woman sauntered into the room. She was carrying a tray, the same silver tray Jennifer had used for cheese and drinks the night we'd met. I locked eyes on the woman, thinking she looked familiar, but I was certain we'd never met. And then I quickly put two and two together, realizing she was the maid. Jennifer had mentioned a maid. She'd told me not to worry about my muddy sandals. The maid came twice a week. And the dishes. She wouldn't let me do the dishes. Bits of information came to me, carried to the shore on waves, depositing seashells of memories on a sandy beach. And this was Jennifer's bedroom and her clothes laid out on the chair. But where was Jennifer?

I watched as the woman placed the tray on the desk. A steaming mug of coffee and a basket of what looked like croissants.

"Café con leche, exactly how you like it," she said. How in the world did this stranger know how I liked my coffee? And then, of course, I realized the obvious. She assumed I was Jennifer. Jennifer Moriarty. I had to set her straight.

"Where's Jennifer?" I asked. The woman laughed.

"Oh Miss Jennifer, I think you had a very good time last night."

"I did, thank you. But. . . is there someone else in the house? Another Jennifer? Am I the only one here in the house this morning?" I asked, struggling to form coherent sentences. She looked at me, her eyebrows raised. I sounded ridiculous to this woman.

"Yes, I believe you are the only Jennifer in the house." The maid laughed and raised her eyebrows. "I don't see another Jennifer here, do you?" she asked. Then she pretended to search under the bed. She opened the closet door and then another door to a bathroom which turned out to be much closer than the one I'd reached in time to avoid a mess in the hallway.

Jennifer's maid continued her search for some mysterious guest who might be hiding. She laughed louder than necessary, the sound exacerbating my headache. "Come out, come out, wherever you are!"

"Sorry. I had too much to drink last night," I tried to explain, placing the palm of my hand to my forehead. I'd play this game with the maid, at least until I found Jennifer. "I'm pretty sure I brought a friend home with me last night, a girlfriend, of course." The maid must have known Jennifer Moriarty was married. She must have met Jennifer's husband, Jim. I didn't want to start rumors about an affair that never happened. Then I thought, *Why the hell not?* It wasn't my life or reputation at stake. Let people talk. What did I have to lose? "I think my friend slept in the boys' room."

"Well, your friend must have left before you went to bed, Miss Jennifer. There's no one in the other bedroom. I've already washed the dishes and cleaned the downstairs." The woman handed me the mug of coffee. "Would you like to have your breakfast in the kitchen while I change the sheets and clean upstairs? I'll carry the tray down for you."

I took a sip of the café con leche. Delicious. Perfect.

"Yes, that's what I'll do," I said. I'd search the downstairs for my phone. I'd find my purse. I'd call Jennifer. She must have stepped out, and she'd probably be back any minute. The maid held my mug as I stood again. I remembered the transparent nightgown I was wearing, feeling uncomfortably exposed in front of a stranger. The maid reached into the closet and handed me a plush robe, a soft turquoise that matched the room's décor. I slipped Jennifer's note into the robe's pocket. My body fully covered, I felt emboldened. I reached out for my coffee.

"What should I call you?" I asked. This seemingly random question elicited more groans and laughter from the maid. Jennifer Moriarty knew her name. The woman believed I was Jennifer, and I had no idea what I might say to convince her otherwise.

"Whatever you want to call me, Miss Jennifer."

"But I want to call you what you want me to call you. As a matter of fact, I don't want *you* to call *me* Miss Jennifer anymore. Call me Jenn, okay?"

"Whatever you say, Jenn. I can do that," she said, rolling her eyes.

"Tell me, please, what do you want *me* to call *you*?" I prodded, trying to sound normal.

"You keep calling me Maria, okay?" Maria. Jennifer's maid had a name. I was proud of my sleuthing skills. But at that moment, I cared more about finding my phone and finding Jennifer.

"Okay, Maria, you're the best, you know?" I said.

"I know, Miss—oh sorry—I know Jennifer. I'm the best. That's what you always tell me. Every time you see me, you always say *Maria, you're the best!*"

Go figure.

CHAPTER 7

I navigated the steep stairs and followed Maria down to the kitchen. I tried to make sense of the note Jennifer had left for me. I kept asking myself, *What happened last night?* The last thing I remembered was a cup of tea. Did Jennifer say it was chamomile? "This will help you sleep," she'd said. "It works like a charm."

After Maria went back upstairs, I swept through the downstairs rooms, clutching my mug of coffee close to my chest. The smooth, strong elixir helped to lift the fog clouding my brain. Not finding my cell phone, I eased into a chair at the small kitchen table, nibbled on a croissant, and tried to focus. The pastry felt like cardboard sticking to the insides of my cheeks. I swept crumbs from the table and rinsed my hands in the kitchen sink.

I returned to the living room, searching once more for my old straw handbag. That's where my phone would be. Where had I left it?

Distracted by a family photograph, I started examining the bookshelves, looking for more clues about Jennifer, her tastes, her family, her life. Devoid of books, the shelves displayed colorful pieces of pottery and one family photograph of a smiling husband, beautiful wife, and two sons. Jennifer had mentioned their names several times. Jason and Martin. One boy was the perfect, older son, and one was the shy, computer geek. Which one kept her up at night? The introverted son, like me.

I studied the photograph for a while, searching for answers. The boys looked nothing alike, as though they didn't belong in the same family. The younger son had dirty blond hair, and he wasn't handsome like his father. His features were not quite symmetrical. Large, wide, empty eyes. He didn't resemble his mother either. His skin was sallow, spotted with acne. His vacant, bored expression seemed familiar. I knew that look from teaching freshman English. I'd weathered my share of storms, standing before a sea of adolescent faces like this boy's. Those faces taunted me with their glazed "I'd-rather-be-anywhere-else" expressions.

The older son, Jennifer had told me, was a high school senior completing his college applications. He was the handsome one, athletic, popular. "God, where did the years go?" Jennifer had lamented. This son was definitely the better looking of the two boys. He'd inherited the best from both of his parents, his father's height and bone structure. He had his mom's coloring—darker hair with golden highlights, a warmer skin tone, and large, almond-shaped eyes like Jennifer. He was smiling broadly in the photograph and I noticed he had our dimple, too. *If I had a son this is what he might look like,* I thought as I studied the photograph.

Other than that one family photo, the living room held no secrets. Everything in its place, no clutter, complete order. I heard Maria's heavy footsteps on the stairs. I rushed back into the kitchen to clear my breakfast tray and place my coffee mug in the sink. I didn't want Maria to think I was lazy or that I expected special treatment. Although perhaps special treatment was exactly what Jennifer Moriarty was supposed to expect from her maid.

"I'm off now," Maria called.

"Thank you, Maria." I felt oddly proud, referring to Jennifer's maid by her first name.

"Have a safe drive back to Coral Gables, Miss Jennifer." Old habits die hard.

"Wait. Maria, please. Don't go yet." Her hand rested on the doorknob. I'd try once more to convince her that I wasn't Jennifer. I'd try once more to get the information I needed. "I know you think I was joking. But really. I'm not who you think I am. I look like Jennifer. I know, but I'm not her." Maria squinted at me, and her friendly smile disappeared, making me feel even more desperate. "Where do you think Jennifer Moriarty might be? Do you have any idea?" I asked, trying one last time.

"Okay, Miss Jennifer. You have a wonderful day," Maria said, shaking her head. I watched the door close, leaving me alone to figure things out.

I found a bottle of aspirin in the downstairs medicine cabinet. I swallowed three of the pills and cradled my aching head in my arms, leaning on the kitchen table, waiting for a hint of clarity. I pulled Jennifer's note from the pocket of my robe and read the words again.

Everything you need is in my purse. . . Her purse. Jennifer's purse. I would search for some clarity there. I grabbed the large, Gucci handbag I found hanging on a hook near the back entrance. It probably cost a month's teaching salary. I emptied the contents onto the kitchen table. A key ring, Jennifer's cell phone, her wallet, and a small makeup bag. A bottle of prescription medication. Xanax. Her cell phone. The items arranged on the table like a bizarre still-life painting, or a strange jig-saw puzzle. What did these puzzle pieces mean?

I had no use for Jennifer's purse. I needed to find my straw beach bag—the same one I'd used for the past eight summers. Where was it? I started to panic, thinking Jennifer must have taken everything that belonged to me. The key to my hotel room, my plane ticket, my wallet. And my journal tucked away safely in that straw bag. *Would Jennifer read it? What would she think?* My mind flashed again to the night before when we were stuffing our faces with spiny lobster, drinking Sangria, joking around, and playing Truth or Dare.

Truth or Dare. Truth or Dare. That silly adolescent game. What did it mean? I looked at the clock on the stove. 11: 45. How could that be? I still had to pack, to check out of the hotel, to catch a plane. And then the awful truth smacked me in the face. My mouth went dry, and my heart raced. My plane had already departed from Miami International Airport forty-five minutes ago. Jennifer Moriarty was on that flight. I'd bet my life on that, and maybe I already had.

Trembling uncontrollably at the kitchen table, I tried desperately to remember the details of Jennifer's question about swapping lives. Pieces of our conversation floated back to me. I struggled to remember that after-dinner dare. Jennifer's dare.

That strange tasting tea. Truth or Dare. It was just a game. I squeezed my eyes shut and willed those amorphous memories back into focus.

"We'll swap lives," she'd said. "Only one month. We can do it. I need you to do this. You said you hated all that back to school nonsense—let me take care of that. No one will know the difference." Did I try to talk Jennifer out of it? Why didn't I refuse? Bits and pieces of the conversation flashed and then evaporated into the ether of what must have been an alcohol-induced state. A pitcher of Sangria. But what I was experiencing was not a hangover. What else had Jennifer given me? The tea. *This will help you sleep,* she'd said. Her voice, hypnotic, reassuring. Why couldn't I remember?

I grabbed Jennifer's cell phone from the table. My hand shook as I tried to enter the first password she'd left me. JENN. It took effort and concentration to force my fingers to cooperate. After three or four tries, I was able to unlock the phone, and I immediately called my own cell number. I heard my monotone, gravelly, voice. *You've reached Jenn Cooper. Please leave a message.* My voice quivered as I left that first message: *Jennifer. What's going on? Call me, please.*

I glanced down at the wallet on the table. Tan leather, as large as a small clutch with a zipper closure stretched tight. I unzipped the top and began to explore the contents. A dozen credit cards. Jennifer's driver's license. And cash, so much cash. I counted ten twenties, followed by crisp, clean, hundred-dollar bills. Sticking together, brand-new. I grabbed the purse, turning it upside down. I shook out thick wads of bills. *Everyone has a price.* I remembered Jennifer saying those words to me. Did I have a price? I'd never swap lives with Jennifer for money. Or would I? Had I changed my mind about that dare? I counted the money. $20,000 in hundred-dollar bills. Was that my price?

* * *

I stared at my reflection in the bedroom mirror. Yes, the remarkable physical likeness fooled Maria. But I'd never be able to manage this charade with members of Jennifer's family. And if Jennifer's husband happened to come by, if he wasn't "traveling," he'd notice the differences. My voice and mannerisms. My body. My vocabulary and syntax. My reactions and affect. Jennifer's sons would know I couldn't possibly be their mother. *What were you thinking, Jennifer?* Was she serious about swapping lives? Was this a practical joke?

I stretched out on Jennifer's bed and waited for the pounding in my head to subside. More swatches of our conversation came back to me. I *had* tried to dissuade my double. "Oh, Jennifer, it's more complicated than you think. I can just about manage my teaching job, and you're not even a certified teacher. Wanting to be a teacher, playing school with your stuffed animals, and teaching freshman English are very different," I'd argued.

Jennifer wouldn't let it go. "Oh, please, anyone can follow a lesson plan. And just think, you can move into my Coral Gables home and have all that time to write. That's what you want, right? My study is waiting for you. You'll love it." We'd tossed the dare back and forth like we were playing with a beach ball. I felt my cares and my doubts melting away as I listened to Jennifer's melodic voice. I remembered something like a lullaby, pulling me into another world, guiding me down a fork in the road, the road that should have remained not taken.

* * *

I forced myself into the shower and leaned my quivering body against the glass mosaic tiles. I stood under the harsh force of the showerhead, the water temperature scalding my skin. Tears mixed with the water droplets streaming down the face of the glass shower door.

I scrubbed my body dry with the fluffy, white towels hanging on the back of the bathroom door. They smelled like summer with a hint of lavender, mocking my mood. Sitting on the bed, wrapped in her Turkish towel, I tried calling Jennifer again. I left another message, more desperate than the first. *Jennifer. I'm begging you. Please call me.*

Finding something comfortable to wear in Jennifer's closet was a challenge. I rejected the short skirts and tight tops Jennifer wore. On the other hand, I liked the way I looked in that silk blouse she gave me to wear, but I couldn't find it. I eventually settled on a demure sundress. It was sleeveless and form-fitting across the bodice. The flowing skirt, belted at the waist, a tropical print with a beige background, was not nearly as flamboyant as other choices in her closet. What mattered was that the dress felt comfortable, and the skirt fell well below my knees. There were several pairs of sandals to choose from, and miraculously they were my size as well, size seven and a half. Miraculous was an overstatement, I told myself. That particular shoe size was common, but still, I marveled at the series of coincidences.

I gazed again in the mirror above Jennifer's dresser. Who was that person staring back at me? Besides the obvious changes from the day before, my reflection appeared subtly different that morning. It wasn't just the clothes. My posture was straighter. My hair was shinier. I looked more vibrant, more like Jennifer Moriarty. Exactly like Jennifer Moriarty. I tried to call her again. Hearing my recorded voice, I started to sob. I left a one-word message for the woman who had caused this misery: *Please.*

* * *

I'd never driven a Mercedes before or any other luxury car for that matter. The model in the driveway looked sporty and brand new. It even had that intoxicating new car smell. Spotlessly clean, inside and outside, like Jennifer's cottage. Creamy beige leather seats, a gleaming white exterior. A ridiculous extravagance.

I fiddled with the key ring, then tried to figure out all the bells and whistles displayed on the car's dashboard. I set the GPS to *Home*, and despite my misgivings, I left the relative comfort and safety of Key West behind.

The trip was going to be a long drive, 160 miles. I'd take my time. The last thing I needed was a speeding ticket. I turned on the radio and discovered that Jennifer had been listening to an audiobook and was somewhere in the middle of the first chapter. A trashy romance novel—my definition of literary torture. By the end of chapter four, I realized that despite my low expectations, the novel's sordid story of adultery and lust engrossed me.

Adultery. Was that something I was heading toward in my life? In Jennifer's life? I hadn't had sex in a very long time. Although I'd told Jennifer it had been eighteen months, I'd stopped quantifying my celibacy. As I listened to the erotic scenes in the audiobook, I remembered what lust used to feel like, and the images brought me back to those familiar urges.

I had normal desires, like any woman my age. But unlike other women, I'd avoided social situations that might lead in the direction of romance. I knew teachers at Dickinson High School who immersed themselves in the online dating scene. It worked for them, but it wasn't for me. A colleague, Andrew Mulligan, once offered to fix me up with his wife's brother, a newly divorced father of three. A dentist. I'd declined the offer. Maybe it was his three kids under the age of ten, or more likely, it was the idea of that man's hands in a thousand different mouths that turned me off.

I stopped listening to the novel and let my mind wander to Lauren D'Angelo, head of the Social Studies department. Lauren had invited me to a speed-dating event in NYC last spring. What a nightmare. I'd spent seven minutes interviewing and being grilled by one prospective match before moving to another table, to talk with another prospective match. Every time the bell rang, every seven minutes, another opportunity presented itself to check out a potential soulmate. Ding, ding, ding. Yes, no, maybe. The experience was beyond humiliating. "Never again," I'd vowed. Celibacy was the tradeoff.

I stopped for gas around Key Largo, mile marker 88, and used the restroom inside the convenience store at the gas station. It might have been my imagination, but the young clerk behind the counter stared at me with a strange expression. It was more like a lustful leer, something I'd not encountered in a decade or more. *It must be the dress,* I thought. The guy could not have been older than twenty-one. He maintained his creepy expression as I paid for the gas with cash. Jennifer had left me more than enough money for this month-long experiment, and I wasn't ready to break any laws by using her credit card. Fraud accusations, a lawsuit, there might be all kinds of unintended consequences. I was already exhausted, knowing I had to scrutinize every decision I made until the nightmare ended. I felt the creepy guy's eyes follow me out to the car, and I forced myself not to look back.

I left the Overseas Highway that linked the Keys to the mainland and concentrated on the GPS directions. For some reason, Jennifer had programmed her GPS with a male voice that spoke with a sexy British accent. I laughed each time the voice gave a new direction in a clipped and formal tone. Jennifer must have had a thing for British men, or it was her sense of humor. Either way, listening to the directions was almost as entertaining as listening to the romance novel.

With every mile marker I passed, I worried I was moving closer and closer to what could be the biggest mistake of my life. The biggest mistake for Jennifer, too. I turned up the car's radio volume, trying to refocus on the wretched story filtering through the car speakers.

Driving closer and closer to Coral Gables, the doubts and terror started filling my chest with what felt like heavy boulders pressing against me, making even shallow inhalations painful. I began to sweat despite the air conditioning that was blasting and set to the coolest temperature possible. My blood pounded in my ears. My mouth dry, my throat parched. I felt lightheaded. *I'm falling apart*, I thought. *I'm having a heart attack. I'm going to die right here on U.S. Route 1, and I'll be buried in a Florida cemetery plot with some other woman's name on my gravestone. I'll be mourned by a husband and two amazing sons whom I've never met.* I pulled over to the side of the road, panting and gasping for breath. I willed myself to inhale deeply, to exhale slowly. *You're not going to die. You're not going to die. You're not going to die. This is not a heart attack. This is a panic attack. You will survive.*

CHAPTER 8

I turned right onto Jennifer Moriarty's shady street. The stately homes in the neighborhood and the wide avenues, lined with live oak trees, tamarind, coconut palms, and buttonwoods, beckoned me into a different world. Manicured lawns and perfectly landscaped front yards adorned the large, stucco, Mediterranean Revival and Spanish Mission houses. Their coral-colored, tiled roofs, their stone and brick driveways, archways, and balconies screamed old money. *You have arrived at your destination,* the GPS announced. And what a destination it was.

I parked Jennifer's Mercedes in the front circular driveway and sat in the car for several minutes, monitoring my breathing, inhaling deeply, exhaling slowly. I closed my eyes, clutching her key ring like a talisman, perseverating on the question that would become a refrain. Was it too late to turn back? Was it too late?

I grabbed the cell phone and tried to call Jennifer again, leaving another desperate message: *I'm in Coral Gables. I'm freaking out. I need you to call me and put an end to this scheme of yours, before it's too late. PLEASE!*

As I stared at Jennifer's key ring, heavy with multiple keys and fobs, my brain spun into a maelstrom of *what ifs* and *what abouts* and self-doubt. What if the teenage sons were home from school? What about sports or whatever extracurricular events filled their afternoons? What if the new school year hadn't begun yet, and I had to deal with both boys as I walked through that door? What if the key to the front door wasn't on that key ring? There were so many details about Jennifer's life I didn't know. Questions I hadn't asked. Answers I never knew I'd need. Why hadn't I asked the right questions? Why had I let Jennifer Moriarty con me into this madness? Was it too late?

My mind wandered, and I started to think about my own key ring and the key to my classroom at Dickinson High. Unlike the southern states, students in my district wouldn't begin classes until after Labor Day. But first, all those back-to-school meetings and workshops for teachers. How would Jennifer Moriarty survive that charade, pretending to be me? Her note assured me she had everything she needed to step into my life. My wallet held most of the information: my license, my credit card, my passwords written on a tiny strip of paper and tucked into a zipped compartment. And all the keys Jennifer needed hung on my key ring. The first term's schedule and lesson plans, my appointment calendar, back-to-school communications from my administrators, everything needed to begin the school year waited for Jennifer on my dining table. All Jennifer had to do was show up. Show up and be Jenn Cooper. For one month. That was the dare.

I pulled a lock of hair around my fingers, twirling it rhythmically, as the heat and humidity seeped into the parked Mercedes, daring me to make the next move. But I couldn't move. Instead, I closed my eyes and imagined my double sitting in the Teachers' Room, struggling through boring faculty meetings, the long convocation in the high school auditorium with its broken seats and inadequate air conditioning, the dull pep talks and welcome back speeches from long-winded administrators, the dreary conversations with colleagues about their amazing summer vacations. While Jennifer handled the back-to-school monotony, I'd have time to begin my novel, four weeks of uninterrupted writing time. In this gorgeous home. Maybe I could pull it off.

As perspiration seeped into the fabric of the sundress, more memories of that game with Jennifer seeped into my consciousness. My doppelganger had dangled her carrot skillfully, hypnotizing me with visions of a dream so real. *Was this the truth? Was this the dare?* The contours of Jennifer's pitch crept into my memory, and then the colorful details followed. "I dare you to swap lives with me for one month. This will be the best thing that has ever happened to you. Trust me." Trust her? I didn't know her.

About to suffocate on my circular thoughts, I finally grabbed the Gucci bag and opened the car door, swallowing gulps of somewhat cooler air. I approached the front door of Jennifer's house, filled with a sense of foreboding mixed with a hefty dose of curiosity. What waited for me behind that door? Would I be able to pull this off? Did I want to?

I reached out and turned the handle. I wasn't surprised to find the door locked. I fumbled with the key ring, trying three random keys before I felt the reassuring click of the door opening. As my breathing returned to something closer to normal, I stepped into the front foyer and shut the door behind me, trying not to make a sound. I stood in the foyer, listening for voices. Listening for music or the sound of a television, or raucous laughter. Nothing. Silence.

"Hello?" I called out. My voice cracked. "I'm home." This seemed to be what a mother would say after being away for a few days. No one answered. I forced myself to breathe deeply again. I lingered in the foyer and listened closely, pulling wayward strands of hair behind my ears as if that might help me hear better. Other than the drumbeat of my heart, I heard nothing. An empty house. An unexpected development and a stroke of good luck. I might have time to explore the place without interruption.

I held onto the cell phone as a drowning swimmer might grip a floating log. Jennifer had to call me back. In the meantime, I'd get my bearings before Martin and Jason and possibly Jennifer's husband returned from wherever they were. Or, I could jump back into the Mercedes and drive back to Hartford, confront Jennifer, and end the insanity. I still had options.

I glided past the foyer through the living and dining rooms. The interior of the Moriarty house was magnificent. Although considerably more formal than the Key West cottage, every room was tasteful and inviting. The impeccable kitchen gleamed with white and gray marble and stainless-steel, high-end appliances. I searched the inside of the refrigerator and freezer. Some frozen vegetables, eggs, butter, low-fat milk, cheese, wilted lettuce in the vegetable drawer. I noticed several tomatoes ripening on the windowsill. Was I supposed to make dinner for the family? It would take only one un-Jennifer-like meal to blow my cover. I wondered how I'd avoid that trap.

I tiptoed quietly through the downstairs' rooms, becoming familiar with the layout. My pulse raced as the fear of what or who I might encounter flooded my brain with chemicals triggering a fight or flight response. I clenched my fists, my senses heightened. I listened acutely, hearing only the insistent pounding of my heart.

I noted the back staircase off the kitchen, but my footsteps on those bare wooden stairs would surely announce my arrival to anyone on the second floor. I wasn't ready for a surprise confrontation with a family member. I moved to the front foyer and crept up the carpeted staircase, feeling like an intruder, which, of course, I was. I looked exactly like the mistress of the household, but playing the part convincingly was another matter.

I stood for several minutes at the top of the stairs. I listened, distracted by the sound of my shallow breathing. I was hyperventilating and becoming lightheaded. I looked around at the heavy, arched, wooden doors on three sides of the upstairs foyer. An open balcony with an ornate banister and railing overlooked the foyer below. Several doors stood ajar.

The first room I entered was obviously Jennifer and Jim's bedroom. A sudden wave of fatigue pressed down on me as I gazed at that luxurious king-size mattress. I felt an overwhelming urge to curl up in the middle of that bed in a fetal position. I craved sleep, wanting to escape into a deep slumber like a character in a fairytale. Like Goldilocks in the Papa bear's bed. That hadn't worked out for Goldilocks. I shook my head and resisted the urge.

Adjacent to the master bedroom was what looked like a guest room with floral touches, too many pillows on the bed, a window seat overlooking the driveway below. The next bedroom belonged to the older son. I noticed a stack of SAT preparation books and college catalogs in a neat pile on the desk. *Was this Jason or Martin's room? Which son was the computer geek? Which son was applying to college?*

Next, I explored the rooms behind the closed doors. I knocked tentatively on each door before trying the knobs. The first room, filled with stacked boxes, was used as a storage space. I read the labels carefully marked with large capital letters. CHRISTMAS ORNAMENTS. MOM'S DISHES. JIM'S BOOKS. I continued down the hallway. Several of the doors opened into bathrooms and expansive linen closets. The fluffy towels and sets of sheets folded and stacked according to color and size.

Finally, I knocked on the last closed door at the end of the foyer, the furthest door from Jennifer's bedroom. I waited and listened. Suddenly, I heard faint movements behind the door. I caught my breath. *Damn.* Apparently, I wasn't alone in the house. I turned toward the staircase, ready to bolt down the stairs, out of the house, prepared to drive away in that white Mercedes. Was it too late? It took every ounce of strength for me to stand my ground.

Instead of running, I knocked again. "Anyone home?" I called out. My voice quivered. My heart beat faster. I listened. Someone was definitely behind that door. I waited a few moments longer. I tried turning the doorknob. Locked.

"Just a minute." I froze at the sound of an annoyed, muffled voice. Jennifer's son. The younger one. I listened to him walking over to his door and fiddling with what sounded like a series of locks. I stepped back, my heart racing as I concentrated on the fumbling and the clicking sounds. It seemed there were at least four locks, positioned from the top of the door to the floor. God, what was I thinking intruding on a teenage boy in the middle of the day? He was probably taking a nap. Maybe he was with a girl or watching pornography.

"It's unlocked," the boy said, his voice fading as I heard him stomp away from the door. It surprised me that this son, Martin or Jason, wouldn't open the door to greet his mother. I turned the knob and opened the door myself, slowly. I peered into a black, cavernous space. Heavy, dark curtains completely blocked the windows and any possibility of sunlight. The one source of light in the room emanated from a large computer screen sitting prominently on the boy's desk. He was the light-haired son, the boy with adolescent skin. The shy, computer geek. Mr. Disinterested-in-the-World. The introvert.

"Hi, honey, I'm back," I said, feigning a warm and loving tone. The teacher in me wanted to reprimand him. *What are you doing in your dark bedroom on a sunny, end of summer afternoon? Turn off the computer and go outside. Play basketball with your friends. Read a book in a hammock.* That was the gist of my message to freshman English students before every school vacation, and that was the lecture I wanted to give their parents who allowed their technology-addicted progeny to remain plugged in for the majority of their waking hours. Clearly, Jennifer was one of those clueless moms. Although when the cat's away, the mice will do whatever the hell they want to do. *That's why mice need supervision.*

"Yeah, I know you're back. I can see that," the boy growled, not looking up from whatever held him captive at his computer screen.

The air in the room repelled me— the sickly-sweet odor of decay. I forced myself to take another small step forward. I hoped the boy would take one look at me and see the truth. I prayed he'd stop me in my tracks and ask the obvious questions. *Who the hell are you? Where's my mom?* Then I'd introduce myself and explain Jennifer's ridiculous dare. I'd put an end to the pretense.

"Any messages for me?" That should have been a safe question to buy myself time. I wondered whether this Moriarty son was in on the dare. Perhaps his mom had already called him. He was probably playing along. Maybe the joke was all on me.

"Dad's pissed you turned off your cell. You said you were coming back last night." Suddenly, the boy looked up. His wide eyes flashed in the glow of the computer screen, his small pupils surrounded by white. He jumped up, knocking his chair to the floor behind him. His fists clenched, his nostrils flared, spittle bubbling on the sides of his mouth. Who was this feral animal ready to attack? Adrenaline rushed through my veins.

"What the fuck, bitch! What's your problem? Shut the door! You're letting the light in!" he screamed in a high-pitched voice, shrill enough to break glass. This sudden verbal attack stunned me, like a sucker punch to the gut. I felt a weakness in my legs as I backed away from the threat in that bedroom and shut the door behind me. Gasping for breath, I wrapped my arms around my waist. I lunged to the top of the stairwell, clutching the railing as I forced myself to walk, not hurl myself down the stairs.

The exchange with Jennifer's son left me trembling. I searched for perspective, trying desperately not to overreact to the profanity, the raw teenage rage. I'd never accept that language at Dickinson High School. This boy's behavior would be grounds for an immediate office referral. A minimum two-day suspension.

What would Jennifer do? That was the wrong question. Jennifer had handed over her car and house keys as well as the keys to her life. Now I was the one sitting in the driver's seat. At least for now. I could do what I felt was right. But what was right? And how would I know? I had no experience as a parent. All I had was some common sense and a significant dose of outrage. I would need to respond to the boy's inappropriate behavior later, but that could wait. First things first, such as remembering to breathe.

I walked into the kitchen where I'd left Jennifer's purse, and I pulled out the cell phone. Not optimistic, just desperate, I tried calling my own number again. My fingers shook as I poked at the numbers. *Please pick up, Jennifer, please pick up.* And then I heard the words that destroyed my last thread of hope for an easy fix to the disaster she'd handed me.

The voice mailbox you have called is full.

I fought the urge to throw the phone at the wall. Instead, I crumbled to my knees on the kitchen floor and sobbed in frustration. Who could I turn to? Who would believe me? With no answers, I gave in to despair. I listened to my muffled moans. *What now? What now?* This was no innocent game of Truth or Dare. That was the one truth I knew in my heart.

After a while, my knees began to throb. I felt hungry, thirsty. I had no more tears to shed. I needed to use the bathroom. I could continue to kneel on that hard kitchen floor as if in prayer, I could give into the inertia, and wallow in self-pity. Or, I could pick myself up and attend to my mundane needs. I could do that much. I could do something. Anything.

I pulled myself up from the floor, shuffled into the powder room off the kitchen, and gazed at my reflection in the mirror. The words came to me from some hidden place. Where had I heard them before? Hemingway? Were they his words? And what did they mean? *The shortest answer is doing the thing.* Was it time to do the thing?

* * *

It suddenly occurred to me to check Jennifer's voicemail. Maybe she'd called while I was still in bed or in the shower that morning. Maybe she'd left me a message. Her passwords, JENN, or *jennifer'spassword,* were not smart from a security standpoint, but they were easy to remember. Propped up on a stool, leaning into the kitchen island, I tried the same password I'd used to unlock the phone. JENN. Just like that, I was in.

Jennifer had a ton of messages: Three from Jim. "Where are you, Jennifer? Call me, I'm worried." The most recent message: "Where the fuck are you?" So, Jennifer's husband was angry. I didn't blame him. I was angry too and for the same reasons. Jennifer had disappeared, ignored his phone calls, and left their monster of a son unsupervised. The woman was a terrible wife and mother. And clearly a horrible friend. What kind of friend would do this to another person?

One message was from someone named Nancy: "It's Nancy, we still on for tomorrow? Pick you up at 9:00 a.m. I'll drive."

Another message was from a woman named Liz: "Where are you? You missed our Monday nails and lunch date. Are you okay? Call me."

The final message was from a Mrs. Dwight from the Coral Gables Public Schools Central Office, asking Jennifer to please call the office at her earliest convenience. They needed to set up a meeting regarding Jennifer's request to continue home schooling Martin.

Home schooling Martin? I felt the blood draining from my face when I heard that last message. *Oh, Jennifer, if Martin is that horrible boy upstairs playing videogames or whatever he is up to on that computer, please do not even think about homeschooling him. I can't be stuck in this house with your son for one month. That wasn't the dare.*

I settled down in a comfortable chair in the family room. I had calls to return, excuses to fabricate. I was a fledgling actor, playing a part with no script, with no director's guidance, with no multiple takes if the first take bombed. And no time to practice my lines. I decided to start with the easiest call first. Liz.

"I'm sorry I missed our appointment," I said when the woman answered on the second ring. "I haven't felt like myself lately?" I tried to emulate Jennifer's speech pattern. The way she ended her statements as if asking a question.

"Jennifer, I worried about you! I waited and waited, but finally, I gave up," Liz said in a reprimanding tone. A familiar tone. It reminded me of Dara Jefferson, Dickinson High's Assistant Principal in charge of curriculum and instruction. No matter how hard I worked, how well my students performed, Dara found something to criticize. As Liz droned on, my mind wandered to an exchange between Dara and me from a few months earlier.

"I expected to see you at the senior play last week-end. You really missed a superb performance." I always found myself searching for excuses, apologizing, feeling guilty in that woman's presence. Liz elicited a similar response.

"I know, Liz, truly I'm sorry. And god, my nails are a disaster." Jennifer would probably say something like that. Although looking down at my hands, I realized my nails truly were a disaster. It felt easier, being honest, but I'd need to be careful. Jennifer's makeover ministrations had ignored this one obvious clue to my identity, my ragged nails. And Jennifer's rings? Where were her diamond rings? Had I left them in the Key West cottage? Had Jennifer taken them with her? I didn't have time to worry about that. I needed to focus on the conversation with Liz.

"You do sound as though you're coming down with something," she said. My gravelly voice, deeper than Jennifer's would be easy to explain. A sore throat. Coming down with a cold. "You're forgiven. You know I can't stay mad at you, Jennifer. Let's try again next week, okay? If you're lucky you might get a cancellation appointment tomorrow, but you know how hard that is."

"I know. I'll have to live with these nails for one more week. I guess I'll survive," I said. One call completed successfully. I moved onto the next with a bit more confidence. Husband Jim.

"Where the hell have you been?" That was Jim's greeting for his missing-in-action wife. I realized he hadn't worried about her at all. The man was simply angry. I couldn't fault him for that.

"I don't blame you for being furious. I'm sorry, truly sorry. I needed quiet time, so I silenced my phone. Then I forgot about it? I haven't felt like myself," I said. That excuse worked with Liz. "When will you be home?" I asked, changing the subject.

"Since when do you care when I'll be home? You come and go as you please. Are you the least bit concerned that Martin has been in that room the entire weekend? You know he won't talk to me. How could you leave him like that? What kind of mother are you?"

"I know. I'm worried too," I said. So now I had the name confirmation I needed. Martin was the younger son, the angry boy behind the locked door. The shy computer geek.

"Jesus Christ, Jennifer. If you're so worried—do something about it," Jim said.

"I will, but. . . I need your help, your support, Jim."

"Since when do you want my help? Never mind. Don't answer that question. I don't trust a word you're saying, Jennifer. Don't wait up for me," he said, right before disconnecting.

I wasn't sure what Jim meant by *Don't wait up for me.* Jennifer had warned me that their marriage was touch and go. Jim's absence gave me more time to put together pieces of the puzzle. More time for Jennifer to check my voicemail messages, call me back, and put a stop to the outrageous dare she'd forced on me.

I decided to ignore the message from Mrs. Dwight until the next day. Someone named Nancy was supposed to pick me up at 9:00 in the morning. I had a busy day to think about, although busy with what I had absolutely no clue. But right at that moment, all I could think about was one thing. Food. I'd had nothing to eat since those few bites of croissant in the morning. I felt weak from hunger.

I crept back upstairs to Martin's bedroom. Without giving my next moves any thought, or analyzing what might go wrong, I knocked on his door with a great deal of force. I called out to him in my most teacher-like voice: "Martin, I'm going to take a shower, and then I'm taking you out for dinner. Decide where you want to go," I said. I waited. "Did you hear me?"

"Yes, I heard you," Martin muttered.

"Fine," I said. "I'll knock when I'm ready." I stayed at his door and listened a bit longer, but Martin didn't respond. He heard me. That would have to do.

CHAPTER 9

I handed Martin the keys to his mother's Mercedes, and I held my breath. I needed to hide my cluelessness for as long as possible, even if that meant handing over the keys to someone even more clueless. At sixteen the boy was old enough to have a license, but whether he could drive was another matter. Unlike me, at least Martin would be able to navigate his way around Coral Gables and find a restaurant he liked without relying on GPS.

Martin had dressed for fast food. Grungy. His faded, ripped jeans and a black T-shirt hung on his frame like limp sheets on a clothesline. I hoped he had an appetite for something more substantial than fast food. I needed a glass of wine with dinner, not a happy meal with fries.

"Where do you want to go?" I asked. Martin adjusted the driver's seat, played with the radio dials until he found an obnoxious station, so-called music with offensive, misogynist lyrics.

As I was about to repeat the question, he mumbled a one-word reply, "Antonio's." And then, "What's wrong with your voice?" *Damn.*

"Sore throat. I'm fighting a cold?" I feigned what I hoped was a credible cough. I should have practiced Jennifer's speech patterns on the drive to Coral Gables. The cough and the Valley Girl accent would have to suffice.

Martin drove way too fast but with an air of confidence. "You know, you're a pretty good driver," I said. Was that something Jennifer might say? I held out an olive branch, searching for a way to connect. I knew all about the importance of building relationships with my students. That was the easy part.

"Tell that to the prick who failed me. That fat fuck couldn't parallel park if his life depended on it." *Nice mouth.* That's what I wanted to say, but I didn't.

"Well, you can always take the test again."

"Yeah, when your asshole husband says I can take the test again." *Why would Martin refer to Jim as Jennifer's husband and not his father?*

"I'll talk to him." I assumed Jennifer played the good cop in the marriage, Jim the bad cop. Jennifer was probably the lenient parent who put up with crude language and bad behavior.

"Fuck that. I don't need a license. I'm not going anywhere." I coughed again, stifling a laugh at the irony of Martin's statement.

Jennifer's son drove beyond his neighborhood, past churches, office towers, a shopping district, toward a less upscale business zone. He turned left into an unremarkable strip mall, peppered with a dental office, a dollar store, a wedding gown shop, and a ballroom dancing studio. The restaurant, Antonio's, was nestled into the corner, adjacent to an empty storefront on one side and a liquor store on the other. Judging by the number of cars in the parking lot, the place seemed popular.

It turned out Martin's choice for dinner, an unassuming pizza joint with an extensive Italian menu, had a full bar. The owner, I heard a customer call him Tony, greeted us with a warm hello. "The Moriarty Family! Long time no see!" He seated us toward the back of the restaurant. As I walked to our table, I avoided eye contact with the other diners, keeping my focus on Martin who was in front of me. I wondered who in this restaurant was a friend, an acquaintance, a foe, a relative. Would they recognize us? Was I walking into a trap? Was this a mistake, taking Martin out to dinner?

Tony brought over a glass of red wine for me, a Coke for Martin. "Thank you, Tony," I said feeling oddly gratified to be on a first-name basis with another total stranger. I was even more grateful for the red wine. Tony knew our drink preferences. Clearly, they were regulars here.

"The usual?" he asked Martin. "Yeah," said Martin, slouching over the cell phone in his lap. I felt a warm flush creep across my face, but I kept my composure. I wanted to apologize for Martin's rude behavior. *I* hadn't raised this ungrateful lout, but still, the owner of the restaurant didn't know that. I gave Tony a shrug, as if to say, "What can I do? You know teenagers."

"And for you, my beautiful lady?" Tony smiled. I almost looked around to see if someone else had Tony's attention.

"What do you suggest tonight?"

"Ah, I have a veal and peppers dish you will love, goes well with the Chianti." I was apparently in excellent hands and appreciated not having to make a decision. Even a mundane decision about what to eat felt beyond my capabilities. I took another sip of the red wine, enjoying the warmth that spread through my body.

Martin maintained his focus on the cell phone he clutched with both hands. I focused on unclenching my tense arm and shoulder muscles. I looked around the restaurant for something, anything, to occupy my attention, while waiting uncomfortably for Martin to finish texting or whatever he was doing on that phone. Finally, I broke the silence, hoping to engage him in conversation. I tried to come up with a safe subject.

"Martin, have you talked with your brother?" He ignored me. I gave him time.

"Martin, did you hear me?" Nothing.

Finally, without looking up from his cell phone, "Why would *I* hear from Jason? We *never* talk to each other." Then Martin swore under his breath and glared at me. "You know that. And what's your problem? I'm playing *Doctrine of Dread*. You made me lose ten points."

What's my problem? My problem was that I had no idea what to say to this boy who clearly did not want to talk with me. My problem was that I didn't approve of teenagers playing violent videogames, ignoring their parents, being rude to friendly restaurant staff, and using foul language. My problem was that I didn't know what I was doing or how I'd survive the next 24 hours, let alone a month of this life-swapping dare. And that was just the beginning of a laundry list of problems.

"No problem. I want to talk to you, that's all. I've missed you. I'm trying to have a conversation, Martin. Tell me about your weekend." Martin ignored me. I wondered how many virtual acts of violence and aggression he would manage to accomplish playing *Doctrine of Dread* while sitting across from his presumed mother at a cozy, candlelit table at Antonio's. He paused for a moment, finally glancing up from his cell phone.

"Mom, did you get it?" Martin's voice was softer.

"Did I get what?"

"Don't be stupid, Mom. You promised. Did you get it? I'm almost out," he said, whining like a six-year-old.

"Let's talk about that later, okay?" I didn't know what Martin was talking about, and so I stalled.

Our food arrived, and we ate our meals in silence, each of us avoiding conversation for different, but I presumed equally compelling reasons.

My hunger abated, I began to panic again. I worried someone would approach our table, want to talk to me, uncover my fraud. I ordered another glass of wine. Why not? I wasn't driving, and I needed it.

"You know, Mom," Martin said as we left the restaurant. He was walking several yards ahead of me, but he turned his head around to make sure I heard him. "I'm not who you think I am."

"Really Martin?" I said. "I'm not who you think I am either. We have something in common, don't we?"

* * *

Later, as I followed Martin through the front door of his house, I told another truth. "I have a splitting headache. I'm going to bed. Goodnight, Martin." Massaging my temples, I didn't wait for a response. I practically bolted up the stairs and escaped into Jennifer Moriarty's bedroom.

I spent over an hour investigating the contents of the double walk-in closets, dresser drawers, the nightstands, and bathroom medicine cabinets. I was in awe of Jennifer's organizational skills. Her clothes and Jim's classified by color and purpose; each piece of clothing had been hung carefully with matching his and her monogrammed hangers. It was like shopping in a high-end clothing boutique without the hovering salesperson breathing down my neck with scorn and disapproval.

Deciding what to wear to bed was no easy task. Did Jennifer usually wear sexy nightgowns like the black one she must have given me the night before at the Key West cottage? I settled on navy blue, silk pajamas that covered everything. I didn't know what Jim would be expecting from me if he did come home. He was angry. He had told me not to wait up for him. What did that mean? Would he show up in the middle of the night? Perhaps make-up sex was something Jennifer initiated. I dreaded that possibility, but to be honest, I was also intrigued by the prospect. Worrying about sex with Jim didn't keep me awake. As my head hit the satin-covered pillows in Jennifer and her husband's king-size bed, I succumbed to utter exhaustion and fell into a deep and dreamless sleep.

CHAPTER 10

I glanced at the clock on the nightstand. It was 8:30 a.m. I bolted upright, suddenly wide-awake. How could I have overslept? I was already late for my 8:00 English department meeting. I gripped the satin sheet that had encased my body overnight and looked around the room, baffled by my surroundings. And then, my fear of being late for a department meeting was replaced by the sheer terror of my new reality. I glanced at the far side of the enormous bed, relieved to see nothing was disturbed. I wondered where Jim had slept as I shuffled to the bathroom, struggling to face another day as Jennifer Moriarty.

I reminded myself that being Jenn Cooper also had its challenges. Some of those challenges I didn't mind avoiding for a few weeks. My teaching schedule at Dickinson High required an early to bed, early to rise regimen. 5:30 a.m. out of bed and out the door of my apartment by 6:15. I typically arrived in my classroom with a hot cup of coffee by 6:45 a.m., giving myself time to prepare for classes and correct a few papers before the homeroom bell. Even on weekends, I rarely deviated from my early to bed/early to rise routine. Something about Florida had corroded my internal alarm clock. Humidity would corrode anything.

I found a stash of unwrapped toothbrushes in a drawer under one of the sinks. As I brushed my teeth, I remembered the phone message from someone named Nancy. She said she'd pick me up at 9:00. I had less than half an hour, barely enough time to get ready. I stopped moving in slow motion and dashed to Jennifer's walk-in closet with a sense of urgency.

I wasn't sure what to wear for that morning's mysterious outing. I opted for a pair of lightweight linen pants and a silk T-shirt. In my life as Jenn Cooper, I had been blissfully unaware of the existence of T-shirts made from silk, but as I slipped the fabric over my head, I understood what I'd been missing.

After getting dressed, I checked the guest room in case Jim had indeed slept at home. I was relieved to see the room untouched, and Jason's room looked exactly as it had the day before. Then, I knocked on Martin's door. No answer. I knocked with more force and called his name. I tried turning the doorknob, but the locked door wouldn't budge. Martin was probably asleep. Or he was being a passive-aggressive little shit, ignoring his mother.

"Martin," I said. "Nancy is picking me up in a few minutes. I'll be back later. Do you need anything?" I heard him moan softly. Then he said something inaudible. I couldn't decipher the words, but I understood the tone. Exasperated, irritated. Annoyed-on-steroids.

"Okay, Martin, Call me if you need anything."

Downstairs in the kitchen, I grabbed a banana and a glass of orange juice. What I really craved was a hot cup of coffee. There wasn't time to figure out how to use the complicated espresso coffee maker built into the wall. *Damn. When did making a simple cup of morning coffee become an art form that required specialized training?* I hoped Nancy, whoever she was, would agree to stop for coffee on the way to wherever we were going. Despite a good night's sleep, I needed a jolt of caffeine to help me navigate the identity traps lurking beneath the surface.

As I waited for Nancy, I called my cell phone, willing Jennifer to pick up. The voice mailbox was still full. My heart sank again, but I didn't have time to wallow in disappointment. I heard a car horn in the driveway and grabbed Jennifer's Gucci handbag.

I was prepared with one urgent conversation starter for Nancy. "I didn't have time for coffee, can we stop first thing?" The words spilled out as I fastened my seatbelt.

"There's coffee at Mom's. Can't you wait fifteen minutes?" Nancy said, with what I presumed was sisterly annoyance. *So, Nancy is Jennifer's sister,* I thought. And we were going to visit our mother. It would take only one wrong facial expression, one use of an unlikely phrase, or one erroneous reaction, to give myself away. I expected everything to blow up in my face on the drive to "Mom's." And a part of me wanted that inevitable outcome.

"Sure," I said, playing the part of agreeable sister. As an only child, I'd never experienced the trials and tribulations of sibling rivalry. I'd never learned the survival skills sisters and brothers acquire at an early age to get through the day. I'd have to fake it until I figured out how this sisterly relationship worked.

My mind raced, putting together random clues like a rookie detective on *Law and Order.* Okay, so we were going to "Mom's," and there would be coffee there. I could have been jumping to conclusions about the relationship. I looked more closely at the woman behind the wheel. Nancy didn't resemble Jennifer. Her stick-straight hair had more than a few threads of gray. The shape of the eyes was different from ours. Nancy's face was fuller than Jennifer's, and she gave the initial impression of a matronly woman, a much older sister. Or, perhaps Nancy was a sister-in-law. Based on her choice of vehicle, a shiny, black, Range Rover, I assumed Nancy had plenty of money, like Jennifer. Not for the first or last time, I wondered why anyone needed a four-wheel-drive vehicle in southern Florida. The inside of the car, as new and sparkling clean as the outside, provided no clues about whether Nancy had children of her own who might need chauffeuring around town.

"I'm worried," Nancy said. "I talked with Dr. Trumbull again, and he told me he's noticing more deterioration in Mom's short-term memory."

"I'm worried too," I said. "What else did Dr. Trumbull tell you?" I tried to stay focused on the conversation, wondering why Nancy didn't notice the stranger sitting next to her. Wondering when Nancy *would* notice, see the truth, and slam on the literal and metaphorical brakes.

"He wants to start her on that new medication he talked about last month. There might be side-effects, but it's worth a trial, don't you think?" I didn't know what to think about a new medication for a woman I'd never met. In any case, the deafening sound of blood rushing in my ears interfered with any thinking at all.

"Let's see how it goes today," I said, stalling. "What else is new with you?" I tried to change the subject. Fishing for information, I cast a wide net.

Nancy glanced my way. Before I left the house, I'd donned a pair of large designer sunglasses I found in Jennifer's closet. They covered a good portion of my face. I felt hidden, safer, Hollywood style incognito. Still, I withered under Nancy's glance.

"What's new with me? Nothing since we last spoke. And what's wrong with your voice? Are you sick or something?"

"Sore throat."

"Well don't breathe on me, and don't get too close to Mom. The last thing she needs is a cold. How's Martin?" An interesting question. Why didn't Nancy ask about Jim or Jason? Or about the condition of Jennifer's appalling nails for that matter? I clenched my fists to hide the evidence. I regarded Nancy's question about Martin as an open door and decided to walk through it.

"Martin? I'm worried about Martin. He's in his room all the time, locks his door, he's so rude to me. Honestly, I don't know what to do."

"Jennifer, I've told you a hundred times, Jim and Mom have begged you, the school has tried to get through to you. You need to get help for Martin. This isn't going away," Nancy said.

"I'm beginning to see that." I stared straight ahead.

"Well, that's good to hear, but surprising. Why the change of heart? This feels sudden." *Great question, Nancy. The change of heart might have something to do with the change in identity.*

"Listen, can we talk about this later?" Back to stalling; back to my new M.O.— avoidance. Nancy pulled her Range Rover into the parking lot of what first seemed to be an upscale apartment building. A row of white rocking chairs flanked the front entrance and made the building look more like a country club or even a New England inn. But then, I read the fancy sign on the front of the building: Westwood Cares Association. This was no country club. It was a nursing home. An assisted living residence.

I struggled to prepare myself to enter the building, to visit the woman who had given birth to Jennifer. Her mother would know I was a fraud. She'd see through the charade. With each step from the parking lot toward the facility, my heart pounded faster. It took all of my willpower to not turn and run in the opposite direction. This outrageous deception could backfire with a raised eyebrow, an awkward movement. How had I managed to avoid disclosure of my identity up until that moment? Jennifer's own child couldn't see me for the woman I was. Jennifer's sister, Nancy, didn't seem the least bit suspicious. Would I get away with it again, this time with Jennifer's mother? The woman who had raised her? The person who had known her the longest?

After we checked in at the main desk, I followed Nancy down the hallway. Several elderly residents sat slumped over in wheelchairs parked outside their rooms. I smelled the disinfectant mixed with the undeniable odor of urine. It brought me back to visits with my father during his final months in a nursing home, where he ultimately succumbed to lung cancer.

He had only himself to blame for the cancer. Years of smoking two packs a day finally caught up with him. At the end, my mother couldn't continue to take care of him and hold onto her job as a bookkeeper. With me still in college, we relied on my mother's income. I went with her to visit Dad almost every weekend. We would bring his favorite sweets from a specialty store. The candies looked like little brown turtles with pecan legs and skinny turtle heads sticking out of their chocolate shells. The caramel beneath the chocolate shell stuck in my father's teeth, making breathing and conversation that much more difficult for him. I refused to eat that candy or anything else in the nursing home. The smell of urine smothered my appetite. Ten steps beyond the lobby I had to breathe through my mouth to avoid gagging. My mom would put a dab of cheap, drugstore cologne above her upper lip. Once we entered Dad's room, the decaying odor of his body overpowered even the cloying, floral scent of that cologne. By the end of his life, my confused father rambled about nonsense, his thinking clouded by pain medication. He didn't even recognize his daughter, his only child.

I followed Nancy into Room 140 where an elderly woman sat in an imitation leather armchair by the window. The woman held a hardcovered book in her lap, open to a page somewhere in the middle, although she didn't appear to be reading. As I moved closer, I realized the book was a bible. The old woman stared at the view outside the window, sitting as still as a painting. The room was sparse, a single hospital bed with railings, a nightstand, built-in dressers, a doorway slightly ajar, opening to a pale green, tiled bathroom. The old woman turned around and smiled. Walking on eggshells, I worried that every step could cause a potential crack. And I still hadn't had my morning coffee.

"Mom, you have visitors," Nancy said in the loving but saccharine voice people use when they talk to newborn babies or puppies. We took turns giving the frail, thin woman air kisses and gentle hugs. Nancy pulled up a chair, and I sat on the bed close to the armchair.

"How are you?" I asked, with as much sincerity as I could feign, given the circumstances. That's when Jennifer's mom looked directly into my eyes with no recognition. We were strangers.

"I'm fine, thank you," she said. Then she looked at Nancy and asked, "Nancy dear, aren't you going to introduce me to your friend?"

CHAPTER 11

"Mom, what are you talking about? It's Jennifer, your daughter," Nancy said, fumbling with the buttons of her mother's sweater. "It's chilly in here, are you warm enough?"

"Nancy," I said. I reached out and squeezed her shoulder, in a loving, sisterly sort of way. "Would you mind getting me that cup of coffee? Give us some time alone, okay?"

I waited for Nancy to leave the room, and then I looked directly into the old woman's cloudy, pink-rimmed eyes. I studied her face and imagined that one day I would look like Jennifer's mother. In thirty years. Our facial structure was similar, and the eyes, they were my eyes. Almond-shaped, deep-set, with a prominent brow. They were Jennifer's eyes.

I had a short window of opportunity to speak privately with her. Nancy would be back soon with my coffee. "Why did you say that? Why did you ask Nancy to introduce us? Do you think I'm *not* Jennifer? Don't I look like your daughter?" I asked, gently, cautiously.

"You do look like my daughter. But you're not Jennifer, are you?" she asked, her voice quivering. I felt a daughter's guilt for toying with the poor woman, intentionally confusing someone who was already fighting a final battle to hold onto her memories.

"Tell me about Jennifer. Tell me about her husband, her kids, her interests. Tell me about your relationship with your daughter." I spoke quickly, desperate for information, and she was the one person in Jennifer Moriarty's universe who didn't have the power to blow my cover. Along with her memories, she had lost her credibility.

The older woman dabbed at her eyes with an embroidered handkerchief she pulled from the sleeve of her thin sweater. "Jennifer doesn't understand. It's not her fault," she said. "She needs help, but time is running out, you know?" She looked up at me with those watery eyes, those sunken cheeks, as if I held the answers.

Time was running out? Were those words the senseless ramblings of an old woman fighting dementia, or an invitation to probe further for a nugget of truth? "I do know. Tell me more about that." I paused, using a favorite teacher strategy that often helped my more reticent students answer challenging questions. *Just wait,* I told myself. *If I wait long enough, she'll reveal more.* The strategy worked well with freshman English students. I waited, but Jennifer's mother began staring out the window again, lost in her own world. I tried a new approach.

"What can I do to help?" I asked. This woman believed I was a friend of her daughter's, someone with influence. Someone who knew the family secrets, someone with knowledge of the deep, dark, mysteries of the family's life. My question pulled the woman's gaze away from the window.

"Yes. You can help. Help Jennifer. Help her stop that boy. Help her stop him first, whatever it takes."

"Stop him? I don't understand," I said.

"Please, it's important. You have to stop that boy!" The fire in her eyes chilled me to the core but also burned through my nagging doubts about the son who locked himself in his bedroom. I knew that boy. I knew it in my gut but needed to hear Jennifer's mother say the name.

"Help Jennifer stop who? Which boy?" I asked her and waited, praying she would say his name before Nancy returned with the coffee.

"Martin. Jennifer's son. Please, I'm begging you to stop him! Stop him first, before it's too late."

* * *

On the drive back to Jennifer's house, Nancy and I were silent, letting the noise from a Miami pop-music radio station fill the void. I suppose we were both lost in our separate worlds, both of us trying to make sense of our visit to the nursing home. As the car turned onto Jennifer's street, Nancy turned off the radio. She pulled into the driveway and quickly broke the silence. "I can't believe she didn't recognize you. She's starting to forget us, Jennifer. Her own daughters. Dr. Trumbull said this would happen. I didn't expect it to happen so soon."

"I think she knows more than we realize. I'm positive she knew me despite what she said." I spoke the truth, of course. Jennifer's mother knew the most important fact about me. She knew that I was not her daughter. Let Nancy assume her sister was in denial about her mom's fading memory. Jennifer Moriarty would be in denial about her mother's dementia, just as she denied her son's precarious emotional and mental state.

Nancy let the motor idle. She turned and placed her hand on my shoulder. "Jennifer, listen to me. I want to say this one thing, and I don't want you to take it the wrong way and get all defensive on me. Okay?"

"Of course. What is it?"

"I appreciate that you're trying."

"What are you talking about?" I hated her patronizing tone. Tempted to flick Nancy's hand off my shoulder, I clutched the Gucci bag harder.

"I'm talking about Martin. I know how hard it's been, and I'm glad you're starting to, well, how do I say this? You are finally beginning to accept that there are serious problems, problems you will never fix on your own." How dare this woman question my ability to handle Martin? I was an experienced high school educator.

I shrugged Nancy's hand off my shoulder and opened the car door. "Nancy, will you please let it go? I know what I'm doing, and you don't know what you're talking about," I snapped, slamming the car door behind me. As I walked to the front door of the Moriarty's house, I reminded myself that Nancy's criticism was directed at her real sister, Jennifer Moriarty, not Jenn Cooper. So much for developing a thicker skin.

* * *

The house was quiet. The kitchen looked exactly as I'd left it. There was no evidence that Martin had eaten breakfast. No dishes in the sink. No crumbs on the counter. Nothing had been touched. I assumed he was still sleeping, following a typical teenager's summer schedule.

In the meantime, I had plenty to do to occupy my time. I decided to check Jennifer's emails before returning the call to the Coral Gables school district's central office. I hoped the emails would reveal more clues about Martin and Jim. I needed information about the other son. Where was Jason? What was his story?

I closed the heavy door of the study. My eyes swept across the enormous space that represented the epitome of perfection that filled my daydreams. If I had a study like this, I believed it would be easy to write the great American novel. At some point in my life, I'd convinced myself that not having a picture-perfect writing space stood in the way of my destiny as a writer. I looked forward to starting my novel in this room. Perhaps that very day. Why not? I might be stuck in Jennifer's world for an entire month. I decided to make the most of my time.

The large window in the study framed a serene view of the backyard, a lush garden, and a swimming pool, its turquoise waters shimmering in the Florida sunshine. I perused the floor to ceiling bookshelves holding thousands of books, hard-covered and old, without a speck of dust. How many of these books had Jennifer read? Based on her audiobook choice, that romance novel I'd listened to in the car, the classics that lined the study walls felt incongruous, fraudulent.

I remembered telling Jennifer about teaching freshman English. It was our first night at the Key West cottage. "I start the year off with Steinbeck," I said.

"I've never read Steinbeck. Isn't that crazy?"

"Really? You should. I assign *Of Mice and Men* in September. It's short, really a novella."

"Oh, I saw the movie a long time ago. Kind of boring. Not enough romance. No action." How would Jennifer ever manage the first week of teaching? She'd be lost, and my students would know she was a fraud.

I sat behind the massive, mahogany desk, feeling profoundly sorry for myself. I folded my arms on the surface of the desk and cradled my head. I actually longed for the loneliness and depression I'd experienced watching television in that hotel room in Key West, stretched out on a lumpy mattress, bemoaning my failings, my dull existence. Those feelings were trivial compared with the total despondency I felt sitting in Jennifer's study. Playing a role I didn't understand, dealing with people whose history I didn't know. Jennifer's maid, her son, her sister, looked at me and saw what they wanted to see. I'd grown accustomed to being invisible, but this was different. This was much worse. And I felt lost without my journal. I'd need to buy a new one. A beautiful new leather-bound journal. I sat up, pushed my shoulders back, and faced the computer screen.

I chuckled as I logged in, using the password *Jennifer'spassword*. Too easy. I accessed Jennifer's emails with a click on a desktop file. I breezed through the ads quickly, deleting those I would have deleted had they clogged my own inbox. Online sales and coupons from Pottery Barn, Nordstrom's, Victoria's Secret, Best Buy, so many things I didn't need from a slew of upscale department stores and companies too rich for my teacher's salary.

And yet, tempted by a Barnes and Noble coupon, I considered spending Jennifer's money on books I'd been wanting to read, titles on hold for me at the public library. It would be nice to have copies for my personal bookshelf back home. Jennifer wouldn't mind, and the books would arrive before the end of the month. I needed new moisturizer too. I couldn't stomach the thought of using Jennifer's skin creams. I'd laughed the night before, when I discovered the stash of cosmetics in her bathroom. She owned a warehouse of skin lotions and balms containing exotic ingredients. Caviar. Snake skin scales. Synthetic horse urine. It was ridiculous. Who would even think of putting synthetic horse urine in a facial lotion?

I considered unsubscribing from all those consumer sites, to deprive her of sales and coupons and great deals. But what was the point? I had a novel to write.

Wasn't that the upside of swapping lives? This dare had nothing to do with spending Jennifer's money or changing her priorities. As for Jennifer, what could be the upside of swapping lives with me? Was she sincerely interested in pursuing a teaching career, her childhood dream? Or did she need a vacation from a broken marriage, from dealing with an aging parent? Did she need a break from Martin? Was that the point?

I refocused my attention on Jennifer's inbox. The promotional emails were easy to delete, but a few of the political messages made me pause. They gave me insight into my doppelganger's life. One email that caused a visceral reaction was the newsletter and request for additional donations from the National Rifle Association. Apparently, Jennifer had been one of the NRA's most generous supporters with a lifetime membership. Why would this have caused even a lowly raised eyebrow? I barely knew Jennifer Moriarty, so why would I care that my double was a gun enthusiast, a big defender of the Second Amendment? This fact about her seemed significant, although I couldn't wrap my mind around the reasons why.

I took a break from emails to examine Jennifer's wallet more thoroughly. Jennifer had left me plenty of cash and numerous credit cards, but I'd been distracted by all that money. I hadn't investigated the side pockets and wallet crevices where people sometimes hide their secrets, their less obvious priorities.

And there it was in plain sight right next to a credit card for Bloomingdales. Jennifer C. Moriarty, a card-carrying member of the NRA. Seeing that card scared me more than it should have. It felt dangerous, especially with teenage children living in the house. Especially with Martin.

I returned to Jennifer's inbox and took my time digging into her email history. I browsed through the sent messages and those lingering in the trash, looking for clues about Jennifer's life, about her relationships, about her family. And then, I discovered one email from Martin to his mother that took my breath away. It referenced a conversation between Jennifer and Martin from several weeks earlier. I read and reread Martin's words carefully, shaking my head in sympathy for that lost soul. The raw emotions he shared with his mother brought on a wave of nausea. I tried to breathe through it.

Am I supposed to thank you? For letting me know what a slut you were seventeen years ago? It all makes sense now. I get it. You're a whore who fucked a stranger after getting drunk at a bar while her husband was out of town. You fucked some ugly dude who looks like me, and you didn't even know his name and then you got pregnant after your one-night stand with a loser. No wonder your husband hates me. No wonder you can't stand to look at me. You're right—you said it, and you're right. You should have had an abortion. You never should have had me. It's nice to finally hear the truth, you lying bitch.

More puzzle pieces shifted into place, helping me see the full picture of the family. I understood why Martin referred to Jim Moriarty as "your husband" rather than his father. I understood Martin's rage. Learning about his biological history and knowing his mother wished he had never been born must have shattered his sense of self-worth. Poor Martin.

Awakened by a heady dose of righteous indignation and compassion for the boy upstairs, I sat up straighter in the desk chair. He needed my help. I had one month to give him. A month to undo some of the damage. Where in god's name would I start? How could I help Martin? I picked up the phone.

* * *

"Hello, this is Mrs. Jennifer Moriarty. Is Mrs. Dwight available? I'm returning her call." I expected the school system to have answers to my questions about Martin's educational needs as well as the history of Jennifer's decision to educate him at home. I wasn't entirely against home schooling in principle. It made sense for some families. And as a teacher, I experienced first-hand the ever-increasing demands and pressures on students and the educators who were fighting in the trenches. Continuous changes, not always for the better, were pushing many of us out of the profession. Every year our administration inundated the faculty with new initiatives, revised teacher evaluation requirements, more frequent lockdown drills, more rigorous high-stakes testing, new standards, new curricula, and new expectations every month. Home schooling had its merits, but not for that boy upstairs, not for Martin. From what I had seen in fewer than twenty-four hours, the last thing in the world Martin and Jennifer needed was the status quo. I might be the one person who could shake things up a bit. I'd at least try to figure out a way to make a difference while I was temporarily stuck in this mad world.

"Mrs. Moriarty, thank you for returning my call. The team hoped to meet with you informally rather than scheduling another Individual Educational Planning meeting," said Mrs. Dwight. The fact that she mentioned an IEP meeting was good news. Martin had serious issues that must have been obvious to his teachers.

Before my call, I'd done a bit of research to familiarize myself with the Florida home schooling and special education jargon. Connecticut used different acronyms and unique terminology for the range of disabilities. Both states understood the importance of camouflaging the true nature of their students' learning challenges, and both states used euphemisms to make labeling kids a bit more palatable for their parents. I was prepared with questions as well as with the right terminology.

"I'm happy to meet with you. I'm also wondering if I could review Martin's files before we meet," I said. "Do you need that request in writing?" I was well-versed in the relevant school law, special education requirements, and The Freedom of Information Act as it related to school documents. As Martin's mother, Jennifer should have had full access to his educational files, report cards, his testing, his evaluations, the myriad of documentation collected since he began his education within the public-school system. Mrs. Dwight paused for a few seconds. Had my request surprised her?

"Do you need an additional copy of the files? I'm sure we mailed everything to you. Let's see—yes, on July 10, a certified copy was sent," Mrs. Dwight said. Those educational files had to be stashed somewhere in Jennifer's house. I needed to say something, a response that wouldn't cause further suspicion.

"Of course, I realize that. Thank you. I don't need another copy of the files. I want to go through the actual files, not the copies. Would you schedule an hour for me before our meeting?" That seemed to be a reasonable request. It might even have been a strategic move, causing the administrators, specialists, and teachers to think Jennifer Moriarty didn't quite trust them. It wouldn't hurt to keep the school district on its toes. I felt almost powerful being on the other side of the table for once.

I'd attended more than a hundred special education meetings throughout my teaching career. I'd encountered more than my share of furious parents complaining about how little the school had done to help their children. And all of those self-important attorneys and arrogant specialists, lengthy reports and vague evaluations, plans and supports put in place to make the problems go away. Too many meetings to count. Yeah, I could play that game blindfolded.

"Of course. That's not a problem," Mrs. Dwight said. "We'll have the file ready for your review at... umm... 8:00 a.m. Friday morning. Looking forward to seeing you, Mrs. Moriarty." And in some strange way, I looked forward to Friday morning as well.

CHAPTER 12

My stomach growled, reminding me it was well past lunchtime. I scoured the pantry and refrigerator for possibilities. I knew I could make a respectable grilled cheese. I studied the ripening tomatoes on the counter, found a half-loaf of stale sourdough bread, and a variety of cheeses in the refrigerator. Since I'd heard no signs of life coming from Martin's bedroom, I decided to check on him. I'd convince him to join me for lunch.

I knocked with enough force to wake the dead. "Martin, I'm making grilled cheese and tomato sandwiches for lunch. How does that sound to you?" I waited. I listened. Was he still in bed? Was he sitting at his computer? Did he even like grilled cheese?

"Fine," I finally heard him mumble.

"Okay, come down in ten minutes. We can eat by the pool. Is that okay with you?" I wanted to get him out of that stale room. It was another steamy day. Hot and uncomfortably humid, but a swim might be a good thing for both of us.

"Martin—is that okay? We could go for a swim after lunch." I waited. "Okay, ten minutes then," I said, giving up on a response.

"Leave it by the door," Martin snarled, louder this time.

Leave his lunch by the door? Was this how Jennifer served her son's meals? I had to decide whether it was more important to get food into Martin or to get Martin out of his bedroom to see the light of day. If I pushed too hard, Martin might become suspicious about the changes in his mother's behavior. I needed to protect my subterfuge for a while longer. And so, I decided to leave a grilled cheese and tomato sandwich by the angry boy's bedroom door.

* * *

Sitting alone at the kitchen island, I devoured my lunch. I kept replaying the scene in the nursing home with Jennifer's mother. I couldn't erase the haunted look in the frail woman's eyes. I heard her quivering voice in my head, her words on a loop. *Stop him. Stop him first.* What did that woman know? What did she mean by *first*? *Stop him first, before . . . before what?* And when would it be *too late*? Was it already too late?

After lunch, a heavy lethargy settled into my bones. My short existence as Jennifer Moriarty was a virtual minefield. I tiptoed from one moment to the next, anticipating the explosion that might blow my cover, expecting an eruption with every move. I decided a swim in the backyard pool might help me escape. At least temporarily.

I searched Jennifer's closet for a bathing suit. There were plenty of options, but her suits were not the cover-everything Speedo variety I was accustomed to wearing at the YWCA in Hartford. Not one of Jennifer's suits had been designed for serious swimming. They were designed to attract attention and a significant tan in sections of my body that hadn't been exposed to sunshine since college.

The water in the swimming pool felt end-of-summer tepid but refreshing nonetheless. I began by counting strokes, then laps. I soon fell into a rhythm that helped clear my mind of everything except the feel of the water surrounding and supporting my body. First crawl and then breaststroke, then back to crawl. I lost count after twenty laps. Eventually, the weight of my arms and a heavy weariness overwhelmed me. I flipped over onto my back and floated in a peaceful, relaxed state. I gazed up at the blue, cloudless sky.

As I drifted aimlessly in Jennifer's pool, my mind began to drift too. I wondered how Jennifer would handle my ninth-grade English classes. Would the new crop of students like her? Would they like Jennifer better than they'd ever like me? And then, my thoughts meandered again, this time to the email from Martin to Jennifer. His rage, the venom in his response to his mother's admission. Her callous stance toward Martin's struggles. My momentary reprieve from Jennifer's reality dissolved like sugar in a hot cup of coffee. I had work to do. I stood up straight in the shallow end of the pool, the warm water dripping down my back and arms, and I gazed up at the ivy covered, stucco walls of Jennifer's beautiful house. I caught a slight movement in a second story window. Martin was watching me from his bedroom. Our eyes met for an instant, and then, he slipped back behind the curtain. *Damn,* I thought. *I hope Jennifer likes to swim laps. Hell, I hope she can swim.*

I stood transfixed in the water, holding my breath, waiting for Martin to return to the window. Finally, I looked away and emerged from the pool, draped myself in a towel, determined to move forward.

* * *

Showered, dressed in a comfortable pair of yoga pants and a clean T-shirt, I locked the door of the study behind me, anxious to locate Martin's educational files. The school had supposedly mailed the file to Jennifer, so it had to be somewhere. I checked the desk first, then all four drawers of a faux-antique cabinet in the corner of the room. The unlocked files contained old insurance policies, a marriage certificate, utility bills from a former decade, old Christmas cards, directions for using small home appliances—a slow cooker, a hand-held clothes steamer. Surprisingly, the Moriarty family didn't seem to have a sensible filing system. Unlike the order and organization so evident in the Key West cottage and the pristine state of Jennifer's closets and kitchen, these files needed purging and organizing. Perhaps Jim Moriarty kept the more important documents such as tax returns and school papers in his office at work.

After an exhaustive search in the study, I was dismayed to find no evidence of Jason and Martin. In fact, based on what I'd seen throughout the house, other than a few artfully posed photographs of an almost happy family, a visitor would never know about Jennifer's two sons. Parents were supposed to keep their children's artwork, their camp letters, report cards, confirmation of their kids' accomplishments, newspaper clippings of their sons and daughters engaged in sports or winning spelling bees. Mementos, tokens, to evoke a past that included their offspring. Instead, this house was a shell of a home, a pristine model in a brand-new housing development, ready for customers to tour while imagining their own families moving in. A blank canvas.

Reviewing Martin's educational file could wait until Friday morning. Mrs. Dwight promised I'd have an hour to review his records before the meeting at the high school. And so, I shifted my attention to a different search.

Given Jennifer's NRA membership, I assumed there were guns in the house. I worried those guns were accessible to the fuming boy upstairs. Thinking about that possibility made my pulse race. If I could find the family's firearms locked up safely, then I might be able to relax and get back to my main concerns: helping Martin and keeping my identity a secret. And starting my novel. Maybe then I'd be able to focus on *my* needs. It was all about prioritizing.

I'd never seen an actual gun, except of course on television and in the movies. I didn't know what to expect. Perhaps Jennifer and Jim had a locked gun cabinet filled with hunting rifles hidden down in the cellar. After opening every closet and cabinet door on the first floor, I realized there was no cellar in this Florida house. I wondered if Jennifer carried a pistol with her for protection. There was no handgun in the Gucci bag. Unless... and that's when the idea first surfaced in my foggy brain. Unless there was something in the glove compartment of the Mercedes. I hadn't thought of searching the car, the most obvious place to search. I remembered Jennifer's note to me, left in the Key West bedroom. *Everything you need is in my purse or car.* I'd focused on her purse and her house, forgetting entirely about the Mercedes.

I sat behind the wheel of Jennifer's car parked in the circular driveway, drumming up the courage I needed to open the glove compartment. I took a deep breath and pushed the button. Nothing—except for the car registration and a few maintenance manuals. Then I popped open the trunk. I walked behind the car slowly, terrified of what I might find.

And there it was. An overnight bag. I laughed at my foolishness. What did I think would be waiting for me in the trunk of her car? A dead body? A bomb? I stared at the titanium carry-on suitcase, the color of smoked salmon. A piece of luggage that probably cost more than two months of my teacher's salary, indestructible, not a scratch or dent on its cool, metal surface. It made sense. Jennifer had left her Coral Gables house for a long weekend in Key West and wouldn't go with just the shirt on her back. Not Jennifer. Naturally, she would bring changes of clothing, some cosmetics, and other essentials with her, perhaps even a handgun.

I imagined Jennifer packing the suitcase the last night we spent together in Key West. I vaguely remembered not being able to walk by myself, so groggy, exhausted, leaning on Jennifer, letting someone else take charge. I had flashes of Jennifer guiding me up those rickety cottage stairs and tucking me into her bed, so comfortable and safe. I imagined Jennifer placing her suitcase in the trunk of the Mercedes before leaving the Key West cottage for my hotel, leaving her elegant lifestyle behind for a one-month stint as a high school English teacher in Connecticut. What clues had she left for me in this suitcase? I lugged the bag out of the car, into the house and up the stairs to her bedroom.

I locked the bedroom door behind me. I sat down on the floor and opened the suitcase. Inside were separate compartments. Shoe bags, laundry bags, cosmetic bags, some built into the interior of the case. I unpacked yoga pants, carefully rolled skirts and blouses, lace underwear with matching bras, a pair of Nike sneakers and, then, there it was. A small, red case in the shape of a pistol. Chinese brocade, with two black handles. Elegant.

I unzipped the case slowly, carefully. I pulled back the rich fabric, revealing a black handgun tucked away in a case so luxurious it mocked the danger hidden within. *So, this is what a pistol looks like up close.* I stared at the weapon, feeling a rush of adrenaline that had something to do with fear, but also a different sort of thrill. An excitement that felt like power, a faint sexual arousal.

I knew that accidental shootings were an all too common occurrence, killing and injuring thousands of children and adults each year. I'd read the statistics for unintentional deaths and accidents, and so I was tempted but reluctant to touch the gun. It might explode in my hand if I pressed something the wrong way or accidentally released the trigger. I didn't know the first thing about how to determine whether a gun was loaded. I zipped up the fancy pistol case and left it at the bottom of the overnight bag, eager to hide Jennifer's weapon for the duration of my stay in Coral Gables. I'd stash Jennifer's bag at the back of her walk-in closet for safekeeping.

Then I noticed one other item rolling around in the bottom of the case. It was an amber-colored, plastic pill bottle. At first, I thought Jennifer might have hidden the bullets for her handgun there, or maybe she had another prescription besides the Xanax she'd left in her purse. Perhaps Jennifer needed medication for a serious medical condition. I carried the pill container to the bathroom and held it up to the light. Small green-colored pills filled three-quarters of the bottle, but there was no prescription label. Thank goodness for the internet. I had research to do.

CHAPTER 13

As I headed toward the stairs, I spotted the lunch tray outside Martin's bedroom door. The plate was empty except for a banana peel. I assumed he expected his mother to clear the tray too. I felt surprisingly triumphant, as I picked it up and carried the tray back down to the kitchen. The boy had eaten something, and that was a win for me.

I logged in to Jennifer's computer once more, ready to search for more pieces of the Moriarty jigsaw puzzle. With Jennifer's cell phone on the desk beside me and my fingers typing away on the computer keyboard, I started digging, like an archeologist. I brushed aside dirt and debris, excavating the hidden history of the Moriarty family.

Much of what I discovered confirmed what I already suspected. Yes, Jennifer's marriage was in serious trouble, and yes, her younger son was a mess. But I was hungry for specifics. I needed to put color and details on the family portrait Jennifer had sketched for me just days ago. Each email and text message exchange revealed another layer of the family's problems and their secrets. The recent texts between Jennifer and her husband made it clear that I didn't need to worry about midnight visits from Jim to his wife's bed.

Jim: I need a break let me know when you're really ready to deal with the MARTIN problem

Jennifer: You can't just walk away from your obligations.

Jim: I'm not walking away you'll get your usual monthly allowance and I'm paying all your bills and household expenses

Jennifer: What about Jason?

Jim: He's happy at Nancy's for now. Leave him alone he needs a break from both of you

Jennifer: When will you be home?

Jim: I'm not coming home and you're still not listening to me. You'll hear from my attorney maybe you'll listen to him

Jennifer: What about Martin? I can't handle him alone.

Jim: He's not my problem anymore. I tried. I'm done.

And that was how things stood. Martin and his mother could suffocate slowly under another layer of isolation, and not a soul would intervene. Jennifer had certainly downplayed her domestic problems while playing Two Truths and a Lie back at the Key West cottage. I recalled my double's bland description of a matrimonial "rough patch." I now understood that Jennifer had left me with a matrimonial black hole.

Searching the internet, I found a site for identification of pharmaceuticals, and it was easy to identify the pills I'd found in the overnight case. I clicked on the color, *green,* the shape, *round,* and immediately the site directed me to oxycodone. 15 mg. A medication used for pain relief and often abused. A big player in the opioid crisis. If the pills were for Jennifer's pain, she would never have left them behind in the overnight bag. Were they for Martin? Is this what he'd been asking for that first night at Antonio's, right before we started eating our dinner? "You promised! I'm almost out," he'd said.

Next, I searched the internet to find out more about Jennifer's handgun. I found photographs that looked like the gun in the brocade case. A Smith & Wesson .380 Semiautomatic Pistol touted as a highly concealable weapon, compact and lightweight, easy to reload, simple to use "even for women." *Ha!* The perfect accessory for Jennifer's personal protection in the wild, wild Key West, or in the jungles of Coral Gables, Florida. A cocktail of Xanax and a concealable gun appeared to be Jennifer's panacea for handling the stresses of everyday suburban life. Home schooling and oxycodone for keeping her volatile son pacified. I sat in front of that computer shaking my head, trying not to hyperventilate. I wondered why Jennifer had left the gun with me. *Was that an intentional decision?*

I pushed away from the desk, annoyed with myself for squandering precious time. Since I first walked into the Coral Gables house, I'd been preoccupied, worrying about guns, pills, and Martin's educational challenges. I could have been writing in Jennifer's gorgeous study, but something kept me away from even starting on that journey. There were more family secrets to uncover, and I had difficulty resisting their magnetic pull.

I worked slowly and methodically, room by room, drawer by drawer. As I hunted for clues, for information, and once more for Martin's educational files, I had to admire the order and cleanliness surrounding me. No odds and ends. Not one junk drawer devoted to miscellaneous stuff.

I thought about the chaotic state of my Hartford apartment, all 950 square feet of space. I needed Jennifer's organizational skills. Or at the very least, more square footage. I was about to give up for the day, perhaps even settle down in the study to start an outline for my novel, when another location for Moriarty secrets occurred to me, giving me a renewed burst of energy.

I entered the garage through the door leading from the mudroom. The space didn't look or smell like a typical garage. I marveled at the comfortable, air-conditioned living room for the family's vehicles. Three times the size and twice as clean as my apartment, I could have eaten off the floor of Jennifer's garage. It wasn't a space designed for accommodating boxes of discarded items, ready for Goodwill pick-up. Everything had a purpose. Everything had a place. There was nothing unwanted in Jennifer Moriarty's house. Except perhaps, the boy upstairs.

The first thing I noticed were two empty parking spaces. A very clean silver jeep occupied the middle space. Once again, I pondered the prevalence of four-wheel-drive vehicles in southern Florida. I dragged my feet as I toured the perimeter of the garage, trying to understand. Trying to make sense of Jennifer's priorities, her life, her family. I gaped at the metal storage lockers, the floor-to-ceiling, built-in cabinetry, and open-shelving as organized as Jennifer's kitchen, with designated and labeled spaces for hand tools, cleaning supplies, athletic gear, gardening equipment, and an entire section for golf clubs. This family owned enough golf clubs to outfit a small country club. A separate set of cabinets held an enormous selection of canned goods and freeze-dried survival meals in bulk quantities. There seemed to be enough food for the Moriarty family to subsist for months. Jennifer had prepared for every conceivable emergency, for any variety of natural disaster, plague, war, Armageddon. Despite the air conditioning, I began to sweat.

Besides the separate, locked entrance from the driveway, there were two other doors in the garage. The door I'd used to enter from the mudroom and one more. I almost overlooked that third door, camouflaged in between built-in cabinets. It was constructed from the same gray metal, but instead of a traditional lock, the door had a keypad entry lever. Jennifer had shared only two password choices— JENN or *jennifer'spassword*. The keypad had numbers—not letters *and* numbers, like a phone. I ran back into the house to grab the cell. I raced back to the garage, breathless, adrenaline cursing through my body. JENN. The letter J, a 5 on the phone keypad. E 3. And N 6. I punched the four numbers into the electronic keypad and prayed to any higher power that might be listening. 5366. I heard the click and pressed the lever downward. The metal door opened to reveal a steep stairwell.

The stairs were carpeted, but not with boring, industrial carpet. These stairs were covered in style, with a beige and black leopard print. Was that a private hunting joke? Did Jennifer or Jim have a wry sense of humor? I propped the door ajar with a golf club and slid the cell phone into my pocket. I wasn't taking any chances. Although I realized my reaction might be overly paranoid, I couldn't shake the premonition that whatever I discovered in the locked loft above the garage might change everything.

I climbed those carpeted steps into another world, a world in which I neither spoke the language nor understood the customs. I stood at the top of the stairs and gaped.

I'd never visited a gun store in my life. In fact, as a teenager, I intentionally boycotted sporting goods establishments that sold firearms. Even then, I had strong feelings about the so-called right to bear arms. In high school I'd written a paper for my American history class, deconstructing the language of the Second Amendment. I'd argued with my father about the easy access and abundance of guns in the country.

"Back in 1791, there may have been good reasons for giving citizen militias the right to bear arms. Like—our country didn't have an army back then."

"Don't waste your time and breath trying to convince anyone against gun ownership in this country," Dad had countered.

"But, Dad, in today's world, do you have any faith in citizen militias, modern-day minutemen ready at a moment's notice to start another revolution? No thanks."

"People want to feel safe, Jenn. They have a right to protect themselves." Case closed. Trying to win an argument with my father was always a waste of energy. And his cancer diagnosis made the man even more intractable.

My dad was right about a universal need to feel safe. My eyes swept across the loft as I tried to take it all in. Is that why Jennifer Moriarty needed all those guns? To protect herself and her family? They could have afforded a state-of-the-art alarm system, and they lived in a low-crime neighborhood. If it wasn't about personal safety, why? Maybe the firearms I discovered in that loft was a hobby for her. Jennifer had a lot of free time. And I assumed the Second Amendment protected gun-collection, hunting, target practice, and other related hobbies.

I switched on the overhead lights and walked around the perimeter of what might be described as an extravagant museum dedicated to firearms and ammunition. The loft above the garage appeared as orderly, clean, and air-conditioned as the space below, but the built-in cabinetry was made of glossy hardwood, not metal. I examined the vast collection of rifles and pistols displayed behind the glass doors. I reached to open one cabinet and was surprised to find it unlocked. *Oh, Jennifer. What were you thinking?* As I opened each cabinet, the lights inside radiated a soft glow, illuminating the pieces displayed with artistry and flair. Someone had organized the collection thoughtfully, creating a timeline of firearms. Antique rifles and revolvers from the 18th century were displayed along the left wall. The rest of the collection was organized by decade around the perimeter of the loft, ending with 21st-century firearms along the right wall.

A large oak table graced the center of the room. On the tabletop, I found a large, wooden tool chest next to bottles of lubricating oil and solvents of some kind, a box of swabs and patches. I returned to the perimeter, taking my time. I read the descriptions of each firearm on labels that had been printed in elegant calligraphy, propped up in fancy brass holders next to the guns inside the cabinets.

Although the historical significance of this massive collection was not entirely lost on me, there were terms I'd never seen or heard. The family owned muskets allegedly used in the war of 1812, muzzle-loading rifles, a Colt Revolving Rifle from the Civil War, rifles with bayonets, carbines, a Winchester rifle, a small-caliber German rifle supposedly used for target practice by Hitler Youth during WWII, big game hunting rifles, machine guns, and even a 3-D printed rifle. In separate cabinets, I found an impressive collection of antique pistols and semi-automatic handguns with corresponding bullet and ammunition displays. I wondered if they had all been purchased legally. But what did it matter? In the hands of the wrong person, the guns were capable of producing the same destruction and heartbreak, no matter how they'd been acquired.

In time my terror subsided, replaced for a moment by a sense of awe for the enormous amount of time and care required for building and maintaining the collection. I'd found what I was looking for, but there were still too many unanswered questions. I wondered if Jim encouraged Jennifer's passion for gun collection. I wondered how much the collection was worth, whether they always kept their firearms behind glass or removed them from the cabinets for reasons other than routine cleaning and maintenance. Did they ever use their guns for their intended purpose, and did they involve their sons in their hobby?

Despite the immensity of the loft space, the four walls and pitched ceiling began to close in on me. I became claustrophobic, and my chin trembled as I whispered one word under my breath: *Run. Run, run, run!* I needed to escape that loft, that life, that world. What was the point of staying? Feeling literally and figuratively sickened by the whole mess of Jennifer's life, I flicked off the overhead light switch and began to descend the carpeted stairs.

Clutching the railing, I glanced toward the bottom of the stairwell. That's when I saw a pair of black sneakers facing forward, their laces untied. With each step down the stairs, more of Martin came into view. His legs, his shirt, his thin pale neck. He stood with one hand leaning on the golf club I'd used to prop open the door, the other hand holding the door open, a wry smile on his face. I froze. I stood halfway down the stairs, exposed, and paralyzed. "Martin," I said. I held my breath and reached for the cell phone in my pocket. "What? What do you want?"

CHAPTER 14

Ignoring my question, Martin turned his back to me and flung the golf club on the garage floor. He sauntered off, leaving the door wide open. My knees buckled as I clutched the railing and slumped against the wall. It may have been a few moments, or a few minutes, or an hour. I lost all sense of time, frozen in space. Finally, I slithered down the stairs, leaning into the railing for support.

The stench of decomposing garbage, of sweat, and decay overpowered me as I reached the bottom of the stairwell. The scent Martin left in his wake felt like a reprimand; this was Martin's house. He had a right to leave his bedroom, to look for his mom in the garage. But it was Jennifer's house, too. Jennifer wouldn't need her son's permission to explore the gun loft above the garage. I reminded myself to act like a normal parent, but unfortunately, I'd lost any reasonable concept of normal.

I reentered the code on the keypad, locking the door behind me, and headed for the kitchen through the mudroom. Despite the hammering of my heart, I willed myself to breathe slowly. I found Martin standing in the kitchen, gazing into the refrigerator, the door ajar.

"Can I make you something to eat?" I asked. I tried to think and to act like a typical mother of a typical teenage boy. Although Martin was far from typical. He looked skeletal, wearing the same clothes he'd worn to Antonio's, the same black shirt, and the same baggy jeans resting precariously on his bony hips. His shoulder blades protruded from his back like sharpened knives, and his pale, hairless arms were twigs, hardly thick enough to qualify as useful kindling for a campfire. He needed food, and as he gazed transfixed into the vacant refrigerator, I had one ridiculous, maternal thought: *I need to put some meat on those bones.*

"Are you hungry, Martin? Can I make you something?" I'd need to get used to repeating my questions, waiting patiently when he tuned me out. I'd already devised a strategy for this reoccurring pattern: First ignore him, next pretend his behavior is normal, then wait, always maintain low expectations, give up, and sometimes try again. I wouldn't let Martin push my buttons. In fact, I was determined to win him over.

"Listen, Martin, I'm going to the supermarket in about half an hour. Tell me what you want or write it down for me, and I'll buy it." I paused. "I'm thinking steak for dinner tonight." *Okay. He doesn't have to respond. I'll get the steak. Let's hope he's not a vegetarian.* If Martin scoffed at my dinner suggestion, I was ready with a fallback position: *I was only joking. Of course, I won't buy steak for dinner. I know you don't eat steak.* I grabbed a piece of paper and a pen from the built-in desk next to the bookcase filled with a collection of what seemed to be brand-new cookbooks. I was about to write the words SHOPPING LIST on the top of the paper but I caught myself. He'd know his mother's handwriting. I put the pen down on the counter.

"There you go," I said, willing myself not to nag him about closing the refrigerator door. That was what my mother would have done. I knew better. With more than two decades of teaching experience, I'd learned to pick my battles. I walked out of the kitchen, never looking back, and retreated to Jennifer's bedroom to catch my breath. To rest my body on Jennifer's bed, to close my eyes for a while, a temporary reprieve.

* * *

Later that afternoon, when I returned from the supermarket with a dozen or so bags of food, I was startled to find a cleaning crew loading supplies into a van parked in front of Jennifer's house. I parked behind the van in the circular drive and got out of the Mercedes. One woman nodded her head in my direction. "Hi, Mrs. Moriarty."

"Hey there."

"You didn't leave any instructions, so we assumed you wanted the sheets changed. Did a load of towels. They're still in the drier."

"Thank you," I said, wondering if I was supposed to have left a check for them. "How should I pay you?" I asked. The woman paused long enough for me to realize I should have known the answer to that question. My ability to read people and situations was fading the very moment I needed it most.

I'd always been proud of that superpower. Reading people had helped me survive teaching freshman English. I could tell when my students were lying. "No, Miss Cooper, you never said that assignment was due today. You gave us an extension, remember?" Or, "Sorry Miss Cooper, my mother was really sick last night; I had to help take care of my baby sister and didn't have time to read." And I could intuit my students' boredom easily, their toxic disapproval, their flagrant ennui, like a flashing neon sign in the room, no matter how hard they tried to hide their feelings. I had to wonder: Why had my power of intuition failed me so miserably in Key West when it really mattered? When I had the chance to walk away? And where was that power now?

"Do you want to change how you pay us?" the woman asked.

"Well, no, not necessarily. Let's keep things the way they are," I said. *The way they are. What did that mean?* "When will I see you next?" More confusion. The woman scowled and tilted her head.

"Twice a week, Wednesdays and Fridays, same as always," the woman replied. I fake-smiled as I reached into the trunk to grab one of the grocery bags.

I considered asking Martin for help. Mothers expect their children to help with chores like carrying bags of groceries in from the car. But asking for Martin's help might be an unexpected and therefore treacherous move. I was only beginning to get the hang of Jennifer's life. The cleaning service, the swimming pool, the built-in coffee machine, and the boy upstairs. Now it was time to get the hang of writing in her beautiful study. With a bit of luck and the return of my power of intuition, I might get there.

* * *

As I unpacked the groceries, I appreciated the Moriarty's magnificent kitchen designed for a chef. I even looked forward to cooking dinner that night. State-of-the-art, stainless steel appliances, an eight-burner gas stove, multiple sinks, and designated food preparation areas, cherry cabinets with gold leaf accents. My god, there were more islands than in the state of Hawaii. The gift of Jennifer's kitchen presented an opportunity for me to escape my culinary heritage of canned soups and frozen vegetables, a heavy hand with the saltshaker, and one-dish casseroles revolving around canned tuna and sausages.

I stopped to peruse Jennifer's colorful cookbook collection. I pulled out Julia Child's *Mastering the Art of French Cooking*. The volume had never been touched. The spine cracked as I opened to a random page.

Watching food and cooking shows on my computer had been a favorite way to unwind after a long day of teaching. I could name all of the celebrity chefs. I watched repeat episodes of *Chopped, Iron Chef, French Chef, Top Chef, Naked Chef, Master Chef,* and *Cupcake Wars*. I devoured cooking programs from around the world, learning about cuisine from Argentina to Zimbabwe. Here, in Jennifer's kitchen, I might be able to apply all of those televised lessons about food preparation. I knew enough to impress a skinny boy, locked away upstairs in his bedroom. Yeah, I'd learned from the best chefs in the world. *The way to a man's heart*, that was the old adage, and I was motivated to test the crap out of that theory. My cooking might make an impact on Martin's appetite as well as his mood. Time would tell.

CHAPTER 15

I didn't want to be late for Friday morning's meeting at Martin's school. I needed to make a good first impression. Although, strictly speaking, this would not be a "first impression" for Mrs. Jennifer Moriarty. According to my GPS, I'd have a half-hour to spare, and so I stopped at Starbucks for a large cappuccino.

Armed with coffee, a yellow legal pad, a list of questions, and an equally long list of demands, I had the necessary tools to handle a team of Florida educators, their pedagogical rhetoric, their euphemisms, and their plethora of acronyms. They were in for a surprise. The new Jennifer Moriarty, Martin's surrogate mother, spoke their language.

Coral Gables High School consisted of an imposing main building. Several contemporary wings seemed out of place, probably tacked onto the main building as the suburban population grew. Like Dickinson High, Martin and Jason's school included the requisite playing fields, tennis courts, basketball courts, and three parking lots; one was for staff and another for visitors. The largest lot, designated for students only, seemed to be overflowing with BMWs, Mercedes, and Audis, all clean and shiny, unlike the older, dusty vehicles parked in the staff lot. The student lot also included an abundance of SUVs, Jeep Wranglers, and a sprinkling of convertible sports cars with tops down. *Welcome to Coral Gables High School, a veritable upscale car dealership.*

Feeling undressed without my teacher badge—a photo ID hanging around my neck on a maroon and gold-colored Dickinson High lanyard—I headed nervously toward the main entrance. Jennifer's Gucci bag felt practically weightless compared with my old, canvas teacher tote, typically overflowing with student papers, books, and a paper bag lunch.

As I entered the building, I had to first pass through the metal detector. Next, I had to verify the purpose of my visit, provide two forms of personal identification, sign in, and make inane but cheerful small talk with the well-meaning security monitor. After those preliminary steps, the monitor searched my bag. Finally, he issued my visitor's pass. As I walked toward the main office, another man, this one in a police uniform, greeted me. "Welcome to Coral Gables High School. May I see your visitor's pass?" he asked. He examined my pass as his German Shephard proceeded to sniff me, searching for narcotics, perhaps. Or, the dog may have been trying to detect explosives. It was ludicrous, worse than airport security, the way the school treated visitors, making us feel like criminals. And yet, I shouldn't have been surprised. That was how things were in schools all across the country and at Dickinson High as well.

I followed the signs to the main office. A long counter separated the office hive from visitors and students, a stark barrier protecting the group of busy worker bees behind the counter from all manner of interruptions. I cleared my throat, trying to get someone's attention. Finally, a secretary greeted me, although her lack of warmth and enthusiasm didn't feel like a greeting in the strict sense of the word. It was barely an acknowledgement.

"Yes?" the woman asked.

"I'm Jennifer Moriarty, I have an appointment?" She directed me to a small conference room down a hallway off the main office. I pulled up a chair at the nondescript table in front of a stack of thick file folders. After a few more sips of my cappuccino, I got to work.

I realized immediately that one hour wasn't enough time to read all of Martin's reports, examine the plethora of academic and psychological evaluations, and review the profusion of communications between Jennifer and the schools Martin had attended since kindergarten.

I scribbled notes as I studied the documents. Martin had been on his teachers' radar since elementary school. His preoccupation with violence became a major concern in second grade. His artwork laced with weapons and blood, his disturbing poetry about murdering domestic and wild animals, his frightening stories of suffocating babies, all pointed to a growing fixation with gruesome violence. I looked away to escape the graphic descriptions and illustrations of Martin's story about a boy who killed and dismembered his grandmother. I pressed my fist against my mouth and pushed my chair away from the table, willing myself to stay calm.

And the school? What had they done to help? They suspended him repeatedly for sharing his inappropriate illustrations and stories with peers. Two-day suspensions, three-day suspensions. Even a ten-day suspension had no impact on Martin's behavior. Although his report card grades were below average, an educational evaluation in grade six reflected a superior intellect, in the high average to gifted range. His school determined that Martin did not qualify for special education services. *How could this happen?* I shook my head at the ineptitude, my disgust turning to rage at the school district as I forced myself to read more.

In seventh grade, the educators must have seen the light. They decided Martin qualified for "an exceptional student education" because of an "emotional or behavioral disorder." The district had ordered a psychiatric evaluation. They used the results to identify his social and emotional disturbances as a rationale for special education identification.

I imagined that particular meeting when the school told Jennifer her son qualified for an ESE because he had an EBD. They probably showered Jennifer with acronyms, designed to sugarcoat the reality of Martin's problems. A jumbled alphabet, secret symbols passed around from specialist to specialist, for the sole purpose of chasing parents off the scent. Keeping everything nice, vague, and a little bit normal.

And then, I discovered a letter from Jennifer Moriarty in that file. Another maddening piece of the puzzle.

To whom it may concern,

We have decided to homeschool Martin Moriarty. I do not agree with your decision to label him "emotionally disturbed." He does not need special education. Martin is an anxious young man, and, as I told you at the last meeting, the unrealistic demands of his teachers and the nonstop bullying by his peers have made his anxiety worse. Besides that, Martin is bored at school. He needs a teacher who is patient and appreciates his creativity. He does not need teachers who keep implying he needs medication. I don't approve of poisoning my son with drugs to make his teachers' lives easier.

Sincerely,

Mrs. Jennifer Moriarty

Further communications between the school and home, made it clear that the district did not approve of Jennifer Moriarty's plan to homeschool Martin, but they believed there was little they could do to stop her. Maybe they were right, I wasn't sure. But Jenn Cooper might be able to do something. I refused to add to the litany of sorry excuses to avoid facing the truth about Jennifer's imperfect, troubled offspring. This time, with my guidance, we were going to help that boy.

The same aloof secretary interrupted me to say they needed the conference room and I should wait in the main office. I gathered my things while she hovered at the door, as if she didn't trust me to vacate the room. Once in the main office, she pointed to a row of chairs along the wall.

I settled in for the wait, twirling a lock of hair around my finger, feeling like one of the potted plants sitting quietly amidst the familiar school office commotion. My mind wandered to Dickinson High. Parents waiting for meetings to begin while teachers and administrators refilled their coffee cups in the faculty room, checked their emails and office mailboxes, visited the restrooms, without a care about how their students' parents were feeling. Waiting, worrying, intimidated by the setting, the staff, and the harsh scent of authority.

I told myself that unlike most parents whose kids attended Coral Gables High School, I was enlightened, a dutiful soldier fighting on the righteous side of the battleground. I was ready for combat. I genuinely worried about Martin. Perhaps not the way a real mother would worry about her son. Certainly not the way Jennifer tried in her misguided fashion to protect Martin from the stress of living his life. Still, I knew how important the meeting would be for Martin's welfare and for the welfare of all the lives he might touch in the future. I'd fight the good fight.

That's how I began to look at my life as Jennifer Moriarty, a short-term job, if not a mission.

"Mrs. Moriarty." I heard the words as background music. Deep in my thoughts, nothing registered at first. "Mrs. Moriarty, are you ready?" I looked up, released the lock of hair twisted around my finger, and I smiled. Although why was I smiling? Would smiling be appropriate? I quickly replaced the smile with a seriously concerned parent expression and grabbed my things.

The woman escorted me into a larger conference room. Five people sat around the table, chatting with each other, laughing, ignoring my entrance. Did Jennifer Moriarty know these people? I noticed laminated cards in front of each individual. Their names and positions were printed boldly in large font. Nice touch. That would be something to bring back to Dickinson High School when I returned to my real job. Finally, the group settled down, and the young woman at the head of the table acknowledged my presence.

"Mrs. Moriarty, as you know, now that Martin has reached the age of sixteen, I believe his birthday was in May, May—let's see, May 19—the state statutes regarding home schooling no longer apply. I have a copy of the law for your review." She handed a photocopy to the woman on her left, who passed it to me. "If you want to continue to keep Martin out of school, he has to sign a notice of intent to withdraw. You will no longer be held accountable for maintaining a portfolio of records and materials. You will no longer be required to keep a log of educational activities, titles of reading materials, samples of worksheets, and that kind of thing." She spoke rapidly, following a protocol intended to move the meeting forward to its pre-determined finality. The other members of the team avoided eye contact with me. I knew that trick, too. Their heads were bowed, studying their notepads, their laptops, or cell phones.

"Excuse me," I said, interrupting the speaker. The title on the woman's name card was Assistant Principal. Mrs. Jill Armstrong. She was attractive, probably in her early thirties. I'd worked with a few younger administrators at Dickinson High. Those educators who raced to the top of the ladder, wearing designer clothing, decorating their offices with exotic plants and black and white photographs of their perfect babies. I wondered how they managed, how they juggled all the demands in their lives. For me, teaching was more than a full-time job. It consumed my weekends, and I stayed up past midnight most nights, grading papers, planning lessons. There was no time for babies.

Sitting at the head of the table, Mrs. Armstrong thought she knew what she was doing. But Mrs. Armstrong didn't have all the facts. The most important fact was that Martin's mother, along with her denial, her lack of good judgment, and her irresponsible history, that woman was not sitting at the table. "I'm sorry for interrupting you, but I have a few questions and some serious concerns." Mrs. Armstrong looked up from her notes, her mouth slack. I had her full attention. "For starters, how have you been holding my husband and me accountable for maintaining a portfolio of records and materials?" I refused to leave Jim out of the responsibility pool.

The silence in the conference room grabbed everyone's attention. Mrs. Armstrong's posture stiffened. She jerked her head back as if an invisible hand had slapped her across the face.

During my online research, I'd familiarized myself with the home schooling laws in Florida. I'd seen no evidence that Jennifer kept anything that even remotely resembled home schooling plans, logs, work products, or records. I'd found no evidence of any such artifact in Martin's files that morning. Unless, playing violent video games qualified as "sequentially progressive educational activities," Jennifer was out of compliance, and Martin had missed two full years of educational opportunities. Perhaps the school district didn't care, and perhaps Jennifer didn't care, but for some strange reason, I cared.

I glared at Mrs. Armstrong, projecting my rage with pride. Along with Martin's parents, the school was also out of compliance, and worse than that, the school district was guilty of severe educational malpractice. Fueled by anger and a surplus of comfort in the school setting, I continued to stare into the eyes of the mystified assistant principal and began to articulate my demands.

"Martin is in no condition to return to this high school setting, but that doesn't absolve you of your responsibilities to educate my son." I referred to my notes, my list of demands bulleted on page one of the yellow legal pad. "First, I am requesting an individual educational plan to include home tutoring and counseling until Martin is able to return to Coral Gables High School." The words on the page began to blur. I looked away from my notes and spoke from my heart. "He is a highly intelligent boy—and yes, he has significant emotional difficulties, but I will not allow this district to shrug its shoulders. Martin has great potential, and if you can't see that potential, if you won't stand up for Martin and his rights, then I will seek and I will retain legal representation. I will fight with every fiber of my soul for Martin. I will fight for my son." By the time I finished my impassioned tirade, my voice and body trembled. I didn't know where all that rage had come from. I did know this: my fury wasn't an act. It was more real than any emotion I'd experienced for a long time.

I felt a hand resting lightly on my arm. "Mrs. Moriarty, may I get you a glass of water?" I turned to the tall man sitting on my left. His expression was kind, and I sensed his sincere concern.

"Yes, please."

"Mrs. Moriarty, what does your husband think about this change of direction?" Mrs. Armstrong asked. Appalled by the question, I gazed at the assistant principal in utter amazement. What did Jennifer's husband have to do with today's outcome? He was absent. He was not sitting at the table. He had given up on Martin. I took a deep breath, and then I took the high road.

"Jim Moriarty and I are separated, but he concurs with everything I've said today." Not that Jennifer's marital status had anything at all to do with her parental rights as far as the school district was concerned. I refused to allow this assistant principal to hijack the meeting, and I directed the group right back to planning for Martin's educational program.

"When may I expect educational services for Martin to begin?" I pushed for a commitment, a timeline, almost daring them to deny my demands.

Mrs. Armstrong referred to an appointment calendar on the table. "Let's see, I can schedule a formal IEP meeting for next Thursday morning. We'll have a more specific ESE plan in place to share with you at that time," Mrs. Armstrong said. Listening to her throw around those special education acronyms, felt like the proverbial fingernails scraping against a blackboard. Inwardly I cringed, but I would not cower from my responsibility as Martin's advocate. I returned to the notes on my legal pad to make sure I'd addressed the most important demands.

"As is my legal right, as Martin's parent, I'd like to provide input regarding his educational programming. I expect it will be a college preparation program including opportunities for honors classes and advanced placement courses. I'd prefer not to seek legal counsel at this time, but if necessary, I will do whatever it takes to make sure Martin's program meets his needs. As I said before, Martin is smart. He can do it, and he will do it." I spoke with more bravado than I felt.

"Of course, your input is invaluable." Mrs. Armstrong had softened her demeanor. She'd adopted a conciliatory tone. I noticed the glass of water in front of me and took a sip. Mrs. Armstrong stood, walked around the table, and reached out to shake my hand. Her handshake was firm, almost painful. I refused to wince. I thanked the other members of the team with a smile and a nod of my head and allowed the tall gentleman who had brought the glass of water to escort me to the conference room door. Together we walked down the corridor. Although I could feel my chin quivering, I focused on slowing my inhalations and exhalations. I was still breathing; a good sign.

The man stopped at the end of the hallway and turned toward me. "Mrs. Moriarty, I didn't have a chance to properly introduce myself. I'm David Allington, the new school psychologist." I turned and looked up, really seeing him for the first time. He was ruggedly handsome. How had I not noticed him during the meeting? "I want you to know that I've studied your son's file carefully, and I want to work closely with you to help Martin. I also want to tell you that you were very impressive during that meeting. Martin is a lucky kid to have you as his mother."

As I walked through the visitor parking lot, my pulse quickened. I felt a flush creeping up my neck, and I couldn't stop grinning. All thoughts of Martin, of Jennifer, of the Moriarty family evaporated. One name, one face filled my thoughts: *David Allington.*

CHAPTER 16

After leaving a late breakfast tray on the floor by Martin's bedroom door, I sat at the kitchen island with a glass of iced tea, figuring out my next moves. I checked Jennifer's phone for messages. There was a text from Jim. IMPORTANT! CALL ME! The screaming, all caps demand had its desired effect. I started twirling a lock of hair, expecting the worst as I called Jennifer's husband.

"What the fuck, Jennifer," Jim said. "Why didn't you talk to Jason when you were at the school this morning? Why would you ignore your son? What kind of mother are you?"

"What are you talking about? I didn't see Jason at school." Although even before the words slid off my tongue, I realized, having only seen a photograph of Jason, it was conceivable that I'd walked right by him in a congested hallway. Even if I physically bumped into him, would I recognize Jennifer's older son?

"Well, he saw you, he even called out to you and you totally ignored him," Jim said.

"My mind was probably elsewhere, Jim. I was at school for a meeting with Mrs. Armstrong and the team, about Martin." Jim's angry tone turned suspicious.

"What about Martin? What the hell's going on with him now?"

"There's a lot going on. Next week the special education team is meeting again. This whole home schooling plan isn't feasible. Not anymore. I made a few suggestions today, and I think the school will be responsive. Martin has special needs, he requires services the school should be providing." Jim scoffed and started to raise his voice.

"Jennifer—what the fuck are you talking about? I've been telling you that for years and you've refused to acknowledge Martin's problems. Is this your way of getting me back?"

"Getting back at you?" I honestly misunderstood.

"Jennifer, our marriage is over. I'm not coming back. You have to know that, right?" I almost laughed when I realized he meant exactly what he said.

"Jim, trust me. This is not a ploy to save our marriage. This is about Martin."

"Trust you? Jennifer, I think it's fair to say you've lost your right to ask for my trust at this stage in the game. As for Jason, you should call him at your sister's house. He won't answer if you call his cell. He's furious. You really fucked up this time, you know." I had to bite my tongue to stop from blurting out what I was thinking; *Jim, you're the father in this household—you really fucked up too.* There was plenty of fault to go around.

*   *   *

I considered carving out an hour that afternoon to start drafting or at least outlining my novel, but there seemed to be a dozen other priorities standing between me and my writing intentions. Instead, I poured my creative juices into answering emails, voicemails, and text messages and snuffing out potential fires. I avoided Jennifer's friend, Liz, who kept leaving messages to remind her about the hospital fundraising gala meeting and to find out how she was feeling. I ignored Jennifer's personal trainer from the gym who left messages wondering why she'd gone missing in action. He tried to guilt her into keeping up with her plank goals. Jennifer's therapist, Dr. Angela Blaine, reminded her repeatedly that the office charged for missed appointments unless given 24 hours advanced notice. Coming up with a million and one credible excuses for dodging people and expectations that I wanted desperately to avoid left me with hardly enough energy for the gargantuan task of developing a suitable academic plan for Martin. I tried my best to focus. I needed to prioritize. The novel could wait.

I picked up my legal pad, a pen, and I curled up on the sofa in Jennifer's bedroom. Solving problems seemed easier with a pen in my hand. I wrote one word, MARTIN, on the top of a clean page. Under that one word, I listed three top priorities.

MEALS

EDUCATIONAL PLAN

MEDICAL PLAN

Other than one dinner at Antonio's the night I arrived, I'd yet to entice that boy out of his room for a meal. Broaching the topic of his education and the proposed changes to his life terrified me. Martin was unaccustomed to the simple demands of typical family life. Getting out of bed in the morning, eating meals at the table, attending school, helping his mother carry bags of groceries from the car into the house, doing homework, acknowledging other people with a semblance of social grace. Poor Martin. He was the opposite of grace. Was there a word for that? Graceless? Gawky might be too kind a word to describe Martin. He had no social life, he had never experienced a positive school life, and now he existed in a lonely world of his own making, a world with no expectations and no purpose. Upstairs in his locked bedroom, protected from the stress of life, Martin was a lost and angry soul. Was he beyond help? And where would I start?

I remembered reading a story in the New York Times about a young boy who had a worm lodged in his eye for months. Finally, a creative ophthalmologist figured out how to lure the one-inch parasite out of the boy's eye using basil leaves as bait, thereby avoiding a risky surgery. Basil. So random. For Martin, I'd need something sweeter than basil to lure him out into the world. Much sweeter. I'd need the perfect bait to sugarcoat the prospect of academic demands, to convince him that life might be worth living despite a little stress now and again. Finally, I came up with a plan that had promise. Forget basil. I'd start with the perfect cupcake.

My theory was that once Martin demonstrated a willingness to emerge from his room for cupcakes, it would be easier to move in the direction of full dinners at the kitchen table. I'd focus on the first bullet on my list of priorities: MEALS. And then I'd broach his educational plan. One step at a time, bite by bite.

I perused Jennifer's library of cookbooks, finally deciding on the perfect recipe. It was touted as the most decadent, chocolatey, sour cream concoction in the universe, with melt-in-your-mouth buttercream frosting. For the next hour, I lost myself in the flour, the eggs, the vanilla extract, and dark chocolate. I reveled in the smooth batter and escaped into the sweet aroma permeating the kitchen.

Later, as the chocolate cupcakes cooled on the kitchen island, I returned to the study to work on the Jason problem. I understood Jim's fury. I'd need to contact his older son and perhaps meet with Jason face-to-face. I dreaded that eventuality, but I needed to fix Jennifer's relationship with Jason, and it had to be easier than fixing the Martin mess.

I'd spent time scouring Jennifer's email inbox, unearthing communications going back months, and I understood the flavor of my double's writing style. I wrestled with the proliferation of grammatical and spelling errors. As an English teacher, *me and I* confusions made my stomach churn, and Jennifer's cringe-worthy abuse of exclamation marks and commas annoyed me. Jennifer would have to clean up her written English under my watch. Although I doubted her family would notice the improvement. I drafted an email to Jason.

Dear Jason,

Dad said you saw me at school yesterday. I didn't see or hear you call for me, honey!! I went to school to meet with the assistant principal about Martin's academic program. I must have been distracted. I probably looked right through you. Forgive me. I miss you! The house is quiet. Too quiet! I understand why you needed to take a break and why you want to stay with Aunt Nancy for now. I don't blame you at all. I hope you'll consider seeing me away from the house. How about dinner at Antonio's next week? Just the two of us? What night is good for you? We can meet there or whatever works for you. I can pick you up if you'd like. Let me know. I love you so much,

Mom XXOO

As an English teacher, those fatuous symbols for kisses and hugs irritated me, but I needed to approach this Jennifer Moriarty role in a credible fashion. That's how she signed off on her emails to her children, as if they were both in pre-school. I supposed that was one way to express maternal love, with symbols, although not necessarily the most effective way. But who was I to criticize? Maternal love was not within my range of human emotions.

I sent the message to Jason and returned to the cooled cupcakes. I frosted and decorated each one with a perfect strawberry sliced to resemble a blooming flower and added a chocolate kiss, tilted at an angle. Each cupcake, a work of art. Subliminal message aside, I wanted Martin to know that I cared. I couldn't vouch for his mother, but honestly, I did care. And I needed his cooperation. I needed him on my side. Given Martin's past dealings with his mother, winning him over would take time, more time than Jennifer had allotted for this crazy life-swapping experiment. Cupcakes might speed up the process.

That evening I placed a dinner tray on the floor next to Martin's door and knocked loudly. "Martin, I'm leaving your dinner here. I tried a new lasagna recipe. By the way, I baked cupcakes today. They're chocolate and really good. The best I've ever made. I'll leave a plate in the kitchen. Take as many as you want. Oh, and there's milk in the fridge too." I waited for a response. I knocked again. "Did you hear me, Martin? I'm going out for a few hours. Let me know if you need anything." Not a word. I waited. I knocked again. "Martin, did you hear me?"

"YES, I HEARD YOU!" he screamed. I recoiled from the door, scorched by his rage. I swallowed the venomous words I wanted to launch back at the ungrateful monster in my charge.

* * *

I spent the next few hours at the mall, trying on comfortable bathing suits, browsing through cookbooks at the bookstore, and remembering how much easier life had been before meeting Jennifer Moriarty. I left the mall shortly before closing time, empty-handed and eager to return home to see if Martin had taken the bait.

As I stepped into the kitchen, my heart soared. Not only had Martin emerged from his bedroom for a cupcake, he had taken the entire plate. He left one cupcake behind on the kitchen table. Was this a peace offering for his mother? I decided the lone cupcake was Martin's way of apologizing for screaming at me earlier. I poured myself a glass of cold milk and relished every decadent bite of the last cupcake.

I had found a way to entice Martin from the prison of his self-imposed exile. I'd hit the jackpot with my very first cupcake made from scratch. I licked the buttercream frosting from my upper lip and finished the last swallow of milk. I leaned back in my chair. Cupcakes alone couldn't cure Martin's anxiety or erase his violent obsessions. But maybe I could help that boy. I could fix part of what was broken in Martin's soul. I could teach him. After all, Miss Cooper could teach anyone.

* * *

Although I fell asleep easily, I awoke in the middle of the night gasping for breath, the terror of my nightmare all too real. I stood in the middle of a forest fire surrounded by flames threatening to engulf the land. I was alone, facing the devastation by myself. I held a fire extinguisher in my hand as the flames leapt closer. I awoke drenched in perspiration, remembering the feel of my burning skin, my throat dry and raw. I didn't need a psychiatrist to interpret my dream. It was obvious. Survival was up to me and me alone.

That morning, buoyed by a strong cup of coffee, I began a cancellation-binge. I cancelled the heavy burden of Jennifer's regular appointments. *Sorry, Jennifer*, I thought. *There is no way I can jump blindly into your psychotherapy with Dr. Angela Blaine while maintaining this grotesque, false identity deception. Any therapist worth a fraction of her exorbitant hourly fee would see right through me. The same goes for your weekly spa appointments and your personal trainer. I will continue to swim in your pool wearing your expensive and uncomfortable bathing suits, but weightlifting, aerobics, Pilates, and Yoga classes will be on hiatus until your return. And my nails will remain unpolished with ragged cuticles. I will manage fine without your weekly manicures.* I felt light and free after cancelling Jennifer's time-killers. *If only I could cancel Jennifer's dare, then I'd truly be free.*

* * *

At 6:00 p.m. that evening, I knocked on Martin's door. "Martin." I waited. "Martin, I'm leaving your dinner in the kitchen tonight. It's on the table. I have a few errands to run. I'll be back in about an hour. You can leave the dishes in the sink," I said. I sounded like any other run-of-the-mill mother, taking care of her son, providing directions and reasonable expectations. But inside I was a tangled mess of wires, worrying about everything that might go wrong.

I'd decided that if I left the house, Martin might be more inclined to emerge from his room, especially for a gourmet meal. No more dinner trays. He left his bedroom for cupcakes, and so I decided he could leave his bedroom for dinner. And even though he hadn't thanked me yet, I believed he appreciated the food. This was no baby step; it was a leap of faith for me and a leap of trust in Martin.

Clearly, Martin wasn't accustomed to a mother who cooked for him. Jennifer Moriarty had more important priorities and demands in her life. She didn't have time to worry about what her family ate for dinner. I didn't blame her. Based on what I deduced from a chain of emails, Jim rarely ate dinner at home, Jason stayed out late, busy with extra-curricular activities, and both kids had pretty much fended for their own nutritional needs.

Well, perhaps I did blame Jennifer more than I was ready to admit. I knew that the ultimate "family dinner" with hungry kids sitting gleefully around the table and nightly *How-was-your-day?* conversations were not even a visible speck on the horizon. Nevertheless, I'd crawl doggedly in that direction.

I left the house and drove Jennifer's Mercedes to an outdoor shopping mall not too far from home. I parked in the multi-level lot and strolled past the familiar stores, window-shopping for inspiration. I finished hatching my plot at the CVS where I purchased a candy bar and then stopped at the mega Barnes and Noble bookstore to pick up reading material for Martin. A book of short stories. Martin would have a surprise waiting for him on his breakfast tray the next morning.

When I returned to the house, I found Martin's empty plate on the kitchen table. Although he ignored my request to leave his dirty dishes in the sink, he'd left his room and eaten dinner in the kitchen, a step forward. Then, I noticed something odd. Next to his plate was what looked like a small piece of paper, folded intricately. As I walked over to the table, I realized it was an origami sculpture, shaped like a handgun, almost a work of art. I gripped the edge of the table until my knuckles turned bone-white. How could something so beautiful have the power to instill such fear?

Even as someone who had no use for guns, I appreciated the artistry. Although an origami crane would have been as appreciated, the paper pistol sent a different message. *A cry for help?* Martin had written words on the barrel of the paper gun. His handwriting so small, I struggled to read the words: *Thx for the food. Where's my oxy? U promised.* So, the bottle of oxycodone in the salmon-colored overnight bag was definitely meant for Martin, not for Jennifer's use. *But why didn't Jennifer get a doctor's prescription for her son?* Clearly, he suffered from anxiety and probably needed a pharmaceutical intervention. From what I'd read, oxycodone was possibly the worst choice for his psychological issues. On the other hand, I could use the pills as bait, one round, green pill at a time. More basil for the worm stuck in that boy's eye. At least until I convinced Martin to see a psychiatrist who would know how to treat him properly. Cupcakes and oxycodone. Baby steps.

I stayed up well after midnight, pursuing the mastery of an art form I'd never paid attention to before: folding paper. I couldn't find much in the way of craft materials in the house, and so I ended up using colorful gift-wrap paper I'd discovered in the mudroom cupboard. I sat cross-legged on the oriental rug in the Moriarty's family room, hunched over the coffee table, perfecting the art of folding origami boxes. Thank goodness for the internet. It took hours of practice, a mountain of crumpled attempts, but finally, I constructed a basic cube. And then another. I created enough boxes for a week and placed one pill in each box. Martin might appreciate my origami efforts, and he might even understand that I was trying to relate to him on some level.

In the morning, I arranged Martin's breakfast tray. Along with the origami box and pill, I prepared an elegant breakfast. Fresh squeezed orange juice, a bowl of mixed berries with a dollop of yogurt, caramel apple muffins made with fresh buttermilk, and a generous slice of spinach quiche. My mother wouldn't recognize the woman I'd become—someone who folded origami boxes and had the patience to bake from scratch. I was proud of myself. It was no small accomplishment to overcome a childhood of tuna casseroles and a young adulthood of sushi takeout.

Next to the origami pillbox, I placed the *Oh Henry* candy bar and the book I'd chosen for Martin's first academic assignment. I placed the assignment inside the front cover. I'd labored for hours over the wording of the final draft.

To my son Martin,

I'm sure you have read some of these short stories, but one can never read too many O. Henry stories, right? I realize that I have not done a very good job as your home schooling teacher. But I believe it's never too late to try harder, to improve. I hope you will forgive me and allow me the chance to do better.

Here's your assignment: Read one story from this collection. Choose one you have never read. Write a short essay (200-300 words) supporting one of these conclusions:

(A.) The story has no relevance to your life, or
(B.) The story has some relevance to your life.

Love,
Mom
XXOO

I placed the tray outside Martin's door and knocked loudly. "Martin," I called. "I made a special breakfast for you today. Make sure you look inside the box. I think it's what you've been waiting for." I didn't have to wait for an answer this time.

"Fine," Martin said. "It's about time."

CHAPTER 17

Swimming laps for an hour provided a much-needed reprieve from worrying about the boy upstairs. With each stroke, I pushed away the warm pool water and the worries about how Jennifer was managing at Dickinson High School.

As an experienced teacher, I'd grappled with juggling the needs of one hundred and thirty students and the constant flow of essays and exams threatening to drown me day after day. *Would Jennifer have the patience needed to deal with the adolescent behaviors, the snarky attitudes?* How much damage might she inflict during the first month of school? I knew I'd have some serious catching up to do upon my return to Dickinson High. From one end of the pool to the other, I tried to sweep away the mounting worries. Back and forth, back and forth, the water enveloped my body in a cocoon of safety, my muscles worked hard to the point of exhaustion.

After a long shower, the pulsing hot water kneading my muscles, I felt ready to settle back into the study—to get back to work. As I made my way down the stairs, the sound of ringing in the distance interrupted my thoughts. It took a few moments before I made sense of that sound. It was the telephone. A landline. I didn't have one in Hartford. I'd given it up years ago like most people in my world. *Who would be calling Jennifer using her home telephone? Could it be Jennifer trying to call me?* I sprinted to the kitchen, grabbing the receiver after the fourth ring.

"Hello, Mrs. Moriarty? It's Dr. Allington. David Allington. From Coral Gables High." I smiled. Despite my disappointment that it wasn't Jennifer, I had to admit I was pleased to hear his voice.

"Yes, hello, Dr. Allington." *So, the guy has a doctorate degree. That's nice.*

"I've been thinking a lot about your son and reviewing his records. I had a few ideas I wanted to run by you before we meet with the team next week. I hope I'm not being presumptuous, calling you at home, but could we get together for coffee? I really want to help Martin."

The prospect of meeting up with David Allington, alone, even for coffee, was an unexpected gift making me feel like some hormonal teenager. I tried to suppress the breathlessness in my voice.

"Yes, of course, let's meet for coffee. I can use all the help I can get with Martin's plan." David suggested a time and place for Saturday morning.

My excitement about David Allington's phone call seemed out of character for me. How strange to be attracted to an eligible man so quickly, so easily, like second nature. Then again, I assumed David was, in fact, eligible. I'd need to confirm his marital status during our coffee date. *Was it a date?* And even more surprising, I had a hunch, that good-looking, employed, and seemingly nice guy with a Ph.D. felt an attraction to me as well. Likely wishful thinking, and yet I felt a warm blush on my face, butterflies in my stomach, and a new bounce in my step. My god, I'd turned into a pathetic cliché.

* * *

After dropping off his breakfast tray that morning, I'd forced myself to keep a safe distance from Martin's bedroom. It was midafternoon when I tiptoed up the stairs, holding my breath, not knowing what I'd find.

As I edged closer to his door, the first thing I noticed was that he had eaten everything I'd given him for breakfast. I smiled like a new mother whose baby finished his bottle of milk. Then I realized the book I'd left for him was gone too. As was the origami box. Feeling triumphant, I leaned down to pick up the tray, and that's when I noticed something that erased my smile and my delusional sense of accomplishment. Martin had left another origami sculpture in place of the box, this time in the shape of a long-barreled rifle. The paper, covered with tiny words, was practically indecipherable. How could a piece of paper hold so much power over me? It wasn't a real weapon. I wasn't in any imminent danger. Why then did my blood run cold and my lower lip quiver? Why did the panic threaten to smother me?

My hands shook as I carried the tray to the kitchen. I felt torn between the temptation to unfold and read Martin's message right then, right there, and a desire to rip the paper rifle into shreds and run like hell. *What had Martin written in such tiny letters? A thank you note for the breakfast and for the pain pill? Or something more sinister?*

With Martin, anything was possible. After reviewing his school files, I'd learned too much about his past to expect a positive response to my assignment. I felt compelled to escape that house and find a safe place, out of harm's way. I slipped Martin's origami rifle inside Jennifer's purse and grabbed the car keys.

I drove to a nearby park I'd noticed a few days earlier and pulled the Mercedes into a space on the far end of the lot, a distance away from the other parked cars. Gardens and walking trails dotted the property. Benches and bridges crossed the well-stocked koi ponds, providing a reasonable facsimile of Monet's garden at Giverny. It felt peaceful there, as though nothing bad would ever happen in that place. I chose a bench close to one of the ponds, far from a gaggle of young mothers and their rambunctious toddlers. I breathed in the quiet, the solitude, the tranquility. Warm breezes brushed my hair away from my face. I slipped the origami rifle out of my purse, unfolded it carefully, and began to read the tiny words.

The Ransom of Red Chief

"The Ransom of Red Chief" is all about my life just like the victim in this story I am an only child I am the only child of Jennifer Moriarty and a one-night stand good old dad is a fucked-up blond guy she hooked up with at a bar in Key West seventeen years ago. My mother's husband Jim is a "prominent citizen" just like Ebenezer Dorset, the victim's father in the story and Jim knows I'm not his son it's obvious. Not just because I don't look like Jim but also because I'm a "sick son of a bitch" who has ruined his life and his real son's life and if someone kidnapped me Jennifer and Jim would refuse to fork over $2,000, like in the story. I'm not worth it.

As I read the beginning of Martin's essay, I found myself distracted by the run-on sentences. Always the English teacher with impossibly high standards, I had to force myself to focus on the content and Martin's crystal clear message.

I gazed across the playground at the young children, listened to their screams of delight as mothers pushed their swings high into the air. *Did Martin ever experience a happy childhood? Did either of his parents love him? Cherish him?* No wonder he suffered from depression and anxiety. No wonder he locked himself in his bedroom. I winced at the reference to his unknown biological father. But I understood why *The Ransom of Red Chief* resonated with Martin. This angry, depressed kid had been rejected by both parents, and he knew he was alone in his pathetic world. He was crying out for help, that much was obvious. I kept reading, looking for clues in Martin's essay that might help me figure out a way to provide the help he so desperately needed.

As for the story it's totally unrealistic. Why didn't the kidnappers kill their stupid victim? He didn't deserve to live. He was asking for it. And why would a grownup like Bill the kidnaper be so afraid of a little punk ass-wipe kid who runs around pretending to be an Indian Chief? If I were one of the kidnappers

I'd have scalped the kid with his own knife and burned the rest of his puny body at the stake like he threatened to do to the kidnappers. What pussys those kidnappers turned out to be. I like the part in the story when the kidnappers threaten to return the kid to his home and he totally freaks out. Here's the quote "Red Chief," says I to the kid, "would you like to go home?" "Aw, what for?" says he. "I don't have any fun at home. I hate to go to school." My life exactly. Yeah that about sums it up in a 200-300-word bullshit essay about a bullshit racist story. Now fork over more pills or I'll scalp you and burn you at the stake.

I squinted at the tiny words, reading the essay again and then a third time, and with each reading, my understanding of Martin's situation deepened. With each reading, the knot in my stomach grew larger, and the muscles in my jaw clenched tighter. Despite the rage between the lines, I was impressed with the thoughtful and revealing content of Martin's essay.

I looked across the playground again and realized the moms and toddlers had disappeared. One abandoned swing continued to sway gently, back and forth. I slipped Martin's essay back into my purse, rubbed the kinks in my weary shoulders, and strolled around the koi pond, stretching my legs, and avoiding my inevitable return to the Moriarty house.

As I walked back to the car, I wondered if Martin expected a grade for his essay. I was feeling generous and decided to give him an A despite his immature writing style. And, of course, the misspelling of "pussies" which, frankly, I didn't want to acknowledge.

At Dickinson High School, I might consider taking the physical threat at the end of his essay more seriously. Zero tolerance was an accepted tenet of that school's culture, like a religious doctrine. But Dickinson High was another world, lightyears away from Coral Gables. I recognized the nuances in Martin's essay. I didn't worry about his obvious reference to the character's threats from the O. Henry story. I appreciated the allusion as Martin's attempt at humor.

Another teacher may have taken Martin's words more seriously, but I pushed aside my nagging fears, convinced I could fix the boy. With David Allington's help, I'd be the caring adult who could mold this young mind. Besides, I had reason for optimism. My student had completed the assignment as I had asked him to do. Martin seemed to like my cooking, and I provided him with the pain-numbing medication he craved. He needed me. He depended upon me. Who knows, maybe he was beginning to like his surrogate mother.

CHAPTER 18

Nancy had left a garbled voice message on Jennifer's cell. "After we visit mom next week, let's do lunch at the Guntry Club. Call me." I listened to the message a second time, wondering about Nancy's mispronunciation. In any event, the prospect of going out to lunch with Nancy held no appeal. I called her back.

"Hey, Nancy. Let's skip lunch. I'm really not up for it." I imagined a white-bread, ultra-conservative, snooty country club with an eighteen-hole golf course designed by Arnold Palmer, a pricey pro-shop, clay tennis courts peppered with wealthy, shallow women showing off their impressive backhands.

"Jennifer, we need this. We'll blow off some steam after we eat, get in some silhouette shooting, some target practice. We both could use the drill, and it's been a while. Don't forget, we need to get ready for the big tournament next month. Besides, it's been too long since the two of us spent time together at the Guntry Club. What do you say?"

I didn't know what to say. Nancy really had said *Guntry* Club in her message, not *Country* Club. I'd never heard that term before, but after experiencing the family arsenal above the garage, I was able to imagine a club like that. I didn't have time to generate a plausible excuse, and so I fell back on a tried and true strategy. I stalled.

"Let's see how it goes with Mom." I wondered what Jennifer might say to her sister. Would Jennifer allow her mother's deteriorating mental state to interfere with a lunch date and a little target practice? Probably not.

"Well, pack a semi-automatic pistol, little sister," Nancy said. "You drive this time. It's your turn." I felt my heart skip a beat when I heard those words. Although now I was able to find my way to the nursing home, I had no idea where the so-called Guntry Club was located, and I didn't even know where Nancy lived. Hell, I didn't know Nancy's last name. There was no way I could pull off being the designated driver.

"You'd better drive. I may have to bring the car in for servicing. I'm hearing a rattle in the engine." I quickly changed the subject to avoid discussion, negotiation, or a sisterly argument about who would drive. "Listen, Nancy, I emailed Jason. Did he mention that to you? I asked him to have dinner with me."

"If you want my advice, I think you need to give him time. I don't think Jason's ready to see you. I told him you were making progress, getting Martin the help he needs. I think he appreciated that. But really, the best recommendation I can give you is to give him space for now." Fine. I'd be happy to give Jason all the space in the world.

* * *

Deciding what to wear for my coffee date with David Allington provided a respite from the pressures of being Martin's surrogate mother. A Friday night shopping spree in that enormous, walk-in closet would save me time in the morning. I wanted to look good for David. I cared too much. How odd for me to be so fixated on what another person thought about my appearance.

Swimming laps almost every day in Jennifer's pool had already made a noticeable and positive difference in my reflection in the full-length closet mirror. My body seemed leaner, more toned. Where were those indentations on my thighs, the changes in my body I'd noticed in the mirror of my Key West hotel? It felt like years ago and yet it was only days.

After discarding several outfits, I settled on a sleeveless silk top. It showed off my muscular arms and the coral color worked well with my complexion. I laughed at myself for making that connection between the color of an article of clothing and my complexion. Ridiculous. Although the white jeans I chose felt snug, they fit well and made me feel confident. I looked in the mirror and smiled, noticing the dimple so prominent on my right cheek, and for the first time in years, I genuinely liked what I saw. And not because I looked like Jennifer Moriarty. I looked like a new version of me, Jenn Cooper.

At eight the next morning, I twirled around the walk-in closet, admiring my outfit again in the wall of mirrors. I'd never looked or felt this sensual, this desirable. I hoped David would agree. Even thinking about David, caused my skin to glow a rosy hue. Blushing made me think about make-up, and so I experimented with bronzer and lipstick, a coral shade, of course, to bring out the color of Jennifer's blouse. And matching my makeup with my outfit gave me the idea to coordinate my sandals and purse. The minutes ticked by that morning until I was perfectly satisfied. I was nervous. My stomach fluttered in a good way. Breathless like a girl on a first date, I jumped into Jennifer's car, entered the name of the restaurant in the GPS, and took off for South Beach to meet with Dr. David Allington.

* * *

I glanced at the clock on the dashboard as I parked the car on Lincoln Road. I was ten minutes late. Being even a few minutes late was not part of my DNA. My father had lectured me throughout childhood on the importance of punctuality. The Coopers arrived early for doctors' appointments, early for school, early for movies. We were the first to arrive for birthday parties, weddings, baptisms, and church services. Once we even arrived before the casket for a distant cousin's funeral. But today, I wanted to make an entrance. Being a few minutes late was part of my plan.

David had chosen a popular restaurant in a hip South Beach neighborhood. The Good News Café. After searching amid the tables arranged on the outdoor patio, I stood by the main entrance.

"Table for one?" The waiter offered me a menu. I looked beyond him and found David sitting at a table in the back.

"I'm meeting someone, a friend. He's already been seated."

I was pleased that David had positioned himself toward the back of the restaurant, away from the heat and humidity of that muggy September morning. For different reasons, I imagined neither one of us wanted to flaunt the fact of our meeting. Hiding out at this back table might have been intentional. Dr. Allington might have been married after all.

David smiled as I approached, folded his newspaper, and put it aside as I sat down at the table. We ordered coffees and studied the menu in silence. I wondered if he was as nervous as I was.

"The vegetable omelet sounds good," David said. "They use organic produce here."

"Hmm. The fresh fruit and cheese platter sounds good too," I said.

"Want to get one of each and share?" And just like that, I relaxed. I was having an ordinary conversation with an ordinary man about what to order for an ordinary breakfast. I glanced down at his newspaper. The New York Times, folded to reveal the crossword puzzle, partially completed. In pen. I liked that. Smart. Confident.

"So, tell me about yourself," David said as we waited for our meals. Although the alleged purpose of the meeting was to discuss the Martin problem, we took our time, meandering through conversations like tourists on an extended vacation. We had all the time in the world, enjoying the detours and admiring the scenery. I tried to steer the conversation away from Jennifer Moriarty, to navigate small talk in the direction of safe topics, books and films, likes and dislikes. David Allington tried to steer the conversation right back to me. To Jenn Cooper, not Jennifer Moriarty. To a woman about whom he had no preconceived notions.

"Okay, besides reading, swimming, and, of course, taking care of your family, what do you like to do in your free time?" I told him about my stalking of famous, dead authors and my visits to their houses. He had never visited the Hemingway House, and he wanted to hear all about it.

"Have you ever been to The Mark Twain House, in Hartford? It's amazing," he said. I clutched the menu to my chest and felt my eyes widen. The Mark Twain House was one of my favorite authors' homes, a short distance from my apartment.

"Yes, I've been there. Several times. Did you visit the Harriet Beecher Stowe House, too? She lived next door to Mark Twain."

"No, I didn't have time. I was in Hartford for a conference and I was lucky to get away for a few hours. I read *Uncle Tom's Cabin* back in high school, and I know Lincoln called Stowe 'The little lady who started the Civil War,' right? Tell me about her house." I noticed that David segued each bend in the conversation with the phrase, *"Tell me about."* I liked that. I glossed over the *Tell me abouts* that might trick me into revealing too much about Jenn Cooper's life or divulge my lack of knowledge about Jennifer's life. I circumvented *Tell me about* where you grew up, *Tell me about* your family, and *Tell me about* how you met your husband. I kept trying to turn the tables on him, using his *Tell me about* probes to uncover some of David Allington's personal history.

As we devoured our breakfast, my curiosity about David's marital status got the better of me. I took a bold, conversational detour. I spread a thick layer of soft brie cheese on a slice of French bread, avoiding eye contact with David. "You know, Jim and I are separated, I think I may have mentioned that at our meeting last week. The marriage is over. And I'm fine with that. We haven't lived as a married couple for a very long time," I said, making the understatement of the century about a man I'd never met. "Tell me about your wife and kids."

"Married once, divorced for four years now," he said. "No kids though. I wanted kids, she didn't. Our problems were deeper than whether we'd have children. We grew apart. I know, that's a trite expression, but in our case, it was exactly what happened."

David's marital history was good news. So far, The Good News Café was living up to its name. I tried not to smile, hoping my facial expression and body language didn't reveal too much. He was single. He was available. He was handsome. I didn't want the breakfast to end. I wanted to sit and talk with David forever, gaze into his dark, brown eyes. Why couldn't I have found someone like him back in Connecticut? Someone interesting, smart, a good listener, and my god, those eyes.

"Let's walk along the beach and talk about Martin. I have a few ideas for his educational program," he said. David tried to pick up the check, but I insisted on splitting the cost of our breakfast. I wasn't ready to cross that line but didn't mind at all that David might be ready. We left The Good News Café like a couple, strolling by the upscale storefronts and restaurants, heading toward the shore. When we arrived at the beach, we removed our sandals and walked along for a mile or more, enjoying the warm water lapping at our bare toes. Everything David suggested for Martin made sense and aligned with my thoughts about next steps.

"I think the plan might include six hours a week of tutoring for Martin, preferably at the public library or at a bookstore to get him out of the house," David said. "He could take his math class online and even a science course at the local community college."

"I could tutor Martin for his English credits. I studied literature in college," I said. "In fact, he completed an essay I assigned, a response to an O. Henry story. It wasn't bad. In fact, Martin can be quite analytical."

One enormous challenge hovered like a threatening rain cloud over my head, impossible for me to ignore. How would I ever convince Jennifer's son to go along with this plan, to accept the help he so desperately needed? Would David have ideas about that too? The two of us would need to be on the same page about everything at the upcoming special education meeting. I'd need David's support.

We stopped by a bench overlooking the wide beach and blue water. I brushed the sand from the bottom of my feet. "What I'm most worried about is getting Martin the therapy he needs," I said.

"You might want to propose twice-a-week counseling with a psychiatrist, someone who can assess his emotional state and prescribe medication for his anxiety," David said. "If you're comfortable with that." Did he know that Jennifer Moriarty had told the school she was opposed to medicating her son? What would he think of me if he learned I had access to medication without a doctor's prescription and was feeding Jennifer's son an opioid to dull the pain of his sorry existence?

"I'm comfortable with that. Definitely," I said. As for finding a way to gain Martin's cooperation, David didn't have all the answers, but he asked a few thought-provoking questions.

"What does Martin enjoy doing? Does he have any hobbies, interests?" Jennifer would be in a better position to answer that question, but I gave it my best shot.

"He's on his computer or using his cell phone all the time, typical of kids his age. But it's not as though he's texting his friends, at least that's not my impression. Frankly, I don't think Martin has any real friends. He plays video games online. They're pretty violent games." I gazed out at the water, embarrassed that I was allowing Martin to waste his time like that. "I realize I need to set limits, but I'm starting to get him to eat three meals a day, and he's beginning to come out of his room more. Progress is slow," I said.

"Why not put parental controls on his computer?" Of course, I didn't know how to go about doing that, and even if I did, Martin might respond with more rage than I'd already witnessed. I worried about what he was capable of doing. I couldn't tell David about the gun collection above the garage. For some strange reason, I felt ashamed about that too. I didn't want David to confuse me with Martin's mother. He was a newly hired employee at the high school and had never met Jennifer Moriarty, the reckless mother who allowed her younger son to go days without eating while she escaped to the family's cottage in Key West. He was getting to know me, Jenn Cooper, someone who had no use for guns, a nurturing teacher who might have been a nurturing mother.

"Parental controls? I'm not sure how to do that, but it sounds like a good idea. To be honest, David, I'm technologically challenged. I can't even use a TV remote," I said, laughing. I regretted avoiding all those professional development opportunities offered at Dickinson High School, workshops designed to build teachers' technology skills.

"It's not hard. I could help you set those parental controls if you'd like." I wasn't sure if David was trying to be helpful or if his offer was a thinly veiled excuse to see me again. I hoped it was the latter.

"I mean, not at *your* home, of course, but if you bring a laptop over to my place, we could figure it out. You'll see it's not rocket science," he said. My pulse quickened as I tried to hide my eagerness. I didn't want to chase him away with too much enthusiasm or read too much into his offer. *Yes, I'd love to meet you at your place,* I thought. *God yes.*

"Let me think about it. I mean, I think I should do it, but it might set Martin off. He has this anger management problem, you know?" Of course, he knew. It was all in the files. David was surely aware of all the gory details of Martin's history.

"What if you used his internet access as leverage? Let him know, if he agrees to therapy, accepts the tutoring help, and takes his coursework seriously, he gets to keep his computer and internet access." That sounded reasonable for the typical teenager-parent negotiation. But then again, there was nothing reasonable about Martin Moriarty and his relationship with his mother. I understood that I might have to resort to these hardball tactics if all else failed. We put our sandals on and headed back to our cars.

"I like your idea. His computer, his cell phone, those are the only things he cares about at the moment. Oh, and one more thing— my cooking," I said.

David stopped walking and grasped my arm for a few seconds. I felt the touch of his fingers on my skin, moving like an electric current to distant places in my body, far removed from my bare arm. "You like to cook?" David asked. It turned out that David loved to cook. And then the conversation took another detour about cooking television shows, famous chefs, and recipes, and eventually looped back to a kind-of, sort-of invitation to have dinner at his place. On the way back to our cars, we made a plan for the following Saturday night.

I stood at the door of Jennifer's Mercedes. "I have to tell you how much I appreciate your support with this. It's big, you know? I've been so worried, and I need someone who is truly on Martin's side. I need someone on my side. I can't do this alone," I said, fighting back tears.

"You're not alone." And for the first time in a very long while, I didn't feel lonely.

CHAPTER 19

Early Thursday morning I entered Coral Gables High School with a heightened sense of awareness. After greeting the security monitor like an old friend, I searched for familiar faces, looking and listening for Jason Moriarty as a mob of students emptied into the hallways in between class periods. I tuned into the dissonant sounds of laughter, cold metal lockers slamming, teenage voices calling out to each other, the overhead announcements barely audible above the din.

I'd studied photographs of Jennifer's older son, although there were only a few scattered around the house. Images of Jason's beautiful, dark-eyed, baby days, a black and white school picture, and a family vacation on ski slopes in the French Alps. Seeing his sweet face change and grow was like watching a tulip bud blooming with time-lapse photography. Would I know Jason Moriarty's face if I saw it in a crowded hallway? Jostled among the hordes of adolescent bodies, I worked my way against the tide toward the main office.

I was a few minutes early, and I was prepared for the inevitable wait. David approached me at exactly nine o'clock with a warm smile. I smiled back, reassured to see a familiar face this time. We shook hands in a professional manner, although I stopped myself, just in time, before reaching out for a friendly hug.

"Sorry, Jennifer, the team is running a few minutes behind schedule. Can I get you a cup of coffee while you're waiting?"

"No thanks. I'm fine." I felt too much adrenaline racing through my veins and didn't need more caffeine.

It was 9:20, and the meeting still hadn't begun. I reminded myself that the new me would be tolerant of a delay. Besides, if Coral Gables High operated like Dickinson High, these meetings were scheduled back-to-back. If we started late, the team wouldn't have time for a prolonged negotiation, and no one would be in the mood to argue with my suggestions for Martin's educational program. That was my theory.

Finally, at 9:30, the secretary escorted me into the conference room. The same players sat around the table behind their name cards, joined by an additional, older gentleman I hadn't met. I took the only available chair at the conference table which happened to be next to David. Mrs. Jill Armstrong, the assistant principal, sat at the head of the table, ready to preside. She flashed her too white, toothy smile at me, as though we were all here for a party and she was the birthday girl.

"Mrs. Moriarty, I don't think you've met our director of special services, Dr. Henry Sternberg," she said. Dr. Sternberg reached across the table and shook my hand. I understood immediately why the director of special services needed to attend this meeting. He wanted to make sure the school didn't agree to anything that would adversely impact the district's special education budget. At least that's how things went down at Dickinson High. It was all about the bottom line. Not a good sign. Or maybe it was a good sign. Too early to tell. I tried to stop looking for signs and reminded myself to simply *be* in the moment. Just *be* Jennifer Moriarty, concerned mom, on a crusade for justice, ready to make demands. And be prepared, if necessary, to fight like hell for her son's educational rights.

"Did you receive copies of my proposed plan for Martin?" I asked. I'd drafted the plan after my South Beach breakfast with David. I'd sent the document to Mrs. Armstrong via email attachment and certified mail. I included a cover letter documenting the decisions made during our previous meeting. I peppered a few legal buzzwords throughout my proposal, buzzwords I'd gathered from the special education statutes and from my experiences as an educator.

"Yes, thank you. This is very helpful," Mrs. Armstrong said, with a tad too much enthusiasm. I glanced down at my copy of the plan and quickly skimmed the main points as I waited for someone around that table to move the meeting forward. I'd labored hours over the wording and the content of the proposal. "Vis a vis our meeting of September . . . *and so forth, and so on*, please review attached individualized educational plan for Martin Moriarty. . . . as per our agreement on September . . . you agreed to review my input as an 'invaluable' contribution to further decisions regarding . . . *etcetera, etcetera, etcetera*." Proud of my efforts, I felt ready to defend the finer points.

Jill Armstrong seemed to be waiting for me to say something. "So, where do we begin?" I asked. I felt the fabric of David's khaki pants brushing up against my bare calf. I sensed his support and relaxed my shoulders, sat up straighter, uncrossed my arms. Mrs. Armstrong turned to the director of special services.

"Mrs. Moriarty, the team has had an opportunity to review your recommendations, and we certainly appreciate the time and effort that went into this draft," Dr. Henry Sternberg said. I waited for the big HOWEVER. It hovered near the ceiling of that conference room like an enormous, invisible balloon, filled with helium, threatening to brush against the fluorescent lights and burst.

"I think we can all agree that your request for tutoring is appropriate at this time, as is your suggestion for online coursework. Is Martin interested in studying a world language? I see he's had Spanish," Dr. Sternberg said, searching through papers in a file folder.

I didn't expect such blatant cooperation, but then again, I wasn't naïve. I wouldn't let down my guard this early in the game. We were in the beginning stages of what could easily turn into a contentious negotiation.

"I honestly hadn't thought of that. Taking a world language this semester might be a good idea. Let me speak with Martin and get back to you. He may be interested in studying a different language this time. Mandarin, perhaps?" I'd advise Martin to study Mandarin. Learning to speak Chinese might help him get into college, further his career opportunities later on. Then again, whatever made me think my advice to Martin would be worth anything? And why was I even thinking about college and career opportunities for Jennifer Moriarty's son? I'd be long gone by the end of the month, back in Hartford, wringing the life out of *A*

Tale of Two Cities. I refocused my attention, realizing the team was waiting for my response.

"I'm sorry, what were you saying?"

"We'll wait for you to let us know, about his world language choice. We think it might be better to start with a lighter load. For Martin's sake," Mrs. Armstrong added.

"I think he can handle whatever any other student can handle. But I'm happy to leave it up to him," I said.

In a matter of minutes, the team had agreed to an online Algebra course, an online computer science course, tutoring for World History, a three-credit Environmental Science class held at the local community college, American Literature with Jennifer Moriarty as his tutor, and possibly a three-credit world language class. This was a full academic load. Fifteen or possibly eighteen credits. Jesus. What was I thinking? The maxim *Be careful what you wish for* immediately came to mind. The district's tutor would also help Martin keep up with his online courses and would meet with Martin three mornings a week. Perfect. I'd won my first battle; they gave me everything I wanted. Now all I needed to do was convince Martin to agree to the plan. All I needed to do was climb Mount Everest, blindfolded and barefoot.

"As for the counseling for Martin," Dr. Sternberg began, "I'm not sure the team is ready to commit to your request until we complete an updated psychiatric evaluation. The most recent evaluation is already several years old. We'd like to have Martin come in to meet with our district's psychiatrist as early as next week," he began. I held up my hand, like a traffic cop, interrupting his train of thought. All eyes around the table were suddenly laser-focused on me. The big HOWEVER balloon was about to burst. Counseling for Martin was the most important component of the plan. And everyone at that meeting knew it.

"No, absolutely not. I am not bringing Martin into this building," I said, shaking my head emphatically and raising my voice. Then David jumped in, backing me up, and I felt my rising blood pressure begin to fall.

"I have to agree with Mrs. Moriarty. From what I've read and heard, I don't believe Martin is ready to enter this building for any reason, let alone for a psychiatric evaluation. I'm wondering if the evaluation might take place in a psychiatrist's office. What do you think about that, Mrs. Moriarty?" he asked, turning to face me. Dr. Sternberg's face turned crimson and he jumped in before I could utter another word.

"Are you suggesting an outside, independent evaluation? We're not ready to support that," Dr. Steinberg said, shaking his head. "The district employs highly competent evaluators, and that's where we'll start." David and I had already planned for pushback and I was ready. I handed copies of a list of proposed psychiatrists' names to Mrs. Armstrong and Dr. Sternberg.

"I have five names of acceptable doctors for both the evaluation and for follow-up therapy," I said. "I understand the district has budgetary considerations. So, I want you to know that all of the doctors on this list are covered by our family's insurance policy," I said, circumventing Dr. Sternberg's objection. I'd fight, if necessary, to have the school district pay for Martin's therapy, but it wouldn't be necessary. If the insurance policy didn't cover the cost of therapy and an evaluation, I'd let Jim Moriarty foot the bill. Martin needed psychiatric help, and that's all that mattered.

The team decided to table the choice of psychiatrist, along with any decision about a world language class, and we scheduled the next meeting. If all went as planned, the tutoring and online courses could begin as early as the day following our next meeting. The community college course began in a few days. Martin would probably miss the first week, even though the guidance counselor promised to complete the registration process. This was really happening. I'd made a difference in Martin's life. I hoped Jennifer would appreciate that I'd accomplished something significant during my short stint as Martin's surrogate mother.

* * *

Back in the safety of Jennifer's car, I shed the façade of confidence and determination that had served me well during the meeting. My hands shook as I started the Mercedes. That sense of urgency that I'd felt a few weeks ago, gazing into Ernest Hemingway's study in Key West, grew like a weed, fertilized by a rising sense of dread. *Jesus Christ, what have I gotten myself into now, and how am I going to convince Martin to accept this plan?* By the time I pulled into the Moriarty's circular driveway I'd stopped shaking, but I was no closer to figuring out my next moves.

CHAPTER 20

Later that evening I knocked on Martin's door. I'd prepared a tray of cheese and crackers and a frosted glass of minted iced tea. "Martin, I'm making a special dinner tonight, and it may take a bit longer than usual. I'm leaving a tray of appetizers for you, to tide you over, okay?" I placed the tray on the floor and waited. I heard Martin moving around the room. "Okay, Martin? Dinner should be ready around 7:30 tonight." I waited, and then I started counting. *One Mississippi, two Mississippi, three Mississippi.* A friend taught me the Mississippi counting trick when I was a young child swimming at the Connecticut shore. When the water felt too cold, I'd jump in quickly and start counting. By the time I reached ten Mississippi, my body would adjust to the water temperature. "Okay, Martin?" *Four Mississippi, five Mississippi, six Mississippi . . .*

"Fine," he shouted. Would I ever get used to waiting for Martin's responses the way I adjusted to the cold ocean water in July?

Back in the study, I sat at Jennifer's desk, hands on the keyboard, pouring words and sentences onto the page. I drafted and revised my letter to Martin, weighing every word, measuring tone, assessing clarity, choking each sentence to an inch of its life. Every word felt ridiculously consequential to me. A matter of life or death.

Dear Martin,

Good news! Starting next week, you will begin taking courses toward meeting your high school graduation requirements. I have worked hard to make this happen for you, and although it will involve a lot of work, I think you'll eventually enjoy the classes. I'm looking forward to being your American Literature tutor. You already earned an A on your first essay. Your other courses (online classes, tutorial, etc.) are explained on the following page.

Here's your next assignment for American Literature, due in two days. (I'm so proud of the A you earned on your last assignment and look forward to your continued success!):

Hemingway wrote his novels and stories based upon his life-experiences including his African safaris, big-game hunting, his experiences as a war correspondent, and travels in Europe. Create a list of topics and experiences culled from your life that might potentially spark ideas for creative short stories. Your list should include a minimum of 10 topics.

Love,

Mom

XOXO

I considered including my own list to inspire Martin. I even attempted to complete the assignment myself. As an English teacher, I'd never ask my students to read or write something that I was unwilling or unable to do myself. Surprisingly, for someone like me who still dreamed of writing the great American novel, the assignment proved challenging. I searched my memory for a few personal experiences that might spark an idea for a fictional narrative. Switching lives with Jennifer Moriarty was probably the only interesting life experience worth mentioning, and I couldn't share that with Martin. The Hemingway examples embedded in the assignment would have to suffice.

I tucked the letter inside another origami box. I was getting quite adept at creating those delicate paper cubes, although not nearly as gifted with origami as Martin. I placed the box next to his dinner plate.

I'd quickly developed a mealtime routine that suited both of us. I usually ate first, and then I stayed out of Martin's way. Sometimes I'd go for a walk or take care of errands. But not that night. That night I planned to deviate from the routine. There was too much at stake, and I needed to stay close and be extra vigilant in case something went wrong. And I realized so many things could go wrong with my plan.

I knocked on Martin's bedroom door at 7:30. "Dinner's ready. I left a plate for you on the kitchen table. I'll be in the study if you need anything." This time I didn't wait for an answer. I didn't count Mississippis. I walked away briskly, intentionally making noise as I stomped down the uncarpeted backstairs. I left Martin's dinner on the table and refilled my glass of Merlot.

In the study, I'd be close enough to hear but not close enough to witness the inevitable shit hitting the fan. I held my ear to the study door until I heard Martin moving around in the kitchen. With nothing left to do but wait, I stretched out on the worn, leather armchair and rested my feet on the matching ottoman.

Contemplating my next move in what felt like a convoluted game of chess, I decided that if Martin declared war against my educational plan, I'd declare war on Martin. *Checkmate, my friend.* If he gave me a hard time, I'd consider withholding the painkillers. Although, I worried he might be addicted to those pills. I'd need medical advice, professional intervention. That part of my plan would come next. Unless Martin agreed to the educational proposal, I'd dial back on the gourmet aspect of the meals I prepared for him. Unlike what his mother may have been doing, I had no intention of starving her son.

And so, I waited. I listened. I glanced around the study and considered searching for a book to read. Sipping my wine, I walked over to the computer to check emails, national and international news, and then I settled into the more important task of refining Martin's American Literature syllabus.

The project pulled me in and wouldn't let go. I lost myself in the forgotten joy of lesson planning, of contemplating how to engage the adolescent mind in the study of literature. The minutes slipped by, unnoticed. When I remembered to check the time on the top of my computer screen it was past nine o'clock. Martin must have finished his dinner a while ago. I'd been so deeply engrossed in planning his lessons, choosing book titles Martin might find appealing—nothing too heavy, nothing too violent—I hadn't noticed any sounds emanating from the kitchen. No clinking of dishes, no stomping of feet, no scraping of chair against the floor. I left the relative safety of the study and crept into the kitchen, wiping my clammy hands against the back pockets of my jeans.

Martin's dirty dishes sat in the kitchen sink, a minor, yet significant victory for me. The origami box, or more accurately, what remained of the origami box, had been left on the kitchen table where I'd placed it. Smashed. Crushed. Flattened. My letter to Martin crumpled into a ball next to the box, told me everything I needed to know. His message was undeniable. A loud sigh escaped my lips. I slumped into the kitchen chair, frozen in time and place.

What in the world had I expected? Of course, Martin would object to new, rigorous academic requirements. He'd fight each one of his mother's expectations. I pressed my fingertips to my temples, squeezed my eyes shut, and willed myself not to cry. I told myself there would be a next step and a step after that. I wasn't ready to give up on Martin.

The angry boy upstairs knew his mother, but he didn't know me, Jenn Cooper. I decided it would only be fair to warn him. If Martin decided to reject Plan A, he'd need to prepare for Plan B. No negotiating, no whining, everything on my terms this time. Before I had time to change my mind, I pushed away from the table and dashed back to the computer in the study. Ready for retaliation, I drafted an email response:

Martin,

If you choose not to accept the academic plan as articulated in my letter, I will be cancelling your cell phone and internet services. You have until 8:00 a.m. Sunday morning to acknowledge receipt of this email and to promise you will cooperate fully. I also want to say that I have been working very hard to make delicious meals for you, and it would be nice to hear a few words of appreciation. Until I know you appreciate my efforts, I will provide more basic (i.e. less gourmet) meals. Also, starting now, there will be no more trays at your bedroom door. All meals, including breakfast and lunch, will be served in the kitchen. Yes, as you can tell by the tone of this email, I'm very angry and hurt. You really didn't need to smash the origami box. I put a lot of time and effort into that. Nevertheless, I love you and only want what is best for you.

As always,
Mom
XOXO

They say never send an email when you're angry. I considered waiting until morning until I'd had a chance to put the incident in perspective. But, ultimately, I didn't give a damn. I clicked on the blue send button and stomped away from the computer.

Back in Jennifer's bathroom, I soaked in a hot bath scented with lavender salts, trying to unwind and calm my jagged nerves. I pulled my body out of the cooling bathwater, still fuming, still blinded by an explosion of rage. I decided lavender bath salts were overrated.

CHAPTER 21

I dragged my aching body to bed. Slowly, my jaw muscles unclenched, the knots in my shoulders loosened, and I gave into exhaustion. I welcomed sleep like a long-lost friend. Instead of the oblivion I craved, my dreams dragged me into a world of swirling colors and vivid textures.

I dreamed I was swimming laps in Jennifer's pool. The warm, turquoise water became more and more choppy and murky. Suddenly, I noticed the pool was filled with children, young children, happily playing tag, splashing, and laughing. I noticed Jennifer and Martin sitting on the edge of the pool, cleaning their hunting rifles, smiling and relaxed. I tried desperately to usher the children out of the water. "Run," I tried to say to them but couldn't form the word. I couldn't form any words. All I could make were the gurgling sounds of a drowning woman. I saw David sitting in a lifeguard's chair at the far end of the pool, wearing dark sunglasses, his hair slicked back, and I reached out to him. "Help," I tried to say, my efforts in vain. He didn't see or hear me. I started to sink into the water which became so deep, bottomless, and as black as the middle of the ocean. The pool and the children had disappeared, and I realized I was alone in the churning waters of an angry ocean, cold and vast. I was drowning, and I thought, *So this is how my life will end*. In the nightmare, I stopped struggling. I let go. I stopped fighting for air, for words, for life. I accepted what I believed was the inevitable end. I almost savored the relief of not fighting anymore, of letting go like that. And then suddenly, I felt something hard and cool on the back of my head. I reached behind me and grabbed onto what felt like a metal rod, thinking there might be hope, thinking someone was trying to save me, to pull me out of the water. Was it the lifeguard? Was David trying to help me? I had to hold onto that lifesaving rod as tightly as possible.

I opened my eyes, slowly realizing the swimming pool, David, the children, my near-drowning experience, had all been part of a horrible dream. I was in Jennifer's bed, not her pool, not drowning in the middle of the ocean. I was in Jennifer's room, in Jennifer's house, unharmed. But the cold, hard metal I'd tried to grasp, the rod that continued to dig into my skull felt all too real.

As I awakened more fully, I sensed without turning my head that Martin was in the room with me. I smelled his unwashed scent. I knew without seeing that Jennifer's son was pressing the barrel of a pistol into my head. I heard his breathing, rough and ragged. My nightmare was starting again. But this time, I was wide-awake.

"Martin, what do you want?" I asked in a hushed, breathless whisper. I wondered what answer to my question would be acceptable. A disturbed son creeps into his mother's bedroom in the middle of the night, puts a gun to her head while waiting for her to wake up. Maybe he wants a midnight snack, or he had a bad dream too and all he wants is maternal comfort. Or, maybe he wants to kill his mother because she colluded with the school district to provide him with a decent education. *Oh, Jennifer. I hope you are suffering wretchedly in Hartford,* I thought. *I hope you are sweating profusely in my sweltering Hartford apartment, despondent and disgusted with your life and with your miserable self. You deserve all that and more. You created this monster.*

"What do I want? I want to know the truth," Martin said. I could barely hear him, his voice muted by the sound of my heart pounding, the roar of blood rushing in my ears. "Who are you this time? I know you're not Jennifer Moriarty, so stop bullshitting me, bitch." I couldn't breathe or think clearly. What did Martin mean? *Who are you this time?* Is that what he said? But what did it matter? There was a gun pressed into my skull. Very slowly and quietly I spoke, barely moving my lips, worried that even the force of my breath might activate the trigger of Martin's rage.

"Move that away from my head, Martin, and I will tell you. I will tell you everything. Please."

I'd never cultivated the habit of praying to a higher power. To be honest, I didn't believe in any human-created formula for choosing those who were worthy of saving and those less pious human creatures chosen to be sacrificed. If the number of hours I'd spent kneeling in church determined my salvation, I was in serious trouble. Nevertheless, I prayed like there was no tomorrow because I believed there would be no tomorrow. I prayed and I waited. I willed my quivering limbs, my shaking body to keep as still as possible, holding my breath for dear life.

The cold pressure on the back of my head began to dissipate. I inhaled a shallow breath. "I'm going to sit up, is that okay?" I asked.

"Fine, but remember, I'm pointing a gun at you, you lying bitch. Don't try anything stupid," Martin growled. I felt like an actor in a cheap horror movie, the camera filming the action from multiple angles. I dragged my trembling body into a seated position, pressing my back against the padded headboard. Martin had left the bedroom door open, letting in enough light from the hallway for me to see the details of the scene playing out in slow motion. Slowly, I turned my head to face the weapon that moments before crushed up against my skull. Martin lowered the gun, now pointing it toward my chest. My skull throbbed, signaling my brain to take things slowly. It was a painful reminder that I'd crossed over from one nightmare to another. Martin slouched in a chair he must have dragged over from Jennifer's dressing table. The chair, Martin, and his pistol were less than a yard away from the bed. Too close for anything approaching comfort.

"You're right, Martin. I'm not who I've pretended to be. I will tell you the rest of the story, but please, point the gun away from me," I said. Martin's hand was steady, not a tremor. His sense of calm righteousness told me everything I needed to know. Even with all his anger, *he* was the one in control. *I* was the one barely holding on, pretending to be strong. Pretending that I had the magic words Martin needed to hear, that I was in charge of my fate, that I had the power to determine whether I lived or whether I died in Jennifer Moriarty's bed. Slowly, I pulled the bedsheet over my chest and crossed my arms, as if my nod to modesty offered protection.

"Martin, how did you know?" I asked, not only from curiosity, but also to distract him. I wanted to communicate a modicum of respect for his intuition, to convince both of us we were simply having a two-way conversation, and to discover for myself whether I was, in fact, paralyzed with fear. It was reassuring to know I was able to speak in coherent sentences.

"You're nothing like Jennifer Moriarty. She hates me, and she doesn't like to swim the way you do," he said. "She doesn't cook, and she laughs all the time, even when there's nothing funny. You never laugh," he said. "Who are you?" I breathed deeply. I had nothing but my life to lose, and so I'd tell him the truth, and together we'd put an end to the ridiculous charade. Together we'd find his mother.

"My name is Jenn Cooper. I'm a high school English teacher. I live in Hartford, Connecticut." I told Martin how I'd met his mother in a Key West bar. He listened, not interrupting with questions. No raised eyebrows, no incredulous smirking. He didn't even shift the position of his body.

"I don't remember all of the details, but your mother and I had both been drinking too much, I'll admit that. And over the course of a few days, your mom hatched this crazy plan to switch clothes and then swap lives but only for a month, not permanently. It was a dare, that's all. A stupid dare."

Martin held the gun in his lap. His facial expression remained fixed as I shared the truth about my identity. He didn't seem surprised or the least bit suspicious. It was as though he'd listened to me narrate a story about my trip to the mall. *First, I parked the car, and then I went to Macy's and bought shoes, and finally in the end, in the end, this is what happened.* Oh god, it did feel like the end to a ridiculous story, someone else's story.

And then suddenly, Martin began to laugh. He tilted his head back and roared with a cruel hilarity that mocked my terror. My eyes were glued to the hand that clutched the gun. I waited for his next move and for the excruciating laughter to stop. Finally, Martin shook his head and sneered. He curled his upper lip and snorted. "There's been a change of plans," he said.

"Change of plans? I don't know what you mean," I said. "I haven't spoken to your mother. We haven't communicated at all since Key West."

"Not your plans, you stupid fuck! I'm talking about my plans. We're done with your plans. Forget whatever agreement you had with that piece-of-shit Jennifer Moriarty. Here's what's going to happen. You're going to stay here with me, permanently," he said. "You're not going anywhere."

This pronouncement terrified me even more than the gun pointed at my heart. That was the moment I realized there was no turning back. No running away. It was too late. Martin had won, and I had lost. I had lost a life in Connecticut, a good-enough job, an apartment, a routine that gave me a sense of purpose if not continuous joy. Martin had won, and Jennifer Moriarty had lost as well. Jennifer Moriarty had a life here in Coral Gables, a sister and mother who loved her, hobbies, friends, even a therapist. Jennifer and I both had responsibilities. This life-swapping experiment was supposed to be temporary. Martin had no right to amend an agreement I'd unwittingly made with his mother. He had no authority to force me to stay here against my will. Then again, he did have the gun, and it was still pointing in my direction. I needed to find my power of persuasion, the right words, my only weapon to get back in the game.

"Martin, listen to me. I'm sure your mother loves you. She'd never abandon you. This was simply a dare. I don't know, an experiment, I suppose." Even as I said the words, I realized that I'd told the most dangerous and implausible lies of all. His mother didn't love him. His mother had most definitely abandoned him. And with those lies, I'd sealed my fate. Martin knew the truth. He snorted again in disgust and sneered at me with pure hatred in his eyes.

And then another truth about winners and losers swam to the surface of my consciousness, presenting itself to me with so much certainty. Jennifer Moriarty knew exactly what she was doing when she colored my hair, applied make-up to my face, and dressed me in her clothes. Jennifer dangled enough bait to hook the one person who had the ability to give her what she wanted most, a get out of jail free card. Jennifer was the real winner in our horrifying drama. She was living in my dull apartment, wearing my bland clothes, teaching my bored students, free of Martin, free of the terror, free of Jennifer Moriarty's life. With my help, with my foolish cooperation, Jennifer had escaped.

"Get used to it. You're going to stay here with me," Martin said more forcefully. The smirk on his face disappeared, replaced with the conviction of his enormous power over me. Martin would be the ruler, and I would be the ruled. "Leaving is not an option. If you go, people will get hurt. I promise you, people will die, and it will be your fault. Their blood will be on your hands. Leaving me will be the biggest mistake of your life." Martin stood, pushing the chair to the floor, his eyes and his gun pointed like lasers in my direction. He inched backward, toward the door, maintaining his aim. He left the room, ghostlike, as I cowered in a cold sweat, terrorized and alone in his mother's bed.

CHAPTER 22

Long after Martin left his mother's bedroom, I couldn't move. My breathing was shallow, and then my leg muscles cramped. Finally, I slowly and painfully dragged my body out of bed. I shuffled across the floor and silently locked the bedroom door, as if that one defensive act might protect me from the horrors of what was on the other side. I'd learned enough about Jennifer's son to believe every word he said. His threat was a sword he held over my head. My delusional confidence about fixing the Martin problem with college prep courses, gourmet recipes, and support from his school district, disappeared into the night. How could I have been so blind to the message of that crushed origami box?

I crawled back into bed and glanced at the bedside clock. It was only 2:15. Trying to control my trembling body, I hugged my knees to my chest. Martin had presented me with a new reality, devoid of feasible options. My thoughts raced through the limited alternatives. No one from my life in Hartford would believe, let alone, help me. I didn't have sympathetic colleagues, loving siblings, a living parent, or even a trusted friend. And there wasn't anyone in Jennifer Moriarty's life who'd be willing or capable of intervening on my behalf. After all, who was I? A delusional woman who looked like Jennifer Moriarty but who now claimed to be someone named Jenn Cooper. Jim Moriarty had already given up on Jennifer and Martin. Jason despised both his younger brother and his mother. And David, poor, clueless David Allington, didn't know what I was really dealing with in the

Moriarty household. Nancy and Jennifer's mother? Not a chance. The school district had already proved to be a dead-end. The system had Martin in its crosshairs for over a decade and had done nothing to stop his rapid descent into a violent, impenetrable reality. The police? My convoluted story about two women deciding to swap lives would be weighed against what was in plain sight: a hysterical mother hoarding an arsenal of guns above her garage versus the empty, veiled threats of an angry teenager. Going to the police could be a dangerous choice. No one would trust my ridiculous story, and worse, if someone did believe me, there might be serious implications. I considered the moral, ethical, legal, and professional fallout from which I'd never recover.

There was no way to retreat back into sleep, my heart was pounding, my mouth was dry. I felt the night crush me like an avalanche, the pressure on my chest painful and overwhelming. Or perhaps I was having a heart attack. I almost hoped for that, at least something more serious than garden-variety panic. I needed a true medical emergency, a one-way ticket out of my nightmare. I pulled myself out of bed again, crawled on my hands and knees into the walk-in closet, hyperventilating, trying desperately to catch a breath deep enough to subdue the adrenaline pumping like a runaway train through my veins. I grabbed Jennifer's small, navy Chanel purse, wedged behind a stack of sweaters in the back of the middle shelf. An effective, albeit extravagant, hiding place for the pharmaceuticals both Martin and his mother needed to get through the day. I grabbed a Xanax, swallowed it whole, and curled up in that closet as I waited for its calming effect.

Although unable to fall asleep again that night, I survived, and by early morning, I was surprised to find myself back in Jennifer's bed. A dim light began to seep into the room from the space between the curtain panels, nudging me forward to face whatever new horrors the day had in store for me.

* * *

I threw on the same clothes I'd worn to Coral Gables High the day before, too exhausted to worry about an appropriate outfit for the Guntry Club. I didn't care what Nancy thought about her sister's fashion choices. In the kitchen I grabbed a quick breakfast, a cup of coffee and a banana. I'd read that the potassium in bananas had a calming effect, and I needed all the help I could find. Tempted to take another Xanax, I decided to break one pill into quarters. I swallowed one of the quarters with a gulp of hot coffee, scalding my throat. "Damn it!" The painful shock made me impatient, and I threw caution to the wind. I swallowed the remaining three quarters with another sip, more carefully this time, cooling the coffee in my mouth before I swallowed.

I ran on a different fuel that morning, pure desperation. I threw together a breakfast for Martin of leftover muffins and juice, leaving it on the kitchen table. I placed his pill on an empty saucer. No more fancy origami boxes and no gourmet breakfasts. Even the stale muffins were more than that monster deserved.

Nancy would be picking me up in twenty minutes to visit Jennifer's mother, followed by lunch at the Guntry Club. My god, I dreaded the entire day. I had time to check emails in the study, and I considered sending a terse message to Jennifer. Something ambiguous. *We need to talk. Will call you this evening.* Something short and vague. What made me think Jennifer would respond to me this time? It might be worth another try. Then I thought better of it. Martin would consider that action, trying to reach out to Jennifer, as "something stupid." I touched the tender spot on my skull again and decided not to risk his wrath.

Nancy arrived right on time. I made her wait in her car, giving myself a few moments to collect my thoughts, to slow my breathing, and more time for the Xanax to kick in. I ignored the rude sound of her car horn. *Let Nancy wait*, I thought.

Nancy's punctuality and a self-righteous glance at her diamond-studded watch as I got into the car felt like a sharp slap in the face. I promised myself I wouldn't let her get under my skin. Not today. I focused on my breathing during the ride to the nursing home. I knew what to expect this time. I knew how to act, and the Xanax had dulled the horror of my predicament.

Our visit began with disappointing news from the Westwood Cares physician, Dr. Trumbull. He escorted Nancy and me into the visiting room lounge. The television blared, and several residents sat slumped over in their wheelchairs, ignoring their visitors and the game show projected on the big screen. Nancy and I huddled together on a small couch. The doctor pulled up a chair, close enough for me to smell a mixture of the man's stale breath and his musky cologne.

"Ladies, I'm so sorry to be the bearer of bad news today. As you know, we began a trial for a promising new medication that we hoped might slow the progression of your mother's disease." Nancy reached over and grabbed my hand. "Unfortunately, there's been no measurable impact on her memory. In fact, without mincing words, I must tell you that I see little hope that her condition will improve," Dr. Trumbull said. "I wanted to prepare the two of you. When you see your mother today, you may detect a noticeable decline since your last visit." I squeezed Nancy's hand as the doctor walked away.

We left the lounge, arms linked, heads down. In silence, we walked down the hallway toward Room 140. Nancy's mother sat in the same chair, looking out the same window. She seemed more docile and even less coherent than the last time we'd seen her. She barely acknowledged Nancy, the daughter she conceived, gave birth to, and had raised since infancy, and she never made eye contact with me, her younger daughter's double. Me, Jenn Cooper, her surrogate daughter. Nancy's surrogate sister. Martin's surrogate mother.

"Mom, it's us. Jennifer and me," Nancy said. "How you doing, sweetie?" Her mother continued staring out the window, ignoring us. I tried to make small-talk.

"It's a beautiful day, Mom. Nancy and I are going out to lunch soon. At the Guntry Club. Did you have your lunch yet?" I held the woman's cool, limp hand, unresponsive to touch. Nancy gazed at her mother, shaking her head, wiping away tears. We stayed for as long as we could bear it, combing the old woman's hair, massaging her dry hands with lotion, talking about the weather, acting lighthearted, and pretending everything in our world was fine.

On the drive to the Guntry Club, Nancy struggled to hold it together. "I'm beginning to lose my trust in Dr. Trumbull. I mean, he's supposed to be a specialist, a gerontologist, right?" she said.

Surprisingly, I shared Nancy's outage. I wanted to know where he went to medical school. I wanted to know how many years of experience he had in the field of gerontology. I'd been too intimidated to ask those questions during our visit. Then again, Jennifer and her sister had probably interrogated the doctor when they first met, and they must have known the answers to those questions. I wanted to make sure the poor woman received the best care possible. Had I been that passionate about my father's treatment so many years ago? My mom was in charge back then and would never have included me in conversations about managing his cancer. How ironic that Jennifer and Nancy now trusted me to help make the best medical decisions for their mother. And how strange that I realized something new about myself. I was worthy of their trust. "I think we need another opinion," I said, certain that Nancy would agree.

* * *

The Coral Corral Shooters Club, aka the Guntry Club, had limited signage outside its gated entrance and tree-lined driveway. Nancy followed the long, newly cobbled road leading to an enormous mission-style mansion. Nancy pulled up to the front entrance, taking advantage of the valet parking. We walked arm and arm, comforting each other from the emotional impact of our visit to the nursing home. We strolled right through the main doors as if we had been there many times before, as if we both belonged.

I'd never been a member of any club. Unless the YWCA counted. My only experience with fancy country clubs was a reception for new teachers given by my school district's board of education. I wasn't impressed with the limp celery sticks and tasteless cheese cubes. I remember thinking that a larger salary would have been preferable to one September evening with an open bar overlooking a manicured golf course. Country clubs were not part of my lifestyle in Hartford and had certainly never been a part of the Cooper family's lifestyle. But there I was standing in the lobby of Jennifer's Guntry Club, taking it all in, acting and feeling strangely at home.

The main lobby appeared to be a typical clubhouse lounge, the kind you'd see on television, upscale and reeking of old-money, with leather couches, enormous widescreen televisions tuned in to the usual conservative news stations, soundless with closed captioning so as not to disturb the members engaged in conversation. I gaped at the inlaid, tabletop chessboards, the round, felt-covered poker tables, and an ornate information counter. Scrawled across the wall behind the counter in enormous and perfect calligraphy, the words of the Second Amendment left no doubt about the club's mission: *A well-regulated militia being necessary to the security of a free state, the right of the people to keep and bear arms shall not be infringed.*

A well-regulated militia. I thought about the cache of guns and ammunition housed above Jennifer's garage and wondered, *Who's regulating the Moriarty militia?* I noticed a sign to my right, directing patrons to the indoor and outdoor shooting ranges, and another sign on my left pointing to the OK Corral Dining Room. I didn't bring one of Jennifer's guns with me that day, although I hadn't told Nancy. I had no intention of prolonging my stay. I wouldn't be shooting at targets or partaking in any other of the activities associated with the Guntry Club. In fact, I didn't think I'd be able to make it through lunch. I felt loopy, probably from the Xanax and lack of sleep.

As if in a trance, I followed Nancy into a luxurious dining room. I expected a swinging saloon door, but the name of the dining room bore no relationship to the elegant décor. I smiled widely and nodded to diners as I followed Nancy and the maître d' to a table. *Who were these people?* I wondered if the strangers we passed were Jennifer's friends or acquaintances. Distant cousins? Best buddies? Sworn enemies? We walked by a round table near the window. Six heavily made-up women were drinking colorful concoctions from martini glasses and laughing loudly, celebrating something. I wondered if they were as young and flawless as they appeared or if plastic surgery had erased their lines and imperfections. I nodded to waitresses dressed impeccably in their black pants and shirts, taking orders, and I dutifully ignored the young men with eyes averted, inconspicuously clearing tables. There were several balding businessmen wearing expensive suits that clung too tightly around their expanding waistlines, deep in conversation while periodically checking their phones for important messages. And then I noticed the more mature singletons, thick white hair gleaming, reading their Wall Street Journals while waiting for their food. I was the only outsider, the only stranger in this strange land, playing my part flawlessly, or so I hoped. I didn't know the language, the customs, or the expectations of the Guntry Club culture, but I'd fake it.

As soon as we were seated, I began to study the menu while simultaneously engaging Nancy in conversation, like any insider. "What are you having?" I asked.

"Oh, the usual." Nancy was no help at all.

"I'm not terribly hungry," I said. "I think I'll have an omelet." I wondered if Nancy would order a drink. Glancing around the dining room, I noticed an abundance of fancy cocktails, wine glasses, and half-filled bottles on the tables. I decided I deserved a glass of something and perused the wine list.

"Hello, ladies, the usual today?" asked the waitress. Nancy and Jennifer were regulars. The woman had waited on them before, many times before. It felt risky to order "the usual," whatever that was, and so I decided to take back control of the situation.

"Actually, I think I'd like the spinach omelet today and a glass of the house Chardonnay," I said, waiting for a reaction from Nancy or the waitress or from both women. A simple act, as benign as ordering lunch, was fraught with danger. I held my breath as Nancy clucked her tongue, disapprovingly.

"That drink won't help your aim later," she said, eyebrows raised. Apparently, the criminal act of drinking and driving was one thing, but drinking and shooting quite another matter. Not OK at the OK Corral.

When the waitress walked away, I leaned in across the table, donning my most serious, forlorn expression. "Nancy, how can you think about target practice after our visit with mom today? I may have two glasses of wine, and then you can take me home. It's too depressing." I teared up, playing offense, playing the woe is me, my poor mother has dementia card.

I'd heard the term "character actor" before, but I suddenly realized the significance of the phrase. I'd become a character actor, living and breathing a role until I could feel the part, until becoming one with the character I was portraying on stage. When had I stopped *pretending* to be Jennifer Moriarty? When had Jenn Cooper become Jennifer Moriarty? I was giving the performance of a lifetime, and apparently, a convincing performance at that. Even the tears were authentic. Even Nancy, Jennifer's loving sister, that woman bereft of hope for her ailing mother, even she seemed captivated by my performance.

"You're right, Jennifer, you're right. I'm sorry. I thought, you know, target practice would be a distraction for us. I think I'll order a glass of wine, too. Hell, let's order a bottle," Nancy said. And that's exactly what we did. We ate, we drank wine, we talked about their mother's prognosis, and between bites of my omelet, I forgot about the Martin problem.

CHAPTER 23

The numbing effect of the wine gave me the courage I needed to return to Jennifer's house that afternoon. Not knowing what to expect when I walked in the door, I made a mental tally of everything that could go wrong. On top of the list was the fear of startling Martin. He might be lying in wait for me with that pistol aimed at my heart, a pistol with a hair-trigger.

I skulked through the kitchen, noticing the muffin crumbs and empty juice glass he'd left for me on the kitchen table. I should have been pleased that Martin was in fact eating the meals I prepared for him and that he was willing to leave his bedroom for food, but my fear and anger snuffed out the possibility of any positive emotion. Even the debris of his breakfast felt like an affront. *Fuck you,* he was saying with that juice glass on the kitchen table. *Fuck you, bitch.* I had no more patience or sympathy for that spoiled, dangerous monster calling all the shots.

Calling the shots—damn, even my language had been corrupted by the Moriarty family. Gun metaphors had penetrated the left hemisphere of my brain. I'd developed a more acute awareness of the language that had always circulated the air around me but had never pierced the armor of my progressive, Connecticut life.

I stomped up the back stairs, trying to make enough of a racket and cause the vibrations necessary to alert Martin that his surrogate mother was approaching. I knocked on his bedroom door. And then I waited. Nothing. I listened. Not a sound. "Martin, I'm home," I called out. Not even the muffled movement of limbs, not the faint sound of an annoyed grunt, not the suggestion of clicking fingers on the keys of his computer. That wasn't the first time Martin had refused to acknowledge a knock on his door. That wasn't the first time he had completely ignored my attempt at even minimal communication. And so, I kept trying and listening, my ear pressed to the door. Not a sound. I even used the appeal of food. "Martin, if you're hungry I'll make grilled cheese and tomato sandwiches," I said. "Okay?" Nothing. "Well, let me know if you change your mind."

Back in Jennifer's study, I tried to focus. I was still feeling the buzz from three glasses of Chardonnay mixed with the morning dose of Xanax. There were thirteen unread emails in Jennifer's inbox, including one from David asking for my input for Saturday night's dinner and providing directions to his place. We were supposed to make a meal together. But after Martin's middle of the night visit, everything had changed. The prospect of pretending to be someone I was not with a man I could conceivably care about, left me with a sense of futility, not the excitement I'd felt the last time I saw David Allington. I'd be wasting my time and his time, continuing this ruse. I considered feigning a migraine. A part of me, not the Jennifer Moriarty character I'd been playing, but the Jenn Cooper person lurking below the surface, that woman wanted to lose herself. I needed the escape, now more than ever. I sent David a few suggestions about the Asian inspired dinner we would prepare together in his condo kitchen the next night, and I told him that I looked forward to seeing him, the absolute truth.

Then I scrolled down to a new email from Martin. As I opened it, my heart pounding, I prepared myself for the worst.

Will accept most of academic plan. No class at community college. I'll think about it for next semester. Going away for a few days, need a break, will be back next week. Will finish Am. Lit. assignment by the time I get back. DON'T DO ANYTHING STUPID YOU WILL REGRET IT!!!!! THEIR BLOOD WILL BE ON YOUR HANDS!

Nothing made sense. His response was the absolute last thing I expected. I didn't think Martin would agree to anything I'd proposed. Especially after his middle-of-the-night visit, I assumed he'd reject all components of the academic plan. Part of me, a very small part, felt a seedling of hope. But as I remembered the gun pressed into my skull, the threat about blood being on my hands, I reminded myself to face the truth. Jennifer's son was a skillful manipulator. The boy was a sociopath. I'd be a fool to believe a word he said, and it would be dangerous to assume positive intent was the driving force behind any of his words or his actions. This kid had held a gun to my head, literally and figuratively. Where was he? Where could he have gone? *He needed a break?* I shook my head at the unfathomable irony. I was the one who needed a break. And perhaps he had given me the break I so desperately needed. I now had the house to myself, a reprieve for the weekend and maybe longer. I might as well enjoy it and worry about the Martin problem later.

* * *

The surprising email from Martin changed everything. Now, I was looking forward to my date with David, and I had plenty of time to prepare. I'd been given the luxury of an upscale closet and enough cosmetics for a Hollywood movie set. I decided to pamper myself the Jennifer Moriarty way. I remembered seeing a walk-in beauty salon at the mall, no appointments required, and I went for it.

After a shampoo and blow-dry, I returned home and curled up in Jennifer's study with a book from her shelf. I hadn't read *Jane Eyre* since high school, but I remembered loving the story and the young heroine who overcame horrific obstacles. Jane had wrestled with her passions and sense of morality. She had figured out a way to balance the pull of the heart with a sense of duty and all those expectations. A relatively happy ending for both Jane and her Mr. Rochester. I needed that. And so, I settled in for an afternoon of reading. I pretended to be the young girl I'd once been so many years ago, engrossed in a classic story, identifying with *Jane Eyre*, a girl with options. A girl with a future.

That evening I put David's address into the car's GPS. I'd even brought a toothbrush with me, although I had no expectation of spending the night, and I didn't think David anticipated anything more than dinner. But I was prepared, prepared for anything. I had nothing to lose.

David greeted me with a quick hug. "Make yourself at home," he said. I admired the open spaces of his condo, clean, modern, and spacious, albeit sparsely furnished. I studied the large canvases of abstract art set off by the almost too white walls. I meandered into the kitchen to watch David prepare dinner.

He'd already completed much of the prep work. The peppers and carrots had been julienned, the garlic and fresh ginger minced, the shrimp deveined, and the green onions chopped. I watched him season the wonton soup while I sat on a stool, sipping a glass of white wine at the counter. He had marinated the chicken earlier in the day, and all of the ingredients, oils, and spices, were measured and organized. God, I really liked this guy and was more than a little impressed with his apparent culinary skills. Watching David was tons more fun than watching a cooking show on television.

"You're in charge of the rice," he said, pointing to the electric cooker on the counter.

I broached the Martin topic even before he refilled my wine glass. "I have good news," I said. David looked up from the wonton wrappers. "It's about Martin. He's agreed to most of the academic plan. His only objection is the Environmental Science course at the community college. Although he did promise to think about it for next semester." David took a sip of his wine and smiled at me.

"Jennifer, that's fantastic. The fact that he's even thinking about a next semester is a positive sign. You should be optimistic. We should celebrate." He raised his wine in a toast, and we clinked our glasses.

"I know. I am optimistic. Cautiously optimistic. Martin's away for a few days, visiting his uncle in Fort Lauderdale," I lied. I didn't want David to know that Martin was out there on his own, missing in action. He didn't need to know that I had no idea where in the world that boy might be. Taking a little vacation. A break from his sorry existence. "So, if you don't mind, I'd rather relax tonight and not think about the situation with Martin." I sounded like an uncaring parent. But David didn't seem to be judgmental. He didn't question my motives. I could tell he liked the way I looked that night. I wanted that to be the only thing on his mind.

"That's a great idea. You must be exhausted. Tonight, we relax, no worries, just the best wonton soup you've ever had in your life," he said with a knowing smile, making me think he had something else in mind for the evening. And then he refilled my wine glass, and I stopped thinking about Martin. In fact, I stopped thinking at all and let my body overcome any semblance of good judgment I had left.

The truth of the matter was this: I wanted to stay the night with David. I wanted to lose myself, to forget who I was, forget who I was supposed to be. I wanted to have sex with that man. My whole body wanted him. I wanted the best sex of my life to happen that night with David Allington.

After dinner, we started on the living room couch and moved quickly into his bedroom. We fell onto his bed and kissed each other deeply and for a long time. At some point, I couldn't get my clothes off fast enough. His hands and mouth were everywhere, and I felt a familiar desperation, needing him inside me, deeper and harder, not caring about anyone or anything. I let myself go, completely. It seemed we'd never get enough of each other. And when we were both physically spent and utterly satisfied, I fell into a dreamless sleep, forgetting who I was. Forgetting my name. Blissfully lost in David's protective arms. Safe at last.

CHAPTER 24

The aroma of coffee drifted into the bedroom, rousing me from a peaceful oblivion. The ceiling fan whirred above me, brushing my skin with cool air. I grabbed the snarled sheet from the end of the bed and covered my naked body, hiding the evidence of my night of pleasure, concealing the shame of dragging David into the mess of Jennifer Moriarty's life.

I realized it would be impossible to continue the affair, especially once Jennifer's son returned from his little vacation. Not possible and not fair to David. I collected my rumpled clothing scattered on the floor and was struggling with the buttons of my wrinkled blouse as David walked into the bedroom with a steaming cup of coffee.

"No sugar, a splash of milk, right?" he said. I smiled. David must have noticed how I liked my coffee at The Good News Café. "Hungry for breakfast?"

"Ah, coffee! Thank you." I reached out to grab the cup. "But, no. I can't stay for breakfast. I really need to run." A hook-up was one thing. It was something I needed. It was wonderful. After all, I wasn't a married woman. David was divorced. This had nothing to do with adultery. But I didn't want to give any indication that I was looking for more.

"Well, if you're not going to stay for breakfast, how about dinner tonight?" I looked up from my coffee. David was wearing a ratty T-shirt and cargo shorts. His hair was just-out-of-bed tousled, and his wry grin sent shivers down my spine. And those eyes. Those eyes. God, what was I thinking? "And if you're not hungry for breakfast, I hope you're hungry for something else." He must have been reading my mind. David took the cup out of my hands, placed it on the dresser, and kissed me. He wrapped his arms around my body, and as he unbuttoned my shirt, I lost my resolve to end our little fling before it went any further.

As I walked out of David's apartment an hour later, I wondered what might be going on in his mind. He had his career to consider and sleeping with a student's separated-but-still-married mother was probably not encouraged by the administration. It might have been grounds for his dismissal. And yet, that didn't stop him. I hoped he thought the risk was worth it.

Back at Jennifer's house, I changed into yoga pants and a faded chambray work shirt. I felt lighter somehow and practically giddy, as though any moment I might break out in a song from a corny Broadway musical. I breathed more deeply with Martin out of the house. I filled my lungs with the oxygen needed to strategize and implement a new plan to extricate myself from this mess, a plan that was beginning to take shape.

But something continued to nag at me, interfering with my ability to focus. I couldn't imagine where Martin had gone for his little "break." Did he have friends? Were there relatives who would take him in without telling his mother? Maybe he went to his father's house or Aunt Nancy's. I told myself it didn't matter. What mattered was the freedom to walk around the Moriarty's house without the responsibility of feeding Martin. Without the fear of running into him unexpectedly on the stairs to the gun loft. Without the disquieting thoughts of Martin watching me as I swam laps in the pool, or worse, as I slept in Jennifer's bed. This freedom, albeit temporary, gave me the resolve I needed to fix what I could in whatever time I had left.

I walked through the mudroom into the garage, considering a new four-digit code for the keypad. Jennifer had made the password so obvious. This would be an easy fix. But as I stepped into the garage, I froze. Something was different, and it took me a moment to realize what it was. The Jeep was missing.

There was room for three vehicles in Jennifer's garage. I'd assumed one space was reserved for the Mercedes even though I never parked there. Since I arrived, I'd been parking in the circular driveway and using the front door to gain entrance to the house. I didn't know which button opened the garage door from the inside of the car, and I'd been too preoccupied to care. Another space in the garage was probably for Jim's car when he stayed in the house. And the third space, the space in the middle, was for the designated extra car. The Jeep. Maybe the Jeep was Jason's. I'd assumed that shiny, silver Jeep was the family backup car for when Jennifer needed something powerful to handle the harsh Florida driving conditions. I didn't know why anyone in that family needed a Jeep, but I remembered it being parked right in that middle spot. It was definitely parked there the first time I entered the garage, the family's just-in-case car. And now, the Jeep had gone missing along with Martin, a boy without a driver's license. I jumped to the obvious conclusion, but then considered other possibilities. Jason had been staying with Jennifer's sister, Nancy. There was a chance Jason had returned home earlier to retrieve the Jeep while I was blissfully unaware at David's house.

Until I got to the bottom of the missing Jeep, I'd be incapable of moving forward. I ran back to the kitchen and grabbed the cell phone. I called Nancy who answered after the first ring. "Hey, Jennifer," she said.

"Hi, Nancy. How's Jason doing?"

"Fine, why?"

"I was wondering about his car. Does he happen to have his car with him?" I prayed nothing in my question or tone of voice would sound an alarm.

"Yeah, he does. Why? Do you need it? Is everything okay?" asked Nancy. I needed to tread carefully.

"Everything's fine, Nancy. Tell me, which car does he have? I want to be sure it doesn't need servicing." Day by day, I was getting more adept at winging it. Living the lie was becoming second nature.

"He has his own car, the Audi, Jim's old sedan," Nancy said, confused. My mind started racing at ninety miles an hour. *If Jason didn't have the Jeep, that meant Martin took it. That boy didn't have a license, and he took the car to go god only knows where for his little vacation break. Jesus. Unless, perhaps, Jim took the car while I was at David's place.* I needed to slow down. I needed to act normal. Whatever normal meant.

"Right. Thanks, Nancy. Listen, what's Jason been up to? I miss him," I said, changing the subject away from car-talk.

"He's busy with school, sports, you know," Nancy said. I didn't know. I still didn't know much about this family.

"Yeah, I know," I said. "Please, Nancy, encourage him to call me or even email me, okay?"

I didn't think Martin would stray anywhere close to his brother, but I had to dig a little to be certain. "Nancy, you haven't heard from Martin recently, have you?"

"Martin? No, of course not. Why? Is everything okay?"

"Yes, everything's the same. I wondered if Martin had called you or reached out to you. I don't know. I'm hoping, that's all."

"Jennifer, I haven't seen or heard from Martin in over a year. I don't expect that will change until he gets the help he needs." And then her voice softened. "Until you *both* get the help you need. Are you taking your meds? Please don't tell me you're skipping your therapist appointments again." I didn't have the patience for Nancy's derisive tone of voice or time for her sisterly advice.

"Stop worrying, Nancy. I'm fine. Everyone's fine. I have to run."

Still needing to confirm my assumptions about the missing Jeep, I decided to call Jennifer's husband. His secretary put me on hold for at least three minutes, and I couldn't stop myself from taking it personally. When he finally picked up, I sensed he was preoccupied.

"Jim, do you have time to talk?"

"What's wrong?" He sounded appropriately alarmed. Maybe he did care about Jennifer and Martin. There could be a sliver of hope for this marriage.

"Nothing. Everything's fine." I lied. "I have a few questions."

"Shoot," said Jim. I'd never escape the gun jargon that infused the Moriarty communication style.

"I'm wondering about the Jeep. Does it need servicing? Should I bring it in?"

"No, the Jeep's fine. Why are you bothering me with this now? You know the business takes care of servicing the cars." My mind wandered. What type of business was Jim talking about? I'd never asked Jennifer about the nature of her husband's work. Not that it was important. I forced my mind to refocus on the purpose of the call.

"It's just, well with our new living arrangement, I thought I should start taking responsibility for running this household. You're *not* here, the car *is* here, you know?"

Jim didn't try to hide his annoyance. "The Jeep is fine. Drive it to the club or the gym once a week or run the motor for a few minutes, make sure the tank is full, the usual," he said. "Is that all?" He tried to brush me off. *Not so fast*, I thought.

"I have news. About Martin." I told him about Martin's academic program. I told him that his son had agreed to start working toward fulfilling his graduation requirements.

"That's good news, Jennifer, really. It's way past time, but finally, some good news," he said. "Listen, I'm in the middle of something, I really have to go." So much for stepping it up as a caring father or husband.

"Well, there is one more thing," I said. I didn't want him to go. I wanted to keep him on the phone. I had this urge to break down and tell Jim everything. Tell him the truth and beg for his help. I wanted Jim to save me, to stop Martin, to find his real wife and bring Jennifer back where she belonged. I wanted Jim to set me free.

"What is it? I don't have all day," he snapped.

"Before you hang up. Umm... I was wondering about the Guntry Club. I think we can let my membership lapse. My heart's not in it anymore, what with my mother's deteriorating condition, and I've been thinking. It's such a waste of money." I actually thought Jim would be happy to hear Jennifer was interested in saving money. He should have been pleased. And even concerned about his mother-in-law's health. There was still the possibility of building this relationship into something close to trust. If we had trust, I could tell him the whole truth. Maybe then Jim would be willing to help me.

"Are you fucking kidding me? You love that place. Since when do you care about wasting *my* money? And since when did you start worrying about your mother's well-being? She has Nancy, one dutiful daughter. Isn't that enough?

That's what you always tell me. Besides, if you quit the Guntry Club, where will you and the boys go for your target practice?" The last question brought me to my feet. *Where would Jennifer, Martin, and Jason go for their target practice?* So, Jennifer's sons were sharpshooters too. Of course. I didn't have an answer for Jim. I was too stunned by the new information, and I had more immediate problems than cancelling my membership to the Guntry Club.

"Never mind, it's not important. Since I had you on the phone, I thought I'd bring it up," I said, before realizing Jim had already disconnected, returning to his busy, important life.

I had wasted time and energy trying to learn the whereabouts of the missing Jeep. All I had to show for my conversations with Nancy and Jim was an excruciating headache.

I dragged myself back to the garage, now even more intent on changing the password on the keypad. I had to keep Martin away from those guns above the loft. Somehow, he'd already gotten his hands on the pistol he used the other night. I wouldn't have been surprised to learn his mom bought that gun for him as a birthday or Christmas gift. Something for target practice at the Guntry Club. His very own gun. One firearm in that boy's possession was already one too many.

Seeing the empty space where the Jeep had been parked, provoked murderous thoughts that were unlike the old me. Thoughts that would have been anathema to Jenn Cooper, the peace-loving, anti-violent English teacher. But those thoughts flooded my brain with images of Martin driving the Jeep off a bridge, smashing it into a tree. I imagined the car engulfed in flames with Martin trapped inside. And then, as if the missing Jeep wasn't enough, I noticed an even more problematic situation in Jennifer's garage. I stopped and stared at the light on the keypad. I froze. The light was green.

Green for OPEN. *Shit!* I'd definitely entered the code to lock the door before I left the garage on Thursday. I remembered being extra careful. I'd made certain the red light was on after I locked the door to the Moriarty gun collection. And now the light on the keypad glowed green.

I opened the heavy metal door and climbed the carpeted stairs, my breaths becoming shallower with each step. I turned on the overhead lights and glanced around the loft. Everything seemed to be in order. I walked over to the right side of the room. I opened each cabinet door, one at a time, examining the contents closely as internal spotlights illuminated the weapons artfully displayed. Everything looked the same as I remembered until I opened the third cabinet. There was nothing there, nothing at all. That cabinet was empty. Even the labels were missing. I tried to remember the firearms I'd seen in that cabinet. Although I couldn't be certain, images of semi-automatic assault rifles and ammunition magazines flashed in my mind. I continued checking the rest of the cabinets. Some of the handguns were missing as well. *Jesus Christ.*

Martin Moriarty had pushed the magic buttons on that keypad, climbed right up those stairs into that air-conditioned arsenal, dipped his hands into his parents' lethal cookie jar filled with armaments of mass destruction, and he took what he wanted. He took what he needed. Now he was somewhere out there with dangerous weapons, war machines, capable of snuffing out so many lives in a matter of seconds, a 16-year-old boy who had experience with target practice, a boy filled with rage and hate and violence. And there was nothing I could do to stop him. The barn door was open, and the horses were long gone. Too late for my plan. Too late to be thinking about changing the password, the lock, or disposing of the ammunition stored in this arsenal. *Now what?* I pressed my hands over my eyes, as if blocking my view of an empty gun cabinet would solve the problem. Was it time to consider calling the police?

Don't do anything stupid. Blood will be on your hands. Martin had warned me. I tried to chase those ominous words out of my brain. Calling the police would be stupid. A wrong move might be a disaster for me as well as for Martin's intended targets. I knew only one other person who might be able to help me figure out how to rein Martin in. His mother, Jennifer Moriarty. She'd tell me if he'd done this kind of thing in the past. Jennifer would know if the danger was imminent or if I might be making too much out of typical Martin behavior. Holding a gun to my head was not exactly typical behavior, I realized that. But grasping at straws seemed preferable to paralysis or even another panic attack.

I ran from the gun loft with only one goal: I needed to figure out a way to contact Jennifer. I had to find a way to get her back. I had to put an end to this nightmare.

It was Sunday, and locating Jennifer would be a challenge. She wouldn't be at school on the weekend, obviously. But I hadn't given up trying to call or text her. I went to the study and sat at Jennifer's desk, staring at her computer monitor, trying to draft the right words. I'd use my Dickinson High School email address. I always read my school emails on Sundays, and although I didn't expect Jennifer would check, there was a chance.

What magic words would bring Jennifer back? *The deal's off. Your son stole some of your assault rifles, handguns, ammunition, and he threatened to hurt many people unless I continue being his surrogate mother. Oh, and by the way, he hates you and doesn't want you back, Jennifer. Thanks a million for this life you threw away. I know you didn't throw it away—you gave it away. To me. Not to look a gift horse in the mouth, but really, what the fuck were you thinking? Did you honestly believe I could do something about the mess you made? I can't. So, get back here and fix this or I'm calling the police.* Finally, I settled on four words, capital letters and exclamation marks: IMPORTANT! PLEASE CALL ME!

After hitting the send button, I tried calling my cell number although I had no real expectation that Jennifer would answer. The voice mailbox was still full, of course. I tried texting my message. URGENT, CALL ME!!!

I poured myself a glass of red wine, sat at the kitchen table unable to think, unable to move. After a second glass I rallied a bit. Tonight, I'd have dinner with David. If I didn't hear from Jennifer by tomorrow morning, I'd call the school. Jennifer would be at Dickinson High on Monday morning, and I'd tell the school office I had a family emergency, the truth. They would surely put me through to the classroom. 9:20 was the beginning of my planning period, and we'd have an opportunity to talk. Jennifer and I would use our planning period appropriately— for planning purposes. We'd plan to fix the Martin problem.

CHAPTER 25

The next morning David nudged me from a deep slumber with kisses on my neck and bare shoulders, and it felt wonderful. It was early, too early for a conversation. Too early for hypothetical questions. But that's what he wanted. I wanted more kisses. David wanted talk.

"You awake?"

"Hmm."

"Good. I've been wondering about something." David stopped kissing me, but unfortunately, he wouldn't stop talking.

"Ooh, that feels nice. Don't stop," I begged. He ignored me.

"If you could be anything you wanted to be in the world, if money were no object, what would you want to do with your life?"

I turned my face toward David's. *He's wondering about this? About what I'd want to do with my life?* "Seriously?"

"Seriously." He was so earnest and adorable.

"Well, money isn't really an object for me at the moment. Of course, that will all change after my divorce is finalized." I couldn't believe I was having this conversation. Too early in the morning. Too early in the relationship. Or maybe it wasn't early at all. Maybe it was too late to be contemplating what to do with my life. With nothing to lose, I decided to go with the truth.

I propped my head on my arm. "But, if I could be anything I wanted to be, well, I'm not sure. I used to think I wanted to be a writer." The real Jennifer Moriarty had always wanted to be a teacher. I wondered if the reality of teaching freshman English at Dickinson High School had tarnished the silver on that dream.

David started stroking the inside of my arm, making it difficult to concentrate on the inane conversation he was trying to have with me. "What would you write?" he asked.

"I'd write novels, I guess. Definitely fiction." I groaned and pressed my breasts against his chest, entwining my top leg around his waist. I wasn't interested in this conversation. I wanted to change the subject. But David wasn't in a hurry. He brushed my hair away from my face.

"What sort of novels? All those houses you've visited must have had an influence on you. Were you looking for inspiration from Hemingway? Mark Twain? Is that why you visited the places where they wrote their literary masterpieces?" David propped his head on his hand, leaning on an elbow, looking at me with so much interest. Staring into my eyes, ignoring my willing body. He wanted to get inside my head. That scared me, but I liked it at the same time.

"Yes, as a matter of fact. Being in writers' homes does inspire me. Sometimes I leave a famous writer's study, thinking, *This is it. I'm ready to do this thing. I'm motivated to put my fingers on the keyboard and take a leap of faith, because I'm convinced that I have a story to tell.*" I pulled away and turned over onto my stomach, resting my head in my arms. I gazed into his dark eyes. He slid his hand onto my lower back. I groaned again.

"Tell me more," he said. God, his hand felt so good.

"I wrote short stories during college. That felt like less of a commitment than a novel." I closed my eyes and thought about David's question; about the book I hadn't even begun. "I don't know what sort of novel I'd write now. If I did know, I'd have already written something. It's probably too late for me."

"Have you ever tried to write a novel or to publish a short story?" he asked. I opened my eyes.

"No."

"Why not?"

"Well, I haven't really had the time."

"Why not?" he asked. I sighed and closed my eyes again, feeling annoyed by his questions.

"I'm busy, David. My days fill up so quickly, with tasks, responsibilities, expectations. Stuff." The conversation was becoming increasingly uncomfortable. I turned toward David again, reached out to touch his chest, trying to distract him. He took my hand in his.

"Jennifer. Are you listening?"

"Ugh! Are you still talking?"

"Yes, I'm talking, and you need to listen. You should make writing a novel one of those expectations."

"Okay, so you're saying 'not having enough time' isn't the only reason I haven't tried to write a novel?"

"I didn't say that, *you* did." I pulled my hand away.

"So, you think I'm scared to write a novel? Afraid I'll fail?"

"Again, those are *your* words. Not mine." David smiled. And when he looked at me like that, I couldn't be mad at him. He pulled me closer.

"I should be careful with you. You're a psychologist. You're analyzing me, right?"

"Is that what I'm doing?"

"Ha! I knew it. And here I thought I could trust you." I pushed him away with enough force to let him know I was feeling playful, not angry.

"You can trust me." David pulled me back to him.

"How do I know?"

"Your body is telling you that you can trust me, right?" His voice was soft, suggestive, while his fingers explored me, gently.

He *was* right. To prove his point, he brushed his lips against my throat, turned me around, and pressed himself urgently against my naked body. He reached around to touch my breast, pulling gently, erasing all thoughts about my writing career. He wanted me. I wanted him. I trusted him, and whether I would ever write a novel was completely beside the point.

After we made love that Monday morning, David hopped into the shower. When he returned, a towel wrapped around his waist, I started to get out of bed, but he insisted I take my time. "Stay. Stay as long as you want," he said. He had to get to school, but on his way out the door, he brought me a cup of coffee and kissed me goodbye. "Don't let this scare you," he warned me, "but I think I'm falling for you." His words didn't scare me, they saddened me. The timing for anyone falling for Jenn Cooper couldn't have been worse.

And yet, I'd never experienced so perfect a Monday morning. I sipped my coffee in bed and daydreamed about a life with David. I imagined we'd begin each day the same way, having conversations, making love. He'd bring me coffee in bed. I'd tell him to have a wonderful day at work, and he'd kiss me goodbye. So corny, I realized that, of course. But still, a harmless daydream. I let my imagination soar, thinking about how I'd have a book-lined study, all to myself. I'd write for hours. I'd take long walks, make myself lunch, read a book for an hour or two, then I'd write some more. David would come home in the early evening, and we'd make love again. Over dinner, David would tell me all about his day, and later he'd want to read the latest chapter of my novel. He'd be my cheerleader, my kind and honest critic. My best friend. My lover. My savior.

I checked the time. 9:00 a.m. My planning period at Dickinson High School was in twenty minutes. I pulled on my clothes, moved into the living room, and curled up on David's couch. I stared at my cell phone, my apprehension increasing with the passing of each minute. 9:16. 9:17. 9:18. So much was riding on that call. I hovered on the edge of the couch, staring at the phone, counting the seconds.

Dickinson High was one of the few numbers I'd committed to memory. I listened to the phone ringing, suddenly worried I'd be trapped in a long series of automated messages and requests. A familiar voice answered. The voice probably belonged to Anne, one of two secretaries in the front office who filled in as receptionist when the office became too busy. I tried to make my voice higher-pitched, more like Jennifer Moriarty's voice.

"Good morning, may I speak with Miss Cooper, please?" Anne, or whoever had answered the telephone, paused. *Damn*, I thought. *She knows it's me.*

"I'm sorry. There is no one by that name working at Dickinson High School at this time." At first, I assumed the secretary misheard me. I tried again.

"I said Miss Cooper, Miss Jenn Cooper. She teaches English," I explained.

"I'm sorry. We have no one by that name working at Dickinson High at this time. How else may I direct your call?" Stunned, I quickly disconnected. I stared at the phone as though the answer I needed might pop up on that small screen if I stared long enough.

This couldn't be happening. Where was Jennifer? What had she done? My worst fear had been that Jennifer would deplete my cache of sick days, waste my carefully protected bank of personal days. I worried about Jennifer not taking the time needed to review my lesson plans. I'd been anxious about Jennifer failing to read the assignments before her students and about her making a fool of herself, a fool of me, for not knowing the content I'd been teaching for so many years. I'd been concerned that my double might fail to stay one step ahead of the students at all times. I worried about my students not liking Jennifer or liking her too much. And all this time I'd been worrying about the wrong things.

I kept staring shell-shocked at the cell phone in my hand, shaking my head in disbelief. What made me think I could trust that woman for even one month of my life? Jennifer Moriarty had quit my teaching job. And now, even if I found a way to escape Martin and his threat, I'd have nothing left, no job, no life waiting for me back in Connecticut. How could I have believed that Jennifer Moriarty would come to my rescue? It was crystal clear, she'd never intended to take responsibility for the role she'd abdicated weeks ago. How could I have been so stupid? Why had I trusted her?

Why? Why? Why? Every violent fantasy I'd ever entertained about Martin paled in comparison to my new fantasies of Jennifer Moriarty's demise. That monster had stolen my life and left me with the smoldering ruins and ashes of her horrible existence. I pulled my gaze away from the screen, and I threw Jennifer's cell phone against the wall. I stared at the indentation I'd made above David's living room couch, marring the white paint. My parting gift to this blameless man. It was a small token of the rage that threatened to consume me.

I dragged myself to David's shower and stood under the force of the punishing, hot spray. Without Jennifer's cooperation, I'd be stuck in Coral Gables as a surrogate mother to the demon son she raised. And Jennifer was now missing in action along with her son. *That bitch. That fucking bitch.*

As I drove back to Jennifer's house, I was still fixated on where Martin had driven with the semi-automatic weapons he'd confiscated from above the garage. I tried to drown out my worst-case-scenario thoughts, blasting Latin music as loud as the car's audio system would tolerate. And then I remembered the feel of David's hands on my body, and thoughts of Martin evaporated. I was falling hard for that man, and despite my better judgment, I feared I'd be back in his bed that very night.

I pulled into the circular driveway and parked the Mercedes, hoping that Martin, wherever he was, took his time. Or better than that, I hoped he'd never return. Or even better, I hoped he'd return with his mother, arm in arm, laughing together about their practical joke. I hoped David would understand. And that was the most unrealistic hope of all. My story was unfathomable. My poor judgment— incomprehensible. My future—unimaginable.

CHAPTER 26

I remembered the directions to Westwoods Cares, and later that day I drove there without needing to rely on GPS. As I walked into Room 140, I was relieved to find Jennifer's mother awake, sitting in her armchair, her withered hands resting in her lap. The woman gazed out the window of her sterile room, as I placed a purple African violet and a coffee cake on the bedside table. I stood close to her, both of us now gazing through the window. "Good morning, Mom." No response. I waited. Without Nancy hovering, I didn't need to rush her.

Besides watching the cars and visitors coming and going in and out of the parking lot, Jennifer's mother could look outside her picture window to enjoy a ringside view of the bold messages plastered across two enormous billboards. They were planted like trees, side-by-side, towering above the buildings, rooted almost in the nursing home's backyard. I hadn't noticed them during the last few visits. How could I have missed those billboards? Today, Jennifer's mom seemed to be mesmerized by the signs. She wouldn't look away, even when I spoke to her again, this time touching her shoulder. "Mom, are you feeling up for a visit?" I tried to attract her attention gently, but the woman existed in another world. No wonder. The messages on the billboards and the messenger were indeed compelling.

"Well, you did ask for a sign." — *God.*
"Seeking truth? Love? Answers? Directions? Talk to me." — *God*

I pulled up a chair, taken aback by those billboard messages. In fact, I *was* seeking answers, and I *was* desperate for directions. If god didn't have time for a conversation, perhaps I'd be able to garner some truth by talking to Jennifer's mother. God might be willing to speak through this woman. Although I'd have preferred a burning bush, I'd be satisfied with a human intermediary. After all, god might have more pressing matters. I stood up and walked over to close the window blinds, blocking the distractions from view.

"I brought you coffee cake and a plant," I said. I kissed my surrogate mother's soft cheek and gave her frail body a gentle hug. I leaned over to cut two thin slices of the crumbly cake with a plastic knife.

I held out a piece I'd placed on a paper towel. "It's good, Mom, try it."

Jennifer's mother continued to gaze at the window although the view was now blocked. Perhaps the messages on those billboards were strong enough to filter through the blinds. I fed the old woman morsels of the cake, as if she were a toddler. Jennifer's mother swallowed tentatively and then opened her mouth for more, like a baby bird, waiting for another worm.

"Should I get tea for us as well? The coffee cake's a little dry. Not enough butter. Or sour cream."

Jennifer's mother looked up in surprise, as if I'd just entered the room, interrupting her thoughts. Her eyes wide, she seemed to awaken, sitting up taller in her chair, her shoulders pushed back, she smiled at me.

"Oh, Jennifer. I didn't hear you come in." She believed I was her daughter. Did she forget that I was the stranger who visited with Nancy? A stranger who happened to look like her daughter? Did this woman even remember my previous visits? "Where's Nancy?" Pleased that Jennifer's mother made the connection between my visit and her other daughter, I smiled and pulled my chair closer. Perhaps her doctor was wrong about the effectiveness of the new medication. Maybe her memory wasn't fading as quickly as he'd predicted.

"Nancy? I'm not sure, Mom. I wanted to spend time with you today, alone time."

"Okay." She turned back to the billboards hidden behind the shades, their magnetic pull, stronger than anything I could say.

"Mom, can we talk about Martin? I need your advice."

"Okay."

I walked back to the windows and pulled the heavy curtains across the closed blinds. *Sorry, god.* I needed her full attention. Now the room was dark, too dark to read the expression in her eyes. I needed to see those eyes and discover any clues they might provide. I turned on the overhead light and sat across from Jennifer's mother. I took a deep breath and began once more.

"I know Jim and I have made mistakes raising Martin. Maybe it's too late to help him. But I want to try. What do you think?" I'd pull Jim into the story at every opportunity. That absent father was not blame-free no matter what he believed. Even if Jim was not the biological father, even if he claimed to have no influence over the way Jennifer raised Martin, at least Jennifer had tried. At least Jennifer had found me, a reasonable surrogate, someone who might have the will and the skills to fix the Martin problem.

I waited for Jennifer's mother to respond with a few words of wisdom. Finally, her eyes widened. "What does God say?" she asked. I dug deep for a reasonable response, and the words dripped slowly off my tongue like honey from a teaspoon.

"God says I should ask *you* for advice." I waited. Martin's grandmother needed time to get this right. I studied her furrowed brow. I got the sense she was struggling to help her daughter. She shook her head, shrugged her shoulders, and finally looked at me.

"I'm sorry, Jennifer. God thinks it's too late. You can't save Martin. But you can save yourself."

I clutched the padded arms of her chair. That wasn't the response I expected. Not even close. I struggled to keep the tears at bay. I needed specifics, a roadmap, a way out.

"How can I save myself?" I sobbed, now frantic for answers.

"Look for a sign, Jennifer."

"What kind of sign?"

"That's up to God. Why are you trembling? What are you afraid of, dear?" The kindness and sorrow in that woman's eyes singed my heart. The physical pain in the muscles of my shoulders distracted me for a moment. I grabbed a tissue from the box near the bed and swiped at my tears. I tried to compose myself. I felt dangerously close to losing all control. I couldn't afford the luxury of falling apart. Not yet.

"I'm afraid someone will get hurt, Mom. I'm afraid Martin will hurt someone." It was a relief to speak the truth about Martin, to voice my fears aloud. Even if Martin's grandmother didn't have the answers.

"So, stop him. That is how you will save yourself. Stop him, once and for all. Do the right thing, Jennifer. Do the right thing for everyone involved." The woman's translucent skin shone like a beacon of hope. Her voice held all the clarity and strength I'd been craving.

Before leaving the room, I pulled the window curtains aside and lifted the blinds, reading the billboard messages one last time.

I stopped by the receptionist's counter near the front door to deliver what remained of the coffee cake. The receptionist looked at my red and swollen eyes with a sympathetic expression. "I know," the woman said. "It's so hard. But don't worry, we'll take good care of your mom. Don't you worry your heart about anything."

Jennifer's mother was right. Whether her suggestion was based on knowing her grandson for 16 years, or whether she'd shared a prophetic message, I needed to take her words seriously. Martin needed to be stopped. I didn't have a blueprint for stopping him. No roadmap for saving myself. I'd have to figure this out on my own.

I returned to the Coral Gables house on autopilot, surprised to find myself pulling into the circular driveway again. With time to kill, I settled into the study and tried calling and texting Jennifer but ran into the same dead-ends. I decided to do an online investigation to discover clues about what Jennifer Moriarty may have been doing since she left Key West. I checked out the high school website, looking for my name under the list of faculty members. Nothing. And then I checked the local online news source called *The Pumpkin Patch*.

The image of pumpkins made me pine for home. I craved fresh cider and donuts, crisp Macintosh apples, the brilliant colors of the maple trees, and the crunch of autumn leaves underfoot. I longed to escape this Florida nightmare in time to enjoy another New England autumn. Exhausted by the humidity, the sultry air, I wanted to start wearing sweaters, black tights and wool skirts, warm socks, and cozy scarves. I hungered for a change of seasons.

And then, a headline from *The Pumpkin Patch* grabbed me like a wrestler's chokehold. I read it twice, then three times, desperately trying to catch my breath and make sense of the words: "Popular high school English teacher vanishes. Foul play not suspected."

I recalled the message on the billboard. *Well, you did ask for a sign,* — *God.* And here it was. A sign. *Thank you, god. Thanks a bunch.*

CHAPTER 27

I rocked back and forth, clutching my arms across my stomach. I felt the room spin as I grappled with the headline. The article must have referred to some other English teacher, I told myself. The headline used the word *popular*. I'd never been a popular teacher. Students *tolerated* Miss Cooper; they didn't *like* Miss Cooper. The article must have described someone else. I forced myself to read the story underneath that headline.

> *A former English teacher has disappeared from their apartment in Hartford. A neighbor notified the police after hearing screams. They found no evidence of forced entry or theft. The teacher had resigned from their position unexpectedly, soon after the start of the school year. Although foul play is not suspected, the police are following up by interviewing friends and family who have requested we not publish the name of the teacher at this time.*

I read the article again and stared at the words on the screen, shaking my head in denial. Those words severed whatever tenuous threads of hope I still held, hope of contacting Jennifer Moriarty. Even though the teacher's name wasn't published, it seemed obvious to me. *No. This could not be happening. Why had Jennifer Moriarty disappeared? Who would do this?* I actually asked myself that question. I entertained the darkest of possibilities. As though there might be multiple scenarios for what happened to the woman who had stolen my life. *Who had motive to harm Jennifer Moriarty? Who had opportunity? Who possessed a weapon?* Only one name came to mind.

The room and my thoughts swirled around me, as if caught up in the vortex of a sudden tornado. My quivering fingers jerked across the keyboard of the computer, searching for answers. I immediately checked Jennifer Moriarty's email. And that's when I found the metaphorical smoking gun with Martin's fingerprints all over it. His American Literature assignment. Martin Moriarty, Miss Cooper's star pupil, had completed his homework as promised. It was practically a signed confession.

10 experiences from my life that could spark ideas for fictional narratives

By Martin Moriarty

1. *I pretended to enjoy whitewashing a picket fence to get other kids to do it for me*
2. *I worked on a steamboat*
3. *I faked my own death with pig's blood*
4. *I took off with a runaway slave named Nigger Jim (Hey teacher-Is it okay to use the N word?)*
5. *I trained a frog to jump higher than any other frog in Hartford, CT*
6. *I had a pap who was a no good drunk and who beat me*
7. *I met a prince who looked just like me so we switched clothes and switched lives (sound familiar?)*
8. *I had a 25-room house built on Farmington Avenue, Hartford, CT, right next to my good friend, Harriet Beecher Stowe*
9. *Some old widow tried to sivilize me, but I couldn't stand it no longer so I lit out*
10. *I was dreadful lonesome being locked up for three days by my pap. I begun to think how dreadful it was, even for murderers to be in such*

*a fix. And so I says to myself, there ain't no telling but I might come
to be a murderer myself, yet, and then how would I like it?*

I read the tenth "experience" again. I wanted to believe Martin was trying to
impress me with his literary allusions, and yet the words turned my stomach. *Tom
Sawyer, The Adventures of Huckleberry Finn, The Prince and the Pauper*, the facts
about Mark Twain's house in Hartford. I was too terrified to be impressed. Clearly,
Martin was trying to send me a message. He was telling me he'd been in Hartford,
Connecticut. He may have visited Mark Twain's home, down the street from my
apartment. He'd probably visited his mother. And like Huckleberry Finn, he
contemplated murder. Unlike Huck, Martin had his choice of guns, even semi-
automatic firearms, a four-wheel-drive vehicle, and a twisted mind.

I began to shake uncontrollably, my mouth went bone dry, and the sounds I
made were those of a feral animal in the forest, fighting for his life. I heard the echo
of my wailing, as if from a faraway place. A dark place, a dank, prison cell. I wrapped
my arms around my body, clutching my ribs, squatting on the floor of Jennifer's
study. Thinking about the woman who had disappeared, a woman who'd resigned
from my teaching position, a missing woman, and in all likelihood, a dead woman.
I rocked back and forth on my heels. Finally, I fell to my knees and curled onto the
hard, wooden floor. I sobbed like a lost child in the woods, helpless and hopeless
and without shame.

Not knowing how much time had passed, I finally pulled myself up off that
floor. I dragged my body upstairs to Jennifer's walk-in closet, grabbed the Chanel
purse, and swallowed another Xanax. Then, I collapsed on Jennifer's bed, curling
up in the fetal position. As the Xanax took effect and my breathing became less
shallow, I considered my options.

I thought about picking up the phone and calling David. I even imagined the
conversation.

Me: *I met a woman a few weeks ago while I was vacationing in Key West. She
looked exactly like me. I mean she could be my double. And I think she*

may have drugged me, and then she tricked me into going along with a ridiculous plan.

David: *A plan? What sort of plan?*

Me: *It was a crazy dare to swap lives. For a month. Her name was Jennifer Moriarty. But now she's disappeared. I think she was killed.*

David: *Jennifer, you're scaring me. You are Jennifer Moriarty.*

Me: *No, I'm not. My name is Jenn Cooper. I'm a high school English teacher and I live in Connecticut. I've been pretending to be Jennifer Moriarty.*

David: *I'm trying to understand.*

Me: *I'm Jenn Cooper. But now I'm stuck in this other life. Because I'm here, I'm alive, and the real Jennifer Moriarty may have been murdered in my apartment in Hartford. She's vanished.*

David: *So, you've been pretending to be someone you're not. Why in the world?*

Me: *I think the real Jennifer Moriarty was trying to escape, to get far away from her son, Martin.*

David: *What are you saying?*

Me: *I believe the real Jennifer Moriarty took one look at me, her doppelganger, a teacher, someone who could help her son, and she figured it was a way out for her. She even told me that I was the answer to her prayers. And I think Martin killed her. Because you see, he had guns and a motive, and . . . David, why are you laughing? Listen to me; this is serious.*

David: *You almost had me there, Jennifer. This is clearly a crazy, made for TV movie script. Or tell me, is this the novel you plan to write? Are you testing this convoluted plot on me? I like it. It has potential.*

The imaginary conversation gave me no comfort. And as I pondered Jennifer Moriarty's disappearance, her possible murder, my own culpability came into focus. I was the one who told Martin where his mother was working, where she was living, the name she was using, all the details he needed to track her down. I should have foreseen that he'd do something horrible to keep his surrogate mother trapped in his life. I was the one who knew Martin had taken the Jeep, had stolen assault rifles, pistols, and ammunition, and I was the one person who knew he was determined to keep me from leaving him. I should have stopped him before it was too late. I was complicit, and David couldn't change that reality. Confiding in David was not an option. I needed to protect myself, to take matters into my own hands.

I hauled my body to a standing position and returned to Jennifer's walk-in closet. I swallowed another Xanax and pulled out the overnight bag. As I packed a change of clothing, pieces of a new plan began to fit together like a jigsaw puzzle.

I placed the overnight bag into the trunk of the Mercedes and sat in the driver's seat, waiting for my trembling fingers to cooperate. Finally, I texted David: *Sorry need to cancel tonight severe migraine going straight to bed please understand.* And then I pulled away from Jennifer Moriarty's house in Coral Gables, heading south on Highway 1. 150 miles to Key West. I'd be there in time for dinner, and for some strange reason, I suddenly felt ravenous. I fiddled with the radio in Jennifer's car and found a classic country-western station. I sang along with songs I'd never heard before. I crooned kick-ass gunfighter ballads with Marty Robbins, cheating heart blues with Patsy Kline, and lonesome love songs with Hank Williams. The miles flew by, one tragic country-western song at a time.

CHAPTER 28

I drove through the historic streets of Old Town on my way to Jennifer's cottage. I had to slam on the brakes of the Mercedes to avoid plowing into a group of tourists, pedaling Floyd's bicycles. Those ubiquitous bikes with their rusty baskets seemed to sprout from the Key West landscape like hibiscus flowers, blooming large during the day.

I let myself into the cottage and collapsed on the living room couch. Finding Floyd's phone number was easy. He had a business, a storefront on a busy corner not far from Mallory Square. I called the number listed for Floyd's Bicycle Tours and left a message. "It's Jennifer. I'm in town, and I need to talk to you. It's urgent. Please call me as soon as you get this message. I'll stop by the bike shop in the morning if I don't hear from you."

I turned up the air conditioning, found a bottle of iced tea in the small pantry, poured myself a glass over ice. I didn't have to wait long for Floyd to return my call.

"Hey, stranger. Good to hear from ya. Watcha doing back in town?"

"I'm here for a few nights. Listen, can we meet? I need a huge favor."

"Sure, babe. Can't make it tonight. And gotta tour scheduled for tomorrow morning at 10:00, but let's meet for breakfast at The Busy Bean. 9:00 work for ya?" I smiled, thinking about what Jennifer had said about Floyd. *Loyal. Trustworthy.* Those were her words. *I can count on Floyd for anything.* I was counting on exactly that.

I went for a long walk and then picked up comfort food from a waterside takeout place a short walk away from the cottage. Curled up on Jennifer's porch swing, I devoured the marinated roast pork, smoked ham, Swiss cheese on Cuban bread. I decided I'd try to make this sandwich, once things settled down. But not for Martin. He didn't deserve a sandwich that good. Plain old grilled cheese was more than he deserved.

At 8:50 the next morning I waited on the steps of The Busy Bean Café down the street from Floyd's shop. Ten minutes later, Floyd pedaled up to the curb grinning from ear to ear. I'd have known him even without his old bicycle. The baseball cap, the tanned, leathery skin, and the way his face lit up when he saw me. Floyd threw open his arms, and I succumbed to a very long and almost painful bear hug.

The coffee shop had only a few customers. Floyd and I carried our muffins and mugs to a table on the porch outside. Already, the heavy Florida air felt suffocating, and although I would have preferred staying close to the overtaxed air conditioning unit inside, we had privacy on the porch.

"So, what's up, Jennifer? What's so urgent?"

"I need a handgun," I whispered, without preamble or small talk.

"Are you kidding? What do *you* need a gun for?"

"Self-protection, what else would I need it for?"

"Really? Self-protection?"

"Yes, self-protection. There've been a few incidents in my neighborhood, and I want to feel safe." I nibbled at my muffin, shrugging my shoulders.

"So, why me? Why not apply for a permit, go legit? It's easy. It's fast. Anyone can get a gun." And that was a big part of the problem, but I wasn't about to get into a discussion about the prevalence of guns in our country. Sure, I had an arsenal of firearms to choose from in Jennifer's loft, but I had my reasons for wanting Floyd's help. All I had to do was convince him.

Something about the adrenaline pulsing through my veins helped me focus. I had acquired the power to fabricate reasonable, creative responses with the speed of a squirrel jumping over a baffle to steal dinner from a birdfeeder. I was feeling ridiculously proud of that superpower.

"You could have said that about the drugs, Floyd, right? I could have asked a doctor for the meds. But you helped me then, you didn't ask questions." He shrugged his shoulders. I looked into his eyes. "You've always been there for me. I've always been able to count on you. That's what I need now. I need somebody I can count on."

I held my breath, watching him swallow the last bite of his muffin and swig his coffee. "Jennifer, we go way back. Your asshole husband doesn't want his wife or son taking medication—legal, illegal—that's all the same to me. I get it. I don't have a problem finding you the meds you need and some weed now and then. But hey, I know you, and I know enough about Jim to worry about your safety. Do ya need protection from your husband? Is that what's going on? Is the abuse getting more serious?"

The abuse? "What are you talking about?" The possibility of spousal abuse had never occurred to me.

"Jennifer, this is Floyd you're talking to. I've seen the bruises. Every time ya come down here, shit, for the past three years, it's something else. A black eye, a broken wrist, a limp. You stay long enough for the bruises to fade, for the bones to heal, and then back ya go for more. I know the signs, Jennifer. When are ya gonna leave that asshole? What's it gonna take?" I wrestled with Floyd's suspicions, trying to fit the pieces into the narrative of what I'd already learned about the Moriarty family. I needed Floyd to understand without knowing what was *really* going on. I needed his help desperately.

"Jim and I have separated. As a matter of fact, it looks like *he's* leaving *me*, and I'm fine with that. The marriage is over. It's been over for a long time."

"That's good news. I'm relieved to hear it. But ya think ya still need protection," he said. "Why, Jennifer? Why now?"

"I want to feel safe, Floyd. This is not about Jim. Believe me." That part of my story was true. "I'm a single woman now, and I want to feel comfortable in my neighborhood, in my home. God willing, I'll never need it. But I think I should have a gun, and I should know how to use it." A well-regulated militia, after all, that's the protection I needed. My Second Amendment right. *Come on, Floyd;*

don't give me a hard time. Not now. I don't have time to argue with you. I don't have the energy to beg.

"Listen. Let me see what I can do. I'll come by the cottage, and we can have dinner tonight. I'll have what ya need." I exhaled, squeezed his hand, and smiled.

"Thank you, Floyd. What would I do without you?" We finished our coffee and moved on to safer topics. Floyd ranted about how his business had taken a hit lately after nasty, online reviews on Tripmaster.

"Fuck those asshole tourists. If they want a boring bike ride up and down Duval Street—wearing their helmets like they're competing in the Tour de France, they can take it someplace else. I guess those flabby tourists don't appreciate me playing Frank Sinatra on my conch shell. Fuck, I was on The Tonight Show once." I started to laugh, I couldn't help it, visualizing Floyd on TV playing *I Did it My Way*, with a conch shell. "These assholes don't know a mango from a papaya. Complaining like babies about how I cut the top of the coconut off with my machete like I'm some Lizzy Borden mass-murderer. How else can ya get the lime in the coconut, right?" He started singing that crazy old song by Harry Nilsson.

I didn't bother correcting Floyd about his Lizzy Borden analogy. Lizzy murdered only two people. That wouldn't qualify as mass-murder. I admired this machete-wielding, bicycle tour guide. Along with his bike tours, he seemed to have a thriving, underground side business, getting pills, pot, and now handguns for suburban women who had nowhere else to turn. Floyd made me laugh even as my whole world was crashing down around me. I marveled at how easy it was to talk with him. He could have given me a harder time, and I appreciated that he never suggested I use one of the handguns the Moriarty family owned. Jennifer probably kept that part of her life a secret, thank goodness, because I had good reasons for needing Floyd as my gun broker. I had a plan.

On my walk back to the cottage, I wondered how I'd missed this Floyd character when I visited Key West as a tourist a few weeks ago. I was too busy chasing after dead authors instead of enjoying the moment, living in the present, noticing those simple joys right in front of me on the streets of Old Town. I might have enjoyed his bicycle tour, exploring the back streets of Key West, away from the bar scene, checking out the flora and fauna and architecture. *Next time*, I thought. With Floyd's help, there might even be a next time. All I needed to do was put the lime in the coconut and pray for a miracle.

* * *

I had the rest of the day to myself. I checked for messages from Martin, hoping for some indication about when to expect his return. Nothing. Not a clue. I couldn't risk his rage. I texted him:

When will you be home? And then I sent an olive branch: *Assignment Grade C-. Nice Effort.* How could I give him an A or B for his Mark Twain inspired list?

If Martin had been a Dickinson High School student, I'd have asked him to wait after class. I might have applauded his ingenuity, his creativity, his literary allusions, even his attempt at humor. Then, I'd have given him the Cooper choice: Either complete the assignment again, the right way, following my expectations or accept a failing grade. I always gave my students do-overs. But Martin didn't deserve one, and we didn't have time. And so, Martin would have to accept the grade I gave him, and a C- was more than generous.

I threw on one of Jennifer's swimsuits and a lace cover-up that actually covered very little. I grabbed beach towels and drove to a nearby state park, Fort Zachary Taylor, where I rented a chair and umbrella. The rocky beach and choppy waves wouldn't deter me from taking a long swim in the warm water. I sidestepped the dead Portuguese Man-O-War washed up on the beach and swam out beyond the buoys, beyond the rough whitecaps to calmer, cooler water. With each stroke, I pushed the seawater out of my way. I pushed away all my fears of Martin, worries about Jennifer, Dickinson High School, and the loss of my former life miles and miles away from the State of Florida. I felt invulnerable to rip tides and to the stinging tentacles of jellyfish. Immune to pain, fueled by a mission more important than any undertaking I'd ever faced.

Back on the shore, I wrapped myself in Jennifer's towel. I collapsed in the beach chair and closed my eyes. My mind wandered back to my conversation with Floyd, the bruises, the broken bones, those injuries. Who had been abusing Jennifer? Was it her husband, as Floyd assumed, or was it Jennifer's son? Floyd had seen evidence of abuse for the past three years. Martin would have been thirteen when he started physically abusing his mother. Where was Jim? Did Jennifer ever tell him about the physical abuse? Was she able to hide it so well from her husband? Was he oblivious to what was going on under his own roof? Or, had Martin learned to be a monster from a master of cruelty, the man who helped raise him? I wondered if my questions would ever be answered. Too late for blame. Too late for analysis. What did it matter?

I focused on my breathing, following each inhalation, each exhalation, finally lulled to sleep by the pounding of my heart and the waves slamming against the rocky beach. This time no one visited my dreams. No one dared.

CHAPTER 29

With an hour to kill before Floyd would arrive, I drafted another American Literature assignment for Martin. I believed he enjoyed those assignments. I'd encountered plenty of students with tough-guy personas over the years, and as much as they complained about homework and my high expectations, when it came right down to it, they wanted their teacher's approval. My assignments gave Martin an opportunity to earn my approval as well. They were an invitation to communicate with his surrogate mother, to express his needs, release his rage, while maintaining his all-powerful, in-control facade. I believed all that was true, or perhaps I was desperate for a positive spin on my impossible situation.

I realized Martin wouldn't have time to read a short story, let alone an entire book on his way back to Coral Gables. I didn't expect him to pull into a truck stop on the New Jersey Turnpike to write an essay. Nevertheless, I wanted to give him something to ponder on his road trip home. I wanted to rebuild a bridge between the two of us, or at the very least, weave an invisible thread connecting our lives, a thread he'd been trying to sever. I squeezed the last ounce of optimism and hope from my heart and sent him one final American Literature assignment.

Dear Martin,

Do you remember the book Charlotte's Web? It's about a spider named Charlotte who befriends Wilbur, a pig. The farmer is planning to butcher Wilbur, and Charlotte becomes his savior. She weaves accolades about Wilbur in her web, words designed to stop Wilbur's owner from killing him, words designed to prove the pig's worth, to keep him alive. "Some pig" "Terrific" "Humble." The author of that book, E.B. White, believed in the power of words. I believe in the power of words, too. And that belief makes me wonder: What words would you want me to weave in a web for you? What words might have the power to save you, to save both of us? I want to find those words, Martin, and I will weave us both a web of threads so strong that nothing and no one can break the bond that ties us together. That is your assignment. Simply tell me the words. I will weave them.

* * *

Later that night, after the sun had set over the beaches and tourists of Key West, Floyd arrived with a rectangular box and a bottle of wine. I'd enjoyed preparing dinner for him. Fresh marinated grouper, with tomato, avocado, and grilled onions with a basil and lime vinaigrette. I'd purchased a Key Lime pie at a local bakery. I was ravenous and still hell-bent on impressing all the key players in my ever-expanding drama.

"Are you hungry? Should we eat first? Everything's ready, but I need to grill the fish," I said, as Floyd leaned against the doorjamb.

"No, let's eat later. And since when do you cook, Jennifer? I thought we'd get take-out." He brushed past me through the small foyer, as though he knew where he was going.

"New hobby," I told him. He threw his backpack on the floor and made himself comfortable in the living room. I'd need to watch myself, even with Floyd. I didn't want to blow my cover.

"Okay. We'll eat soon. But first, I have something for ya. I need to explain everything before we drink this." Floyd handed me a chilled bottle of white. "Oh, and I brought us a little treat for dessert," he said, producing a small plastic bag of weed and rolling papers. I hadn't smoked marijuana since college. "But first things first." He placed the box on the coffee table. "Have a seat." I didn't really have a choice; the man was in control that night.

"Okay, Jennifer. Ya need to understand what's in this box. It's powerful, reliable, and specifically designed for women." Floyd used his words like weapons. He reminded me of a boring high school teacher, the way he lectured me. I tamped down my irritation as he droned on. "Not all guns fit comfortably in a woman's hand, which is typically smaller than a man's hand." *Unbelievable.* I wanted to lash out. I wanted to grab that box right out of his hands and send him on his way, but I kept my cool.

"Yes, I get it, I know. Women's hands are smaller than men's hands. So, let's see the gun," I said, with more of an edge in my tone than I wanted to convey. I felt like a powerless teenager the way he spoke down to me. And, like a bored teenager, I tuned him out.

Floyd would be the sort of teacher who wouldn't call on you even if you had a burning question, even if you were one hundred percent sure you had the answer to his stupid question, and your arm was about to fall off because you were waving it wildly in the air for twenty minutes. Floyd would be that teacher who blathered on and on and on in slow motion. On and on and on, putting students to sleep, like a pain-numbing opioid, like a lullaby without meaning, without love. God, I hoped my students didn't think of me as that kind of teacher.

"This is important. Are ya paying attention, Jennifer?" he asked, dragging out the question, one plodding syllable at a time. "This gun is easy to conceal and to operate, and it won't malfunction when ya need it, *if* ya need it. Even when you're under stress, you'll be able to operate this gun, okay?" He was speaking deliberately and articulating each phoneme, as if he thought English was not my primary language. It was maddening. I wanted to tear my hair out by the roots.

"Okay, that's good." *Come on, come on, just give me the gun.* My patience was waning. That should have been clear, but Floyd seemed oblivious.

"It *is* good. But here's the thing, Jennifer. This handgun is only as good as the person using it. You know what they say. *Guns don't kill people. People kill people.*" I wanted to argue and tell him the truth. I wanted to explain that people with guns kill people. I wanted to lecture him about the widespread incidents of gun deaths from suicide and accidents and murders and mass shootings. I wanted to point out that people who lived in other countries, countries with common-sense gun laws, had fewer homicides and almost no mass shootings. But I didn't think Floyd was interested in the truth. And after all, the man was doing me a favor. I ignored his false platitudes and kept my mouth shut. But it wasn't easy.

"Trust me, Jennifer. You're gonna need to practice. Ya need professional training."

"But you just said it's easy to use. How much training will I need?" I stared at the box, silently willing Floyd to get to the point.

"Well, ya need to experience what it feels like to hold it, to shoot it. Where to aim if you wanna kill the intruder or if you only wanna wound him, like if he's unarmed. We're talking about self-defense against an intruder, right? We're not talking about your husband." Floyd raised his eyebrows, flared his nostrils. He saw right through me.

"That's right," I assured him. "This has nothing to do with my husband. I told you we're separated. It's over."

"Okay. That's good. Now look, there's not a lot of recoil with this handgun, but ya need to know what that feels like too." Recoil. I didn't care about recoil. I wanted to get the gun, have dinner, and send Floyd on his way. Finally, he unwrapped the box, and with something akin to reverence, he lifted the handgun up in the air like a newborn baby and handed it to me.

I held it with confidence, as if I knew what I was doing. He explained about the ammunition. He had brought a fifteen-round magazine, which held more bullets than I would ever need. I assured Floyd that I'd find someone in Coral Gables to train me properly. He would have been stupid to believe me. We both realized we were engaging in an illegal transaction now that I had an unregistered weapon in my possession. Floyd recommended YouTube videos for me to watch back home, and I promised I'd at least take the virtual training seriously.

Floyd uncorked the wine. I grilled the fish. We sat in the comfortable armchairs flanking the coffee table. It was after dinner, after the Key Lime pie, after more than a few tokes of Floyd's weed, and after draining the bottle of wine. "So, Floyd, how much do I owe you for this handgun?" I asked. I reached for Jennifer's wallet still flush with cash.

"Oh, Jennifer, don't be ridiculous," he said. Floyd leaned over, pulled me onto his lap, and pressed his mouth against mine, knowingly, with confidence, his tongue exploring me. So, that was how things worked with Jennifer and Floyd. Why hadn't I anticipated that? There would be no turning back now. All I needed to do was live up to his expectations and give the performance of a lifetime. And that turned out to be easier than it should have been.

CHAPTER 30

By the time I awoke early the next morning, Floyd had disappeared. Relieved to find myself alone in Jennifer's bed, a layer of guilt clung to me, mixed with the scent and sweat of my night with Floyd. As I stood under the steaming shower, scrubbing away all sense of remorse, I tried to put the evening in perspective.

My relationship with David Allington was new, fragile, and already doomed, even without Floyd in the picture. The night before had little to do with passion or even appreciation for the handgun. It was about playing the role of Jennifer Moriarty who still loomed large in my increasingly tenuous world. I needed to keep the Jennifer persona alive a while longer.

Later that morning, I drove the Mercedes on autopilot, under sixty miles per hour, all the way back to Coral Gables. With an unregistered gun in my possession and the vestige of an illegal substance lingering in my bloodstream, I was determined to play it safe. My thoughts, on the other hand, flew much faster than the speed limit.

When I stopped for gas I listened to messages and read texts. There was one message from David, checking to see how I was feeling. Messages from Nancy, from Jennifer's therapist, Angela Blaine, and someone named Eleanor, wondering how Jennifer was doing. Two furious messages from Jennifer's husband. The tone and word choice were classic Jim. *Where the fuck are you?*

The only message that gave me some semblance of comfort was the one from Martin. Just two words: *HOME THURSDAY.* Although he'd ignored the latest American Literature assignment, he'd taken the time to let me know when to expect him home. Of course, I didn't completely trust that Martin would be back on Thursday. And if my theory about the purpose of his road trip proved to be true, it would be impossible for him to drive to Hartford, cause the disappearance of his mother, visit the Mark Twain House, complete his earlier assignment inspired by Mark Twain, and drive back to Coral Gables all in less than a week. It defied logic. But then again, everything about my predicament defied logic.

* * *

I found the Coral Gables house exactly as I'd left it, uninhabited. The Jeep was still missing, and the door to the arsenal above the garage was in its locked position. The red light on the keypad glowed reassuringly. Martin, true to his word, had not yet returned, giving me more time to prepare.

I played with the idea of giving in to my desires, tempted to spend one more night with David. I realized that would be my last chance for a while. I could explain and be forgiven for not returning his calls. He'd believe the migraine headache excuse. I imagined losing myself again in his arms before dinner and then again after dinner. I craved those feelings of safety and acceptance. But my good judgment had the upper hand for a change. Running back to David would be a risky move. What if Martin returned earlier than expected? Besides, it wouldn't be fair to David to string him along, not now. I needed to end the relationship before it went any further.

I'd been composing my message to David on the car ride back, trying out different phrases aloud to hear how they'd sound. And before I gave into temptation, before I had time to change my mind, I typed my message and hit the send button.

Dear David,

As difficult as this is for me, I've made the decision to stop seeing you. My life is complicated right now and getting more complicated by the minute. I followed my heart, my personal needs. Right now, my desire for a relationship with you must take a back seat to Martin and his needs. I wish we had met at a different time in my life. I can't ask you to wait for me, because I don't know what the future will bring. I hope you will understand, and I hope you know how much our brief time together meant to me.

Jennifer

I reread the email after sending it, regretting that it was too late to take it back or even change a few words. I realized immediately what pathetic tripe I'd written. If this message to David represented my writing ability, why would I ever consider writing a novel? But my email to David wasn't about drafting the great American novel. It was about survival. Ending things with him was the right thing to do, the hard thing to do. If nothing else, I'd poured truth into my final message to David. The only lie was how I signed my message. Jennifer. That was the lie. I wiped away my tears, stopped feeling sorry for myself, and then I got to work.

I stood outside Martin's bedroom door and knocked out of habit. I tried all the extra keys on Jennifer's key ring. None of them fit either the cylinder deadbolt or the lock on his door handle. All of the upstairs doors were heavy, constructed from exotic-looking wood. Jennifer Moriarty was single-handedly responsible for destroying a few rainforests for the sake of her exquisite doors. Each one had traditional raised panels, six of them. I knocked on different parts of Martin's door, listening to the reverberating sounds. As predicted, the wood was not nearly as thick within the panels.

I went downstairs and made myself a strong cup of coffee. I settled back into Jennifer's study, wondering how I'd have managed without the internet guiding me every step of the way. I typed my question: *How do you kick down a door without hurting yourself?* I quickly discovered that breaking into Martin's room would not be as easy as it looked on TV. Using my body weight against that heavy wooden door was out of the question. I'd most likely break a foot if I tried to kick down the door, and the online warnings ruled out using my shoulder the way I saw it done in the movies. After reading a few more articles, I became an unlikely expert in the field of interior door construction. In my previous life, this would have been trivial and unnecessary information. But in this life, learning about door construction meant survival, and ultimately this knowledge led to the perfect solution, the simplest, most efficient way to break into Martin's bedroom. I began my shopping trip in the Moriarty garage.

The unused hand tools hanging neatly from pegboards would be useless for the task I had in mind. I wondered what purpose those gadgets and gizmos might have served the Moriarty family. Perhaps, along with the arsenal of guns and freeze-dried meals, Jennifer wanted to feel prepared for any imaginable disaster. Breaking into Martin's bedroom was probably not on her list of imaginable disasters. It should have been.

But I needed a tool with muscle, a power saw. I studied my options online. There were so many choices: a jigsaw, reciprocating saw, scroll saw, a miter saw, a band saw, a chain saw. I didn't need to cut down a damned tree, just a door. Finally, I decided on the perfect choice.

After a quick trip to a local hardware store, I returned to the house, ready to follow the complicated directions for using my brand-new state of the art circular saw.

I didn't care that Martin would return home to discover that his surrogate mother had invaded his privacy. Martin had invaded my privacy by traveling to Hartford, and although I had no proof of what really happened when he confronted Jennifer, my theory seemed reasonable. People don't vanish into thin air. Jennifer was duplicitous, granted, but she wouldn't disappear on me. We had an agreement, didn't we? This was supposed to be a dare, for one month, a lark.

My arms shook from the vibrations as I pressed the sharp blades into the lower panel, but I managed to penetrate the thickness of the wood without breaking a sweat. As I worked, my anger towards Martin's mother took a turn.

In spite of everything that had happened, I was prepared to forgive Jennifer for quitting my teaching job. Part of me understood that decision. I was even ready to forgive Jennifer for deceiving me into taking over the life she had forsaken. Jennifer Moriarty was wrong, of course she was wrong, but she didn't deserve to die, not at the hands of her son. All those thoughts swirled around me as the hissing sound of the circular saw provided a soundtrack for the horror of what I might soon discover on the other side of Martin's door.

Once I traced a route around the perimeter of the lower door panel, it took little effort to push the wooden panel through to the other side. One swift kick and I completed the job. I peered through the hole but saw nothing beyond the blackness. The room was even darker than the day I'd arrived, the day Martin had unlocked the multiple interior bolts on this same door allowing me to enter his lair. I thought about the first time I stood in the doorway pretending to be his mother, that terrifying moment when I first experienced Martin's violent outbursts. Was that simply a few weeks ago? It felt like a lifetime.

I gazed into that black hole, into the abyss of Martin's life. Unless I mustered the courage to squeeze my body through the opening to see for myself what appalling secrets were hidden behind that door, both Martin's room and his surrogate mother would remain in the dark.

CHAPTER 31

Sprawled on the hallway floor, I pressed my back against the wall adjacent to Martin's room. I twisted my body toward the door and stared blindly into the murky space between me and that black hole. It may have been minutes, it may have been hours. I wasn't sure how long I'd been sitting there, the heavy saw cradled in my aching arms, cementing me to the floor. Suddenly, the piercing sound of the doorbell penetrated my inertia, jolting my body as if nudged by a cattle prod. The reverberations rattled my bones and breached my state of limbo.

I had to see what was in that bedroom, and I was running out of time. I knew I needed to get rid of the uninvited visitor as quickly as possible. I wondered if the echoing peal of a doorbell was another sign from god, a signal designed to awaken me from my stupor. And yet, I didn't want to move forward. I wanted to move backward, backward in time and in space. But the doorbell kept drilling holes into my skull.

I disengaged my rigid arms from the saw and placed it on the carpet. I staggered away from the hole in the door and clutching the banister for support, I slowly made my way down the stairs. I felt my head splitting in two as I swung open the front door without even looking through the fish-eye lens of the peephole.

"Thank God," Nancy said. "Where have you been? I've been trying to reach you for hours! You look horrible, what's wrong? Why haven't you called?" Nancy pushed past me into the foyer, peppering me with questions.

"Another migraine, and then I went to Key West, to get away for a bit, and then when I got back, Martin took off in the Jeep." I rambled on and on, as though a floodgate had been lifted. The words poured out of me. "He said he'd be back today or tomorrow, and I need to get to the store to buy food for him, the refrigerator is empty." I molded the words like clay, to create some semblance of meaning for Jennifer's sister. Something plausible.

"Jennifer, let's sit down," Nancy said. "You're not making any sense. We need to talk." Normally those four words, *We need to talk,* would have the power to instill a sense of imminent dread. But not for me. Not now. My brain had been marinating in a cocktail of adrenaline and cortisol, my neurochemistry was off-kilter. My blood had run cold with terror for weeks. *We need to talk* news from Nancy had no power to diminish or increase the terror. I'd already hit rock bottom.

I followed her into the living room. "I have to tell you something, and I don't know how you're going to take it," she said. I didn't have time for Jennifer's sister. I didn't have the patience, and I felt the energy leaking from my body with each passing moment. But I sat down next to her on the small sofa, waiting for more drama, more complications, and more obstacles in my path.

"It's about Jim," Nancy said.

"What about Jim?"

"He came to visit Jason the other night, took him out to dinner, and dropped quite the bombshell." I feigned interest, hoping Nancy would get to the point and leave. "Apparently, Jim's met someone new. It's serious this time, Jennifer. I didn't know if I should tell you, but I think you need to be aware of what's going on. He's planning to move to Seattle to live with his girlfriend."

I let the news sink in for a moment, processing the implications and coming up with a Jennifer-like response. Nancy had said it was serious this time. Seattle? Okay, that's fine. Let Jennifer's husband run away to Seattle. But please, make him take Martin. Jim may not have been Martin's biological father, but he raised this disturbed child along with Jennifer. It was Jim's turn to bear the burden. It was Jim's opportunity to fix the Martin problem. Would Jennifer be surprised? Devastated? Furious? Really, I wanted to laugh at the absurdity of the news. Close to hysteria already, I didn't need Nancy's forlorn expression pushing me over the edge. If I started to laugh now, it would be impossible to stop. I even pinched my thighs, hoping the pain would help me focus.

I stood up from the sofa and started pacing the floor. "Seattle?" One word was the best I could come up with while maintaining a semblance of incredulity. "Seattle?"

"Jennifer, you need to use the same attorney I used. She's a tough one. She'll get you everything you deserve. You know what a great settlement she got for me. George's attorney was an asshole. He didn't stand a chance against my lawyer." So, Jennifer's sister was divorced and happy with her settlement. She liked her attorney. Good to know. But really, it didn't matter. "I already called her, and she's willing to squeeze you in. She can see you the day after tomorrow. I made an appointment."

I kept pacing, avoiding eye contact, my arms crossed in front of my chest, holding myself together. "Oh, Nancy, I don't have the energy for this. I don't want to fight with Jim, I don't deserve anything, the house, the car, I don't care about any of it."

"I thought you would say that, Jennifer, and that's exactly why you need to see my attorney. Deborah Thompson. She's the best matrimonial lawyer in the Miami area. Trust me. You don't need to fight with Jim; you let your attorney do the fighting for you." Nancy walked over to me, held me firmly by the shoulders, interrupting the momentum of my pacing. Then she brushed the hair away from my face with sisterly tenderness.

"Nancy, you don't understand," I sobbed. Of course, Nancy didn't understand. She didn't have the facts. She didn't know her own sister, Jennifer, had disappeared, was probably dead. She didn't know what was lurking behind that bedroom door upstairs. I didn't know either, which is why I needed to get Nancy out of Jennifer's house as quickly as possible.

I swiped my arm across my face, soaking up tears with my sleeve. I stood up straighter and took a deep breath, placing my hands on my hips with new resolve. "Okay, Nancy, listen to me. I'm not all that surprised about Jim. I saw this coming, I did. The marriage has been over for a while. I'll go to your attorney. I'll hear what she has to say, but I have to get groceries for Martin, and I'm so tired right now. I need to be alone, to take this all in."

"I understand, Jennifer. Call me later or I'll worry, okay? And thank God, you're listening to reason for a change." *Thank god. Yes, god's been so busy lately looking out for us. Need to remember to thank him for sending Nancy, for making her ring that doorbell.*

"Yes, I'll call you later. I promise," I said.

"Good. And be ready for our appointment with the divorce attorney. 8:30 the day after tomorrow," Nancy said. "Don't make me wait this time. You know how much I hate to wait, and Attorney Thompson is doing us a big favor squeezing you into her busy schedule."

I practically pushed Jennifer's sister out the door, thanking her for being there for me, for taking care of things, for being the best sister ever. Nancy was my guardian angel. I even told her that. I used those exact words. "You are my guardian angel," I said. *Isn't that what Jennifer Moriarty would say?*

CHAPTER 32

As soon as Nancy walked out the door, I raced up the stairs. Without giving myself the chance to change my mind, I squeezed my body through the rectangular hole in Martin's door. It seemed as though I was plunging myself into a gaping wound. I clutched a flashlight in one hand, using its beam to penetrate the blackness. I must have stood up too quickly because the room began to spin. I brushed one hand against the wall to locate a switch for an overhead light but found nothing. Daylight from the hallway seeped reluctantly into the space near the door, casting ominous shadows. Using the flashlight to guide me, I shuffled cautiously to the windows. With every step, I bumped up against the detritus of Martin's little world, strewn haphazardly across the floor.

I drew the dense curtains aside and raised the heavy roman shades. The Florida sunshine poured into the room as a thick dust resettled into the illuminated spaces. Clearly, Jennifer's cleaning crew had avoided Martin's bedroom for months if not years. The staleness hung in the air like an old man's sour breath, pungent and overpowering. I opened a window to access fresh air. I inhaled deeply and then choked on the dust and fear of Martin's world. I coughed and gagged, struggling for composure. Finally, I lowered myself into Martin's desk chair and inspected my surroundings. The room, the boy, the wasted life. How had all of this happened?

I knew that kids often rebelled against perfectionist parents, but Martin's room personified something well beyond adolescent rebellion. Besides dozens of empty water bottles, candy wrappers, pizza boxes from Antonio's, and take-out containers from various Coral Gables fast-food restaurants, the surfaces, the floor, and the four walls of Martin's bedroom were covered with a blueprint for disaster.

The crumpled sheets on his unmade bed were illustrated with baby blue dinosaurs. They were probably designed to be adorable and appropriate for a six-year-old child. I wondered if Jennifer had failed to notice Martin was no longer a six-year-old child, no longer her innocent baby. The sheets were an ironic backdrop for the three semi-automatic assault rifles lined up like soldiers, reporting for duty on Martin's single bed. My body started shaking uncontrollably as I stared at those weapons.

I pulled my gaze away from the rifles on his bed and studied the surface of the desk. I rummaged through a stack of video games, creatively titled to entice would-be assassins from all walks of life. The descriptions on the back of the games promised simulated experiences of inconceivable violence, gore, dismemberment, cannibalism. An appalling way to while away the hours of a life without purpose. Entertainment for a tortured soul, a sick mind. Jennifer's son, still a weak little boy, slept protected amid an artificial world of blue dinosaurs at night and awoke to another universe where he could be the big bad carnivore, the powerful T. Rex in the room, ready to take down his imagined enemies. Martin awoke each morning prepared to wage war, a real man fighting the good fight against his own extinction.

The closet door had been left ajar. Combat gear dangled from hangers. There were army boots, military-style jackets, even a camouflage vest designed to hold ammunition, with pockets surrounding the midriff. Other than a wicker basket on the floor, partially filled with folded, clean laundry, I saw little evidence that Martin possessed a civilian wardrobe.

The bedroom furniture was sparse. Besides the desk and the bed, there was a small nightstand and a large chest of drawers. I stood up from the chair and moved closer to the dresser, seeing the scene more clearly with each reluctant step. Art supplies and scraps of paper were scattered on the floor, but on top of the bureau, Martin's skill for origami was displayed in all its horror. A miniature scene of carnage created from folded paper. I backed several steps away from the scene, wanting to close my eyes. It was like passing a multi-car wreck on the highway. I couldn't turn away.

Martin had created an array of pews within this diorama world, with a large raised pulpit at one end of the box. An origami minister stood at the altar, holding a perfect origami rifle pointed at his paper congregation. Bodies were splattered everywhere, hands clutching pieces of tiny origami bibles. A large cross glued to the wall behind the pulpit, shredded bible pages and origami body parts splattered with red paint littered the sanctuary. The exterior of the box had been painted clapboard white. Miniscule arms, legs, torsos and heads, folded and bleeding red with agonizing precision, protruded grotesquely from the church's spire like a surreal weathervane.

It was all too much for me. I began to gag again, grabbing my midriff with both arms, I whimpered into the void. I struggled to make sense of what I was seeing, the meaning behind that repulsive display, not ready to put the pieces of the puzzle together. The semi-automatic assault rifles on the bed. The diorama. I was too terrified to face the implications. I turned numbly toward the wall opposite the bed.

At first glance, my mind registered a type of contemporary, mixed media collage or an overly busy wallpaper covering the expanse of the bedroom wall. I stepped cautiously around the garbage littering Martin's floor, moving toward the wall for a closer inspection. I quickly realized the scene before me had nothing to do with wallpaper and nothing to do with abstract art. And yet, I understood immediately that the wall was a labor of enormous magnitude. Here was Martin's magnum opus of sorts, another window into his twisted inner self. Here was his dissertation, an oeuvre that must have taken months if not years, a blueprint for a scheme that may already have been launched. I stood there at the epicenter of another predictable tragedy that had played out in too many places, with too many victims. The survivors' cries for help and change had been swept aside too many times.

A cold and tingling numbness seemed to fill my bones as I followed the timeline Martin had created. Beginning with Columbine, the documented terror crept across his bedroom wall. The photographs, newspaper articles, an enormous graph, maps, and headlines, from rampage to rampage, moved steadily into a terrible future Martin had imagined with precise details. A strategic plan. Calculated mayhem. Bright red, pushpin flags identified the locations of the more infamous mass shootings, the well-known, headlined tragedies, displayed on a huge map of the United States of America, plastered on Martin Moriarty's bedroom wall. Columbine, Tucson, Aurora, Newtown, Charlestown, Fort Hood, Virginia Tech, Parkland. And there were so many other pushpin flags—places of carnage I'd never even heard of. I hadn't been paying attention. Mississippi, Illinois, Nebraska, Hawaii, Alabama, from sea to shining sea. Red flags of heartbreak covered the map of the USA. And above the map, scrawled in Martin's cursive handwriting were the words from Emily Dickinson's poem. Those words, so deeply embedded in my memory, would become a new headline ready for the world to read, embedded in this timeline across a disturbed boy's bedroom wall.

How did Martin know? How had he discovered that particular Emily Dickinson poem, of all poems, of all quotations? Why had he chosen the very poem that I'd memorized as a child, the words that still haunted me? It was too much of a coincidence, and yet, I couldn't deny the message scrawled across the wall. *I shall not live in vain.*

Those words pulled me back to the poet's homestead. I heard echoes of her ponderings about the meaning of a life well-lived. I felt her loneliness, her sorrow, like heavy hands on my shoulders. And yet, Emily had her immortality. Is that what Martin craved?

Suddenly, my rambling memories of Emily Dickinson's homestead evaporated. The musty heartbreak of her life, replaced by the pungent smell of Martin's unwashed body. I felt the boy's leer a second or two before I heard his voice.

"Worth an A, don't ya think?"

CHAPTER 33

A wave of revulsion brought me to my knees. "Are you impressed?" he asked. My muscles froze. I couldn't turn around. My eyes were glued to the timeline and graphs plastered on Martin's bedroom wall. The years going back to 1999, the dead, the maimed, the movie theaters, malls, streets, clubs, concerts. And the schools. And places of worship. And here I was at the altar of Martin's madness, kneeling, praying for a miracle.

"Martin, what do you want from me?" The words so soft I wasn't sure he'd hear them.

"For starters, cover the windows and the fucking hole you made in my door." His voice oozed with venom. Martin had all the power, as if his hands were on the controls of a horrible videogame. "I have to admit, I never thought you'd have the balls to break into my bedroom. I guess I underestimated you right from the start," he snarled. "Clean up this mess. Make me a grilled cheese sandwich. And then, we'll see," he said. "I think you'll be interested in what I have planned. I can't wait to tell you all about it." I assumed he was being sarcastic, although, a part of him may have wanted my admiration. Martin strolled deeper into the room, creeping slowly behind me. I flinched when I felt his breath on my neck. "You'll appreciate the effort. That's important to you, right? Effort?"

I struggled to make sense of his words, to find a seed of hope amid the horror. He had a plan, and he was ready to share it with me. He was hungry and wanted a grilled cheese sandwich. These facts were fragile threads connecting me to a tenuous survival. And still, I could not will myself to look in Martin's direction. Was he holding a gun? Was it pointed at me? I would do exactly as he told me to do. I would cover the windows, the hole in the door, and I would make his lunch.

I sensed him walking back to the bedroom door and fiddling with the locks and then opening the door wide. I thought he was intentionally making it easier for me, so I wouldn't need to crawl through that hole again. I followed the sounds of his footsteps as he settled into the chair at his desk. As he clicked away at his computer, I pulled my wobbly legs to a standing position and began my work.

Floating like a silent apparition, I closed the drapes. Although Martin's attention seemed to be on his computer screen, I felt his eyes laser-focused on me. I left the bedroom to search for supplies, moving swiftly through the house, hell-bent on accomplishing a surreal mission. I found large, black garbage bags in the pantry and duct tape in the garage. I took my time covering the hole in the door from both the inside and the outside of Martin's bedroom. I was about finished when his voice startled me.

"Hey, bitch! Clean up the mess in here," he said, waving at the empty containers, wrappers, and water bottles, the garbage of his pathetic, squandered existence. I grabbed more plastic bags from the upstairs laundry room.

As I stuffed the garbage bags full of Martin's trash, I was under no delusion that a clean room would help him. I understood that no wave of a maternal wand could make a difference. It was too late for that. Cleaning up the debris of his sorry existence wouldn't change anything. Even my mercy, my kindness, my cooking, my American literature assignments—none of it had the power to activate a morsel of humanity where none existed. No one had *that* kind of magical power.

And as I filled the third garbage bag, Martin mumbled words I couldn't quite understand. ".. the movie.. the book."

"What did you say?"

"I said, I saw the movie, never read the book." It took me a moment to make the connection.

"Oh, you mean *Charlotte's Web*," I said. "The book's better than the movie. That's usually the way it is."

"If you say so."

"I'll make your lunch now," I said.

"Knock yourself out." I grabbed the bags, sweeping my gaze one more time over the walls and surfaces of Martin's world. The combat clothing, the diorama of the church massacre, the map of the United States covered with pushpin flags, the graphs, and the newspaper clippings on the wall, the words of Emily Dickinson's poem, and those three assault rifles perched on Martin's bed. And then, with certainty in my heart, I went down to the kitchen to make Martin's lunch.

The last two tomatoes on Jennifer's counter were a deep crimson color, spotted and split open, the juices bubbling through discolored skin. They'd been sitting out on that counter since last week, and I should have discarded them. I'd neglected the kitchen since Martin's trip to Hartford. I used a sharp knife to remove the discoloration. Cutting into those overripe tomatoes may have been the trigger, the exact moment when my resolve hardened into a pillar of stone. I remembered Lot's wife, how she'd turned into a pillar of salt. But unlike Lot's wife, I would not look back. I remained focused on making Martin's lunch and nothing more.

The bread was also past its sell-by date. I melted extra butter in the frying pan thinking he wouldn't know the difference. I prepared Martin's tray with as much care as I'd ever given such a mundane task. I cut the sandwich into quarters as if he were a toddler, arranged a sprig of parsley on the side of the plate, wilted but still green, a glass of juice, a small bowl of potato chips. A simple meal.

I carried the tray upstairs to Martin's room. He must have closed his bedroom door after I left to make his lunch. As if that would keep his surrogate mother away. As if closing that door would keep him safe. I knocked. "Martin, I'm leaving your lunch outside your door." I knew he heard me because I heard him. The plastic garbage bags hardly muffled the sound of Martin's fingers moving rapid-fire across the keys of his computer. I walked away from the door, ten paces forward, ten giant steps. I turned around and sat cross-legged on the carpeted hallway floor, facing Martin's bedroom. I waited. Patient, resolute, determined.

The sandwich must have still been warm a minute or two later when Martin unlocked his door. Although the hole in the door, now covered with black, plastic garbage bags, seriously compromised his privacy, he had taken the time and made the effort to lock his door from the inside. Was it habit? I sat transfixed as Martin reached down for his lunch tray, and I saw him grin like a hungry toddler. As he stood, our eyes locked for an instant. Martin's eyes were wide and round. The whites of those eyes encircled his small, dark pupils.

I pulled the trigger once, aiming for Martin's chest, the area above the lunch tray, the largest part of him. The easiest target. My hand was steady. I didn't expect that. I watched Jennifer's son hugging the tray to his chest with both hands and then falling as if in slow motion. I heard him groan, and he clutched his shoulder. Blood seeped into the grilled cheese sandwich, or was it the red juices of the overripe tomato? I wasn't sure. I had to be certain.

I stood and stepped closer until I was standing over Martin's writhing body. This time I took my time, aiming directly between his round eyes. Those surprised, pleading eyes were looking up at me.

"I can't help you, Martin," I said. "I tried, I really tried. I can only stop you." I pressed the trigger again, handling the recoil easily, as if it were second nature. And then I turned around and walked away.

CHAPTER 34

I left the front door of the Moriarty's house unlocked and slightly ajar. I knew Nancy would come by at some point. I promised I'd call her. She'd worry when she didn't hear from her sister. And when she came to pick me up for the appointment with her attorney, she'd walk into Jennifer's house, call Jennifer's name, and notice something amiss. She'd discover Martin's body upstairs, and I trusted her to take care of all the details.

Without a glance in the rear-view mirror, I drove away in Jennifer's white Mercedes. I wasn't aware of an intended destination. No conscious plan. I floated free-style, locked outside my body, watching the action as a spectator, as if sitting safely in the front row of a theater. I watched an actor I didn't know place Floyd's handgun inside Jennifer's Gucci handbag, now perched innocently on the passenger seat next to me. I watched that same actor drive the car. I may have been sitting in the driver's seat, but I felt like a passenger.

I even felt empathy for that stoic woman who wasn't me, the hero of the story who had stopped Martin from committing his deadly rampage. The woman who had put an end to his plans for mass murder. Who was that woman? No one would believe that Jenn Cooper, a middle-aged, English teacher from Connecticut, would be capable of stopping Martin. Jenn Cooper didn't know how to use a gun and didn't have a violent bone in her body.

Escaping Jennifer's house and the tree-lined streets of Coral Gables, I tried to erase the images of Martin's lifeless body, the blood seeping into the carpet. Those images flashed in my mind, throbbing with each beat of my heart. They were too vivid to be a delusion, too intense to be a dream.

Driving aimlessly, well within the speed limit, I kept my hands on the steering wheel, taking control of my next moves. I remembered the workout clothes stuffed in a gym bag in the back seat of Jennifer's car. Well beyond the neighborhood, I pulled into a lonely gas station, grabbed the gym bag, and headed to the restroom at the back of the building.

I tried to avoid looking into the mirror above the grimy, porcelain sink. I removed my bloodstained clothes and stuffed them into the bottom of a large garbage pail under the sink. I scrubbed my hands, my arms, my face, with soap and scalding hot water. I pulled on the spandex yoga pants and coordinated top from the gym bag, took a deep breath, and finally glanced at my reflection in the mirror. I looked presentable; no trace of what I'd done, not on my clothes, my skin or in my eyes. I left the restroom feeling cleaner than I had a right to feel, and I hit the road again.

I followed the entrance onto the highway, heading south. About twenty miles from Coral Gables, I pulled into a dockside restaurant and bar called Bobby K's.

Sitting at a small table near the water, I focused on a lone, white ibis a few yards away who was standing inconceivably on its long, thin legs. Wading in the shallow sand flats, the creature looked up at me, perhaps begging for food. Why else would it wander so close to this waterside bar? What did that bird expect from me? I had nothing left to give. I ordered a burger and the bar's signature drink, a blue and fruity concoction laden with various liquors. I felt strangely at peace, or was it simply the absence of fear?

After lunch, I returned to the car and continued on my way. After a while, I noticed signs for a popular Everglades visitor center located about halfway between Miami and Key West. This would be my next destination.

As I pulled into the parking lot, I thought I might have been to the park once before, in another life. The landscape felt strangely familiar. A place where tourists and families hiked safely on solidly constructed boardwalks and paved walkways.

Almost Disney World but with living, breathing, untamed wildlife hovering in the air, on the land, and in the marshy waters. I paid the admission fee with cash, bought mosquito repellent in the gift store, along with a map of the trails. I planned to spend the next hour hiking and birdwatching. Despite the oppressive, ninety-degree Florida heat, I would lose myself in the beauty of the natural habitat.

The trail felt peaceful and calm. I scoured the air and the grounds for wildlife, noting a great blue heron, a group of cormorants fishing for their dinners, and great white egrets going about the business of survival in the Everglades. Although a popular destination during the winter months, the final days of summer must have been the quiet season for tourists but not for wildlife. Summer vacation was officially over, children and parents were beyond the back-to-school hump of readjusting to their frenetic schedules. The State of Florida could catch its breath before the snowbirds and vacationers returned in time for the Thanksgiving holiday.

Far from the visitors' center, I stood on a boardwalk looking down into the marshy wetness below, beyond the tall grasses. I knew they were there, camouflaged by the murky water. They were floating like logs close to the surface, mouths at the ready, suddenly gaping and wide jaws snapping. I reached my hand into Jennifer's purse. As if in slow motion, I hurled the gun like a discus, sending it flying across the marsh. It landed with a discreet splash, sending ripples across the water, not even troubling the wading birds nearby, disturbing nothing and no one. The gun disappeared, as though it had never been.

I completed the short, circular trail, slapping mosquitoes that were woefully undeterred by the chemicals smeared on my neck and arms. I returned to the car feeling lighter, unencumbered, looking forward to the hot shower waiting for me in the Key West cottage. I breathed deeply, wiped the perspiration from my neck as I waited for the coolness of the car's air conditioner to do its magic.

* * *

Back on the road, heading south, I turned on the radio and quickly found a classical station. I let the music seep into my pores. Was it Chopin? The melancholy piano prelude in a minor key filled me with regret, shattered my resolve. The music unleashed the torrent of heartache I'd managed to suppress earlier that day. Bitter tears stung like tiny wasps poking at my eyes. Suddenly, sobbing and gasping for breath, I pulled the Mercedes into the lot of an abandoned gas station, parked the car on the side of the property away from the useless pumps. I turned off the engine and breathed in the silence.

It was too late for second-guessing, and so I tried to convince myself that I'd done the right thing—the only possible action given the situation. I didn't have a choice. And yet, the tears streamed down my face, the sobbing intensified. I had to get control of myself, and so I focused on my breathing, promising myself the luxury of falling apart once I arrived safely at the cottage in Key West. For god's sake, I couldn't sit there crying all day.

Reaching into Jennifer's purse, I groped for her cell phone. I'd check my messages and then be on my way. Ignoring voicemail, I went right to the unread text message. I stared at those words on the small screen. Two words, like daggers, pointed at my heart, ripping through my resolve.

Martin had completed his last assignment. Hadn't he told me that morning, he had seen the movie, *Charlotte's Web*? He'd thought about my question: *What words would you want me to weave in a web? What words might have the power to save you, to save both of us?* Martin had sent his response, this last text message, moments before his surrogate mother had carried that grilled cheese and tomato sandwich to his bedroom door. His final plea. Two simple words for the web. Exactly what I'd asked for, the words Martin needed me to weave for him. And there they were. Urgent and heartbreaking in their simplicity. *HELP ME.*

I dropped the cell phone onto the seat next to me. I covered my mouth and dry heaved into my hands. Rocking back and forth, I sobbed hysterically. I pulled at my hair and muttered the words over and over again. *What have I done? What have I done? My god, what have I done?*

Finally, after what seemed like an eternity, I closed my eyes and leaned back into the headrest. I'd never remembered feeling that tired. I tried to fight the blanket of despair and lethargy that hovered over me like a dark cloud, but I felt myself losing that fight. I never stood a chance.

CHAPTER 35

Jennifer Moriarty opened her eyes, wondering how long it had been since she'd dozed off with her head cradled in her arms, resting on the steering wheel. She was so tired she could barely keep her eyes open. The air inside her car was stifling hot. She struggled to breathe.

She gazed outside the car window at the desolate setting. Jennifer remembered this gas station when it had been alive and well years ago, a welcome rest stop for her family's frequent trips to the Key West cottage and home again to Coral Gables. She could still hear the boys in the backseat, arguing about anything and everything. They were so young. Where had the years gone? And now, the rusty pumps stood like crumbling gravestones in an ancient cemetery.

Someone had scrawled an attempt at humor in the thick dust of the glass garage doors: *FIGHT APATHY. OR DON'T.* Were the windows of the convenience store boarded up the last time she had passed this way? She craved a candy bar and a diet coke. Something to jolt her awake. She would need to push through without the caffeine. For now.

Jennifer looked down and noticed her phone next to her on the passenger seat. She picked it up, and she stared at the text message on the screen, not understanding. *What in God's name was Martin talking about now?* she wondered as she read the latest nonsense from her son. *Help me? Help him do what?* She felt too weary to deal with this latest garbage from Martin. She'd never understand that boy. Her thumbs flew over the keyboard, sending a hasty response to his gibberish. *See you in an hour or so, on my way home from Key West XOXO.*

As Jennifer pulled the car out of the abandoned gas station toward the intersection that would lead her back to the Overseas Highway, she caught a glimpse of her fingernails. Raggedy with chipped polish. My God, how long had it been since her last manicure? She shook her head in disgust. And where were her rings? Had she left them in the Key West cottage? Or God forbid, at Floyd's place the other night? Jennifer stopped at a red light, checked her reflection in the rear-view mirror, and gasped. Her eyes, red-rimmed and swollen, her hair dry and frizzled. She was a total wreck. She tried to pull her fingers through the snarled mess but it was hopeless. She'd call the salon in the morning to see if they would squeeze her in. She could use a massage too. But first, she needed to be home, back in Coral Gables, take a long, hot shower, and crawl into her bed.

Jennifer couldn't remember the last time she had experienced such intense exhaustion. Not since, not since. . . when was it? Had it been two years already? Three years? She'd slept for days after that last incident. That breakdown, that's what Dr. Blaine and Nancy had called it. Just a nervous breakdown.

The light turned green. Jennifer followed the sign and turned onto Route 1, heading north back toward Miami. She turned on the radio. *Classical music? Strange,* she thought. She turned to a country station and sped down the highway at 75 miles an hour. She'd be home in no time.

* * *

Jennifer pulled the Mercedes into her garage. She left her bag in the trunk of the car, too exhausted to lug it upstairs to her bedroom. Dragging herself from the garage into the mudroom, she craved only two things: a hot shower and sleep. Martin would be in his bedroom. Jason was staying with Nancy. Jim would be, God knows where. No one would bother her. It felt good to be home again.

The house was silent as usual. Jennifer left her Gucci bag by the backstairs and made her way into the kitchen. *My God.* Hadn't the cleaning service been here while she was away? There were dirty dishes in the sink, a greasy frying pan and spatula on the stove, a half stick of butter sitting on the counter uncovered, along with a knife and cutting board coated with tomato seeds and juices. Jennifer was in no mood for this mess. At least Martin had eaten something. She shouldn't be aggravated with him, but she felt so damn tired. She needed sleep desperately, and yet, Jennifer knew she would never be able to close her eyes with this disaster waiting for her. Leaving a messy kitchen had never been in her DNA.

Jennifer pulled on her rubber gloves, and she scrubbed the dirty dishes, dried them with a clean dishtowel, and put each item away. Everything in its proper place. As she worked, she worried about her younger son. He was getting so thin. She wondered at times if he had an eating disorder, although anorexia was mostly a problem for teenage girls, not boys. Martin relied too much on her for takeout, pizza, and fast food meals he insisted she deliver to his bedroom door. Leaving him for the long weekend had been a good decision, despite risking Jim's anger. Martin needed to develop some independence. And this proved her theory. When push came to shove, Martin could fend for himself. Now, if only he would clean up after himself, her life would be perfect.

Jennifer noticed two cookbooks sitting open on one end of the kitchen table. *Strange. Why would Martin be looking at cookbooks?* She put them back on the shelf in the exact places where they belonged, alphabetical order by author.

Finally, with the kitchen back to normal, Jennifer dragged her aching bones to the front foyer, willing her tired legs to climb the stairs. Halfway up the stairs, she looked back for some reason and noticed the front door slightly ajar. She sighed and shook her head, annoyed with her younger son for being so careless. It had always been a safe neighborhood, but still, an unlocked door was practically an invitation. She trudged back down the stairs to close and lock the front door.

Perhaps Martin was getting out of the house a bit. He'd locked himself in his bedroom for so long, and it was becoming more difficult to lure him out into the world or even to communicate with him directly. She understood that Martin felt uncomfortable with face-to-face conversations. It was all about emails and text messages with his generation. But his anxiety seemed to be getting worse. She had tried to ease his stress, but even the medications she gave him didn't seem to be working as well as they used to. And yet, while she was away, it seemed that Martin had left the house. Things were looking up. Maybe she'd need to get away more often. Floyd would like that.

Jennifer reached the landing at the top of the stairs and turned right, heading for the tranquility of her bedroom. She felt too exhausted to check on Martin. Why bother? She would knock on his door and he would ignore her. Why waste her time? Jennifer began to close her bedroom door behind her when she sensed something awry, something amiss within her peripheral vision. She turned her head around, glancing toward the end of the hallway, expecting to see the same view she always saw from this angle, a view of Martin's locked door.

At first glance, the scene didn't register meaning for her. His bedroom door was partially open, something that looked like a black plastic bag covered the bottom panel, and there was Martin, face-up, his feet and thin legs protruding into the hallway. Was he sleeping on the floor? She saw a tray near his body and what appeared to be tomato juices seeping from his head and shoulder. It made no sense, what she was seeing. And then, as a moment or two passed, and Martin didn't move his body, Jennifer felt the blood drain from her face. Her legs buckled and she wrapped her arms around her abdomen, gasping for breath.

Hunched over, she crept toward Martin's still body. Step by step, the horror of the scene revealed itself to her, gradually, like a curtain rising on a stage. Her son, her baby, her little boy, Martin. Who would do this? How could this happen? She fell to her knees next to his body. She shook him, tried to wake him, and then she prayed that this was all a tragic mistake, a horrible nightmare. She wailed, *"God, help me, help meeeeeeee,"* and then she tried to bargain with Him, to reason. *"God, why? Why Martin? Please don't let this happen, anything but this, give me another chance, please God,"* she wailed, looking upward to a magical place where a higher power might be listening.

Jennifer clutched her son's lifeless body, as her tears washed over her baby. And yet, even the piercing sound of her mournful keening proved unable to awaken the dead boy. Why would God let this happen to Martin? Her beautiful son didn't deserve this. Gently, she let her baby's body slip back onto the carpet. She kissed the palm of his hand, and she curled up beside him in the fetal position and shut her eyes. She prayed for oblivion as an addict begs for the narcotic to mask his agony. The pain would still be there in the morning. Grief would be an uninvited guest scraping at her heart for the rest of her life. But for now, she would close her eyes and try desperately to escape into a world where hope was still possible.

CHAPTER 36

The piercing sound of the doorbell chimes wrenched Jennifer from a catatonic state. She opened her eyes, lifted her head from the carpet, aware of a stench she couldn't identify. Her joints and muscles ached, her skin felt raw as though she had slept on a surface of crushed gravel. At first, she didn't know where she was, or who she was, or what had happened. And then, as she sat up and looked around, she saw Martin's lifeless body next to her. She heaved, pressing her fist to her mouth as if to obstruct a scream. She tasted the iron of her son's dried blood on the skin of her knuckles. The doorbell chimed again, catapulting her from the protective cocoon of her fugue state into the horror of the moment. Jennifer lunged away from Martin's corpse toward the landing, and she stumbled down the stairs. "Noooo," she screamed. "No, no, no," she moaned, over and over again. She unlocked and pulled open the front door, not knowing, not caring who was on the other side.

"Jennifer, what is it? What's going on?" Nancy asked. Jennifer's body shook uncontrollably as she collapsed into her sister's arms.

"No, no, no, no, no," she wailed. Her sister dragged her into the house where she crumbled again, onto the hard, marble floor of the foyer. "Nooooooooooooooo!"

"My God, Jennifer. There's blood all over your arms, are you hurt? What happened?" Nancy slid down to the floor near her sister, her hand gently rubbing Jennifer's back. "Talk to me, Jennifer. Where's Martin?" Jennifer crammed her fist back into her mouth, as if to stifle the horror, and she continued sobbing.

Nancy tried again, raising her voice to get through to her sister. "Jennifer, where's Martin? Did *he* do this to you? Did he hurt you again? Is he upstairs? I'm calling 911 this time." Nancy reached into her purse as Jennifer grabbed her arm.

"Nooooo!" That one word, drawn out like a viscous strip of flypaper, grabbed Nancy by the throat. She froze, her hand stopped groping for her phone, and she stared at Jennifer in wide-eyed terror. As if she knew. As if somehow, she knew.

"What? Tell me. What did you do?"

"Nancy, it's too.. it's too late. He's . . dead. Martin's dead," Jennifer whispered. "He's upstairs." She pointed to the staircase. "Someone killed him. I found him. Who? Who would kill Martin? Who would do that?" Nancy stared at her sister. Jennifer's eyes were wild, like a rabid animal caught in a trap. "Who would hurt my baby?"

Nancy withdrew her hand from Jennifer's back, as if recoiling from her sister's pitiful face. She covered her mouth with both hands and looked up the stairwell, gaping at a scene she couldn't see. A scene she could imagine but didn't want to see. Jennifer followed her sister's gaze, as if the two of them were expecting Martin to appear on the landing to reassure them both he was alive and well, and this was a sick joke. Nancy reached again for her cell phone. Jennifer didn't stop her sister this time as she dialed 911.

* * *

For days, Jennifer hovered between consciousness and oblivion. Her heavy eyelids felt glued shut as she tried in vain to push through the darkness. Snippets of Jim's angry whispers filtered through the thick fog. "There were no other fingerprints, Nancy. No signs of forced entry. There's no other explanation." Jennifer heard a swirl of random words, trying to find their rightful places, like a poem by e e cummings without punctuation. The meaning of those words just out of her reach.

"There has to be another explanation. My sister is not capable of murder," Nancy said. "And lower your voice, Jim. She'll hear you." Jennifer fought the blackness, trying to make sense of what they were saying. Were they talking about her?

"I don't give a fuck if she can hear me. It's about time she woke up. Or maybe she's faking this too, pretending to be asleep so she doesn't have to answer any questions."

"No, Jim, she's not faking. They've sedated her. But I think whatever they gave her is wearing off," Nancy whispered.

"Good, because Detective Anderson wants to know more about the last time this happened. Dr. Blaine won't give him any information. Not without Jennifer's consent."

"Please, don't talk to the police again, not before we find the right lawyer for her. As for the last time this happened, she never hurt anyone. It was a coping mechanism—that's what her doctor said. She needed a break, a psychological break, and so she took one. A few weeks in New England, that's all it was. A late summer vacation."

Jennifer struggled to open her eyes. "Did you see that? Her eyes flickered. I think she's waking up," Nancy said. Jennifer groaned, desperately trying to push against the glue that kept her eyelids shut. She was confused by the heavy fog wrapping around her brain. Her husband and sister stopped talking for a moment as she moaned, trying desperately to speak.

"Don't worry, she's still under," Jim whispered. "Nancy, they're searching the entire house, and they won't even let Jason and me get the rest of our things. I mean the house is a fucking crime scene. I can't believe this is happening. This is a nightmare. It's. . .oh my God, it's not real."

"She can stay with me until all this gets sorted out. I mean, when she leaves the hospital," Nancy said. Jim scoffed. Jennifer remembered that sound all too well. The sound of Jim scoffing would always feel like a slap across her face.

"Are you kidding? They're not going to let her leave the psych ward. They think she fucking killed her own child for Christ's sake. They think she killed Martin! And you know what? I think that's exactly what happened. I'm planning funeral services for that monster son of hers, Jason's freaking out, and my consulting business is hurting. Do you get it, Nancy? Do you? This kind of publicity is poison!"

"Quiet down, Jim. I think she's opening her eyes. Look. She can probably hear you," Nancy said.

"I honestly don't give a fuck if she hears me. I hope she hears me." Jennifer winced at the sound of metal scraping over the floor close to her bed. She groaned again.

"I'm out of here," Jim said.

"Jim, wait, please!"

"She's all yours, Nancy. I'm done." Jennifer listened to the sound of footsteps fading, and then she heard nothing at all, not even her heart beating. The silence, the blackness, welcomed her again. A temporary reprieve.

CHAPTER 37

"Jennifer, you need to eat. Please, listen to me," Nancy said. She held a soup spoon in her hand. "You have to cooperate. Besides, they won't let you starve yourself if that's your goal."

"That's not my goal." Jennifer held up her hand and leaned away from the bowl of lukewarm chicken broth on the bedside tray. "I'm not hungry." She pressed the button at her side, lowering the head of the hospital bed to a fully reclined position. Jennifer curled away from her sister, drawing her knees up close to her chest, closing her eyes. "I'm tired. I want to sleep. Go away. Go." Her monotone voice seemed to echo against the barren walls of her small hospital room. Nancy reached around, pushing a wisp of hair out of Jennifer's eyes.

"I'm not going anywhere, and I'm not giving up on you. We need to talk. We need to talk about what happened. About what's going to happen next." Nancy rolled the tray away, pulled down the guardrail, and lowered herself onto the bed next to her sister. "I'm going to brush your hair, it's a disaster."

"Leave me alone." Jennifer covered her head with her arms. "Just go. I'm tired. I want to sleep."

"I won't leave you alone. I can't force you to eat or talk to me. But I'm going to talk to you, and you're going to listen." Jennifer turned onto her back and opened her eyes just wide enough to see her sister folding her arms across her chest. Nancy seemed to swallow the frustration in her voice, donning a patient, a more understanding tone. "You're my baby sister, and you need me now more than ever."

Jennifer squeezed her eyes shut again, but she let her sister's words filter through veils of stubbornness and curiosity. "Attorney Cohen is preparing for your competency hearing," Nancy said. "He's using the court-appointed doctor's diagnosis of Multiple Personality Disorder. What do they call it now? Dissociative Identity Disorder. DID. He's going to argue that you aren't competent to stand trial. But Jennifer, it doesn't matter if he wins or loses at the competency hearing. Both sides want to settle. No one wants to see your case go to trial." Jennifer wished she were sleeping, comatose, or even dead. She prayed Nancy would leave, and yet, a small part of her wanted to hear more.

Nancy kept talking, as if hacking away at a brick wall with an ax of words. "I mean, they hardly have a case. The prosecution doesn't even have a murder weapon. They've accounted for all the guns from above the garage, and not one of those guns was used to kill Martin. All they have is circumstantial evidence. And a theory. I mean, the prosecution thinks this is all an act. But a trial? It's not worth the risk for them or for you."

Jennifer pulled herself to a seated position. She opened her eyes and turned toward Nancy. "Do you think I want a trial? I don't. I want one thing. I want to know what happened to Martin. I want to remember." As Nancy readjusted the position of the bed to support her sister's back, as she fluffed the pillows behind her head, Jennifer wailed. "I want my son back." Her face seemed to melt as tears streaked her hollowed cheeks. Nancy started to reach out, as if she wanted to put her arms around her sister's body and hold her close. But something kept her away. She looked at Jennifer as if she didn't really know the woman sitting in the bed beside her. As if she didn't trust her.

Jennifer wondered what Nancy believed. Did her sister think she was truly capable of killing her son? How could she not remember something like that? Did Nancy believe what the specialists said about multiple personalities? Dissociative identities? What did that even mean? Was she faking? Even Jennifer wasn't sure. Nothing made sense.

"You may never remember. With or without treatment, Dr. Wright says your amnesia may be permanent. And Jennifer, that's a good thing."

"Nancy, you don't understand. It's not a good thing! I *need* to know. Who did this? Did Jenn Cooper kill Martin? Is Jenn Cooper in my head, or is she real? I need to know. Did I kill Martin? I don't remember. I can't remember." Jennifer sobbed into her open palms.

"There's no way you would have killed your own son. Jenn Cooper, she doesn't matter anymore. She's gone. The psychiatrist told us that personality has disappeared, maybe for good this time."

"What does that mean, *this* time?" Jennifer clutched her sister's hand too tightly, her eyes wide, terrified. Nancy grimaced at the sudden pain in her knuckles. "This has happened before? Jenn Cooper has been here before?" Nancy looked down at the faded green blanket on the bed. She seemed to be debating how best to answer Jennifer's questions. "Nancy, please. Answer me. Has Jenn Cooper been here before?"

"Yes. One time. You left home for two weeks. You told your attorney you have no memory of that time. But Jenn Cooper left a journal about her New England trip. The police found it in Martin's closet." Nancy pulled her hand away from Jennifer's firm grasp. Jennifer didn't know what her sister was talking about. *New England? A journal?*

"The doctor says you're having short and long term memory problems. You probably don't remember talking to Attorney Cohen about this, but he told you about the journal you wrote." Jennifer looked at Nancy, mesmerized, as more words swirled around her head like confetti. "The court-appointed psychiatrist read excerpts from the journal you wrote. Or, I should say your alternate personality, Jenn Cooper, wrote. You don't remember your trip to New England, visiting all those dead writers' homes, do you?" Jennifer closed her eyes tight. She wanted her sister to stop talking nonsense. What was she even saying? Maybe it was the sedative they gave her or the shock of Martin's murder. What did Jennifer remember? What did she ever know?

"I don't remember. I'm trying. Can't you see I'm trying? What kind of sister are you? Why aren't you helping me? I tell you I don't remember, and you keep talking at me, like I'm a lunatic."

Nancy sighed, shrugging her shoulders, as if giving up. "Oh, really? You're trying?" The frustration in Nancy's voice tore at Jennifer like the claws of an angry bear. "What kind of sister am I? *I* was the sister you called that September morning, when you woke up in a strange town in Massachusetts, clutching a book of poems by Emily Dickinson." Jennifer shook her head, covered her ears with her hands. Nancy spoke louder. "What kind of sister am I? *I* was the sister who brought you back home and convinced Jim to give you another chance." Jennifer sobbed loudly, failing to drown out the fury in Nancy's voice. "And now, here *I* am again. Your big sister, picking up the pieces of poor Jennifer's shattered life." Nancy looked down at her wrist. "Never mind," she sighed. "It's getting late. There's no point, is there? I have to go. In case you're interested, I'm visiting Mom again, and I don't want her to worry. But you don't care, do you? You never really cared." Jennifer looked up with swollen eyes.

"I do care. She's my mother too."

"Mom was so agitated yesterday, asking for you. Wondering how Martin was doing. Of course, we're never going to tell her what happened. There are times she's lucid, so with it. And other times... well. I guess that's to be expected." Nancy rolled the small, bedside table closer to her sister. "And Jennifer, you want to know what kind of sister I am? I'm the kind of sister who cares enough to tell you that you need to eat something." Jennifer turned away again, curled up in the fetal position, and listened to her sister's rapid footsteps fading into the distance.

* * *

Weeks later, or perhaps it was months—she'd begun to lose all sense of time—Jennifer sat in the armchair opposite Dr. Angela Blaine for their weekly session. The light poured in through a window set close to the low ceiling of the small, basement office. Mesmerized by the dust particles dancing madly like drunken snowflakes on the rays of sun, she had to remind herself what she was doing in that basement office. Dr. Angela had visiting rights at The Miami Institute for Psychiatric Disorders. She had agreed to continue therapy sessions as part of Jennifer's inpatient treatment plan. But really, what was the point? Jennifer reached for another tissue from the small, end table next to her. "I can't stop crying," she said. "Why can't I stop crying?"

"You're grieving, Jennifer. It will take time."

"How long have I been here?"

"You ask that question every week. As of today, it's been four months. Four months and five days. You're doing well. You're making progress."

"They watch me. All the time. They're waiting for me to hurt myself. I'm *not* going to hurt myself. Please tell them to stop watching me." Her longtime therapist nodded her head, waiting. Was she waiting for Jennifer to say more? That had always been Dr. Angela Blaine's strategy with Jennifer. She never interrupted her, never hurried her. But Jennifer had nothing more to say. She would refuse to let her therapist manipulate her. She shifted her gaze back to the dust particles.

Dr. Blaine leaned in, interrupting her reverie. "Jennifer, I'm optimistic. I trust the treatment you're receiving. Your medications have been stabilized, you've been participating, albeit reluctantly, in your group therapy sessions, your work with your medical team here is going well."

"But I'm still crying." Jennifer reached for more tissues.

"Yes. You're still crying. You're still grieving."

"Will they keep me here until I stop crying? Will they keep me here until I can remember? Until Jenn Cooper and I . . . what did you call it? I keep forgetting that word. Until our two personalities fuse?"

"We've been through this before, many times. You may never remember the weeks before, during, or immediately after Martin's death. Right now, the grief, the depression, the headaches, the post-traumatic stress—that's what your medical team is focusing on. It will take time. You know you may be here a long while."

Distracted again by the rays of sun, the particles of dust, Jennifer Moriarty tried to focus on her therapist's words. She'd been trying for months. Four months and five days.

"I'm going to be here a long while? What does that mean?" Jennifer asked. Dr. Blaine droned on, as if trying to break through Jennifer's impenetrable shield of confusion. Each week, she would remove a chink or two, dislodge a memory, and the next week, the shield would be repaired, refortified somehow. Dr. Blaine tilted her head to the side, furrowed her brow, and reached out to touch her patient's hand. Jennifer forced her gaze away from the light that filtered through the window. The dust motes scrambled for their lives and finally settled on surfaces. It was all so random.

"You agreed to this commitment, Jennifer. No criminal trial. That was the choice you made. An extended stay in a psychiatric hospital. And Jennifer, that was the right decision for you, for your family."

Maybe she should have opted for the trial. She had that right. Some days, The Institute felt like a prison to Jennifer, a prison sentence with no end in sight. Four months and five days felt like ten years. Would she be here for the next ten years?

She studied her therapist sitting across from her. Dr. Blaine's furrowed brow was familiar, that concerned expression she wore like a mask. "I need to remember," Jennifer said. "I need to know what happened after I met Jenn Cooper. I remember sitting next to her at the bar. I know we went back to the cottage. I remember that part. I liked her. I trusted her to fix everything. I believed she was the answer to my prayers. Sent by God. Why was I so stupid? I need to find her, to talk to her. I need to stop crying." Jennifer broke into convulsive sobs.

Dr. Blaine handed her the box of tissues. "I know that's what you want. And, as we've discussed, your alter-personality, Jenn Cooper, may never reappear. You may never fuse. But one day you will stop crying."

Jennifer looked at the clock on the side table. Her session would end in a few minutes. And yet, there was one more question. She'd wanted to ask Dr. Angela this question for weeks. If she asked now, there would be no time to hear the answer. The timing was perfect.

"Dr. Angela, there's something I want to ask you. You don't have to answer me right away. In fact, you can think about it and give me an answer next week. It's important."

"I'll answer your question if I can. What is it you want to know?"

"Did Jenn Cooper..." Jennifer swallowed, struggling to find the words.

"What about Jenn Cooper?" Dr. Angela asked. Jennifer looked up at her therapist with red-rimmed eyes, blinded by tears.

"Did Jenn Cooper do the right thing?" Her words floated in the air between them, swirling madly with the dust motes. "I mean, Jenn Cooper was trying to protect me, to protect all the innocent people Martin planned to hurt. She had to stop him, right? She did what was... she did what was necessary. Right? I mean, she didn't really have a choice." Jennifer squinted. She looked at her therapist, knowing there was only one answer she could live with.

"Did Jenn Cooper do the right thing?" Dr. Blaine took her time. She jerked her head to one side, that familiar tic, a sudden twitch signaling she had stumbled on a moment of clarity. Jennifer felt it coming. "That's an interesting question. I have different questions." Jennifer wiped her eyes with another tissue. The wicker trashcan next to her chair was now filled as it was at the end of every session. She took a deep breath. She waited.

"I think they're more important questions than the one you're struggling with right now."

"What? What are they?" Jennifer shifted in the chair, grabbed another tissue. Dr. Blaine waited for her full attention.

"Can you forgive her? Can you, Jennifer Moriarty, forgive Jenn Cooper? And can Jenn Cooper forgive you?"

"What do you mean?"

"What I'm trying to say is there's plenty of blame to go around. Even beyond you and your alter, Jenn Cooper. You don't have to shoulder all of it. Have you considered that?"

Jennifer was too stunned to even contemplate an answer. She didn't know forgiveness was an option. "And it could be you're not ready to answer those questions. But I want you to think about them, Jennifer. Will you do that?" Dr. Blaine glanced at the clock. "Our time is up. We'll talk more about that next week." Yes. She would think about it. She had all the time in the world to think about it.

Dr. Blaine opened the office door and gently touched Jennifer's elbow, leading her down the dark corridor, up the stairs to the locked women's ward. Jennifer shuffled along, thinking only of the river of endless tears streaming down her face. Yes. She had so much to think about, if she could only stop crying.

EPILOGUE

Six years later

"We're looking for someone who can commit to fifteen hours a week at the gift shop but also fill in when one of our tour guides calls in sick." Jordan Green, the assistant director of The Ernest Hemingway House and Museum, couldn't have been much older than twenty-five.

"Fifteen hours a week would be ideal." Jennifer Moriarty didn't need the money. She needed to keep busy, stay active. That's what her new therapist, Dr. Gary Jepson, told her. And she realized he was right. She had way too much time on her hands.

"The tour guide training is offered in the evenings from 6:30-8:30 p.m. There are two sessions, next Monday and Wednesday. Unfortunately, we won't be able to pay you for those hours. But once you complete the training, we would pay $100 per tour. And of course, that would be in addition to tips from the tourists." No, it wasn't about the money. Jim had covered all of her legal expenses. He never complained about paying the bills not covered by insurance at a pricey psychiatric residential treatment center. And after all that, Jim left her with enough alimony to manage.

Despite the divorce attorney's advice, despite Nancy's urging, Jennifer had no regrets. She'd refused to ask for anything beyond basic living expenses. Jim was generous, allowing her to live in the Key West cottage for as long as she needed a place to stay. Now that he'd remarried and was living in Seattle, he had no use for the cottage. And after everything that happened, Jim wanted no connection to the State of Florida. Jennifer had understood there'd be no money for a personal trainer, no weekly massages, no cleaning service, no Guntry Club, no nail salon, not even a gym membership. A roof over her head—that was enough. She didn't deserve more. And now, a part-time job to keep her occupied. To keep her sanity.

"I understand, and that's completely fair," she told the assistant director. Jennifer had dressed with care for the interview. She wanted to look the part. Conservative, professional, tasteful but not flashy. Closed-toe espadrilles, a khaki-colored, safari dress, belted, the hem falling mid-calf. She thought the look was Hemingway-esque, if there was such a fashion trend.

"Tell me why this position interests you." She'd prepared for the interview, and she expected a question like that one. She crossed her legs and leaned forward in her chair.

"I've recently relocated to Key West. Now that my son has left home, I'm reentering the workforce. Jason lives in Seattle, and he graduated with an advanced degree in Education. I'm so proud of him. He's going to be a teacher," she said, suddenly realizing she'd digressed. "So now, I have time on my hands, and I've always loved The Hemingway House. I visited here many years ago, and I can't imagine a more magical place to work."

"I agree. It's a special place." The young director smiled at her. He probably assumed they had something in common. A love for Hemingway. The truth was, Jennifer Moriarty had never visited the Hemingway House, but she'd read about it online. She'd even studied summaries of Hemingway's novels in case the assistant director wanted to talk about the author's books.

"I'm fascinated by his life, the house, the six-toed cats, and, of course, his novels. I guess you might say I'm a big Hemingway fan." Jennifer had done her homework.

"Do you have any questions?" he asked.

"I don't think so. Do you?" He laughed. Jennifer could be charming, especially when she was nervous. A positive trait for a tour guide.

"One more question. When can you start?" They both laughed. Jennifer shook her new boss's hand.

She practically danced in the streets of Old Town on her walk back to the cottage. She had nailed the interview, and Jennifer was in the mood to celebrate. Dr. Jepson would be happy. She was moving on, determined to live a productive life. A meaningful life.

Back in the cottage, she poured herself a glass of iced tea and settled into one of the rocking chairs on the front porch. She picked at a flake of peeling white paint. The chairs needed a new coat. Maybe tomorrow she would start that project. She pulled out her cell phone and called her sister.

"Nancy? I got the job!"

"That's wonderful! I'm so happy for you. When do you start?" Jennifer filled her in on the details. They spoke on the phone a few times a week, but their conversations were always short. Jennifer didn't have much to say, and Nancy was stingy with news about Jason. Then Nancy said, "I'm on my way out the door, but we'll talk soon. And Jennifer, I'm proud of you."

Jennifer sipped her iced tea, soothed by the back and forth motion of the rocking chair. She looked out on the quiet street, thinking about Floyd, wondering if she'd see him again, riding his rusty old bicycle down her narrow road. He refused to pick up where they'd left off so many lifetimes ago. She'd called him when she returned to Key West, but he told her he couldn't handle it. "You've changed so much, Jennifer. You're not the person you used to be," he'd said. "I don't even know who you are, and I can't be part of this." She didn't blame him, but sometimes she heard the echo of his rusty old bicycle bell outside her door. Some nights she almost felt the warmth of his strong arms around her, making her feel safer than she had a right to feel.

She missed Jason, too, of course, but Nancy let Jennifer know her older son was doing well. He didn't want to see her. He wouldn't even talk to her. But the pain of missing Martin hurt her the most. The tears returned at sunset, as the darkening sky unleashed new waves of sorrow. She didn't miss the Martin who had locked himself away from the world, not the boy she'd left in the hands of a surrogate mother. She missed the sweet little child who curled up next to her on his bed each night, chiming in when she read his favorite book, *Goodnight Moon*. Sometimes she would read the book twice or three times when he pleaded for more. "One more time," Martin would demand. She could never refuse him. Perhaps that was her downfall. *"Goodnight comb and goodnight brush,"* Jennifer would read. And Martin would join her, *"Goodnight nobody, and goodnight mush. Goodnight to the old lady, whispering. . . .."* and then Martin would whisper in her ear with his darling voice, *"Hush."* What happened to that Martin?

* * *

It was a beautiful, sunny day with low humidity. Today would be Jennifer's first group tour, and although she'd successfully completed the training and had studied the thick manual like a college student preparing for a final exam, she was a bundle of nerves.

She called her sister in the morning. "Do I seem ready? Do you really think I can do this?"

"Of course, you're ready. They wouldn't let you lead a tour if you weren't ready." Nancy was right. And Dr. Jepson had assured her she could take a Xanax for her anxiety if she needed one. She definitely needed one.

Later that afternoon she stood with a small group of tourists outside Hemingway's study. They crowded together on the small landing above the carriage house, behind the velvet rope, looking in. She couldn't relate to these tourists as they breathed in the Hemingway air and as they stood in awe of Hemingway's genius. They gaped at the writing studio where he wrote *For Whom the Bell Tolls*, taking in the original furniture, the paintings on the wall. These tourists practically worshiped at the altar of Hemingway's typewriter.

She took advantage of their wonderment. "See that typewriter? Those keys are probably still smudged with Hemingway's DNA," she told them. She was proud of herself for remembering that detail from the manual. The tourists were staring at her, perhaps impressed with her Hemingway knowledge. But the sun beating down on Jennifer Moriarty as she stood outside the study with her tour group, made her feel lightheaded. Suddenly, she became distracted by the heat, by the buzz of conversations swirling around her.

Or maybe it was her thoughts of Hemingway that distracted her. It was Hemingway who made her think of Jenn Cooper and wonder about the novel Jenn talked about wanting to write. Suddenly, she felt Hemingway's presence, hovering near her, like a flicker. The flicker turned into a flame, and the flame consumed her. She stood there motionless and feverish, miles away and lost. How long did she stand there, burning, sweating, staring into Hemingway's study, gazing into another world? Was it minutes? Could it have been weeks or a month?

"Excuse me," a woman interrupted. "Excuse me. The Ladies Room?"

"Yes?"

"The Ladies Room? Can you tell me where it is? I mean, the tour's over, right?" The tourists stared, glancing sideways at each other, clearly confused.

"Oh, sorry. I'm not sure where the Ladies Room is located. I've only been here once. I think it's in the main house." The group descended the steep stairs leading back into Hemingway's garden, whispering and directing their surreptitious glances toward the landing outside the study.

"Umm. That was weird."

"There's something definitely wrong with that woman."

"Did she have a seizure or something?"

"Should we tell someone? Maybe she needs medical attention."

* * *

After purchasing a leather-bound Hemingway House journal at the museum gift shop, I walked back to the cottage with a renewed energy and sense of purpose. I stopped at a package store and bought a cold bottle of Chardonnay. Back at the cottage, I changed out of my dress and slipped into a comfortable pair of yoga pants and an old T-shirt I found in the back of Jennifer's dresser. I poured myself a glass of wine and grabbed a pen from her writing desk. Curled up on the porch swing, I listened to the whining of the rusty chains as I rocked back and forth. I placed my wineglass on the rickety end table. Then I picked up my pen, and I began to write. I was finally ready, and I had a story to tell.

The Surrogate

By

Jenn Cooper

Prologue:

Florida was her first mistake.

THE END

ACKNOWLEDGEMENTS

I would like to thank my friends and family who read early drafts and provided support and insight every step of the way: My critique partners, Kelly Kendra Hughes, Beth Brody, and Pam Kelly, you continue to make me a better writer. Steve Kaplan, Mark Ritter, Susan Seider, Bert Kaplowitz, Ken and Bonnie Robson, Michele Miller, and June Glaser, you gave me encouragement when I considered abandoning this manuscript. Marty Plaine and Phyllis Holtgrewe, my amazing sister-cheerleaders, I'm so lucky to have you both in my corner. Samantha Holtgrewe, Comma-Queen, I thank you for always being an email away. And most of all, to RBK, my best friend and soul-mate. Thank you for believing in me and all my crazy dreams.

ABOUT THE AUTHOR

Lynn Katz is a former teacher, curriculum writer, and school principal. She writes adult and middle grade fiction in Connecticut where she lives with her husband.

NOTE FROM THE AUTHOR

Word-of-mouth is crucial for any author to succeed. If you enjoyed *The Surrogate*, please leave a review online—anywhere you are able. Even if it's just a sentence or two. It would make all the difference and would be very much appreciated.

Thanks!
Lynn Katz

Thank you so much for reading one of our **Psychological Thrillers**.
If you enjoyed our book, please check out our recommendation
for your next great read!

The Tracker by John Hunt

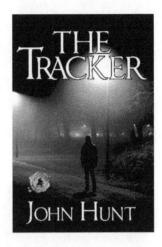

"A dark thriller that draws the reader in."
–Morning Bulletin

"I never want to hear mention of bolt-cutters, a live rat and a
bucket in the same sentence again. EVER."
–Ginger Nuts Of Horror

View other Black Rose Writing titles at
www.blackrosewriting.com/books and use promo code
PRINT to receive a **20% discount** when purchasing.

CPSIA information can be obtained
at www.ICGtesting.com
Printed in the USA
FSHW010311100221
78461FS